A Debt of Death

Jonathan Dunsky

A Debt of Death
Jonathan Dunsky

Copyright © 2017 by Jonathan Dunsky

Cover by Dan Van Oss – CoverMint

Cover photograph © mandritoiu/shutterstock (street)

ISBN-13: 978-1979578707
ISBN-10: 1979578702

Visit JonathanDunsky.com for news and information.

Books by Jonathan Dunsky

Adam Lapid Series

Ten Years Gone

The Dead Sister

The Auschwitz Violinist

A Debt of Death

For Keren

Chapter 1

The dead man was lying facedown in a puddle of blood and rainwater.

I didn't think he was dead at first. My initial impression was that he was a drunk who'd had five or six too many and had stumbled to the curb and passed out. It was the positioning of his body. It didn't look like dead people often do, with their limbs sticking out at angles that no living soul could tolerate. He looked peaceful, relaxed, like he was in the midst of a deep sleep.

It was only when I crouched down beside him, meaning to nudge him awake and off the wet pavement, that I noticed the blood. I had missed it at first, partly because of the dim lighting afforded by the streetlight five feet away, and partly because the blood had mixed in with the water in the puddle, which had diluted its natural redness to a barely discernible lilac.

I didn't know it was Nathan Frankel until I turned him over and saw his face.

His eyes were open and, as bad luck would have it, they were staring right at me. I swore, and for some inexplicable reason I had chosen to do so in German. This made me swear again—this time in Hungarian.

His mouth hung slack and open, and there was blood

on his lips and chin. His tongue had sunk back toward the rear of his mouth like a rolled-up sock. His face was bleach white, and when I removed my right glove and pressed two fingers against the artery in his neck, the skin felt cold.

There was no pulse. I hadn't expected to find any. I had seen more dead people than most morticians were likely to lay eyes on over the course of their career. I could tell by his face that Nathan Frankel was quite dead.

I suppose it was groundless hope that led me to check his pulse anyway. And as experience had taught me, when all you have left is groundless hope, you might as well start grieving.

Catching sight of his eyes again, I noticed that they held not the glassy, vacant stare common to the dead, but a mixture of expressions that I could only guess at. Fear, imploration, resignation, accusation?

I muttered another profanity, a particularly juicy Hebrew one I had learned recently and that for some reason had stuck in my mind.

Running my eyes down from Nathan's face, I noticed the bloodstains on his jacket. It was unbuttoned, and when I drew it open, I saw his drenched shirtfront and the two stab wounds in his torso.

One was on the right side of his stomach, just under the ribs. The other was lower and almost dead center, about where his navel would be. They were bleeder wounds, the sort that wouldn't kill you fast, but rather would leak out your life drop by drop until you croaked.

Looking around the body, I noticed that there wasn't

as much blood as I would expect there to be. I raised my head, scanning the sidewalk past the body and spotted a trail of red droplets snaking its way north up the pavement. So he had been stabbed somewhere else and had managed to stagger all the way down here.

Was he coming to see me? If so, he had fallen short by about thirty meters. I shook my head in anger. Goddammit. Without a conscious thought, I curled my right hand into a fist and brought it down hard on my thigh.

Suddenly I heard a sound behind me. I whipped around, ready to launch myself up from my crouch, fist cocked. But it was only Greta. She stood wide-eyed and slack-jawed, grasping my coat in both hands.

"You left this behind, Adam," she said in a tremulous voice, her eyes on Nathan's body. "I saw it and ran out after you..." Her words trailed off and she gulped, closing her mouth with a smack. "Is he...?"

I nodded, lowering and unclenching my fist. "He's dead."

"Are you sure?"

"Yes. You better call the police."

She had installed a telephone in the café two weeks earlier and now went to put it to good use. It was past eleven at night and the air was dry and very cold. I slipped my glove back on. I looked up and down the street, but there was no one in sight. Knowing I had a couple of minutes at most until Greta returned, I squatted by Nathan again, studiously avoiding his eyes, and quickly went through his pockets.

One trouser pocket yielded a ring of keys and a pack of mint chewing gum; the other a cigarette lighter, a near-full pack of Camels, and some change. I put everything back where I'd found it and started working on his jacket.

No gun, no knife, no weapon of any kind. In his right-hand pocket was a ticket stub to a movie at Migdalor Cinema, dated eight days ago. The left-hand pocket was empty. The wallet I found in the inside breast pocket.

I took it out and did a quick search. ID card, which listed an address on Arlozorov Street; ration strip; a receipt from a radio store; what appeared to be an old grocery list written in a tight, cramped scrawl; and a wad of banknotes in the bill compartment. I counted them. Two hundred and thirty-two liras.

I removed two hundred liras, folded them, and stuffed them in my pocket. The thirty-two remaining liras I slipped back into the wallet and then returned it to the pocket from which it came.

I had just about finished doing that when I heard a woman gasp. I turned and there was Greta, looking at me as if she was seeing the real me for the very first time, and what she saw was dirty and immoral and depraved.

"I can explain," I told her.

She said nothing.

"I did not steal this man's money, Greta. You need to trust me on this."

Still she said nothing. I could see the struggle in her face. She desperately wanted to believe I was not a thief, yet her eyes told a different story.

I let out a sigh, got to my feet, took Nathan's money

out of my pocket, and held it out to her.

"There're two hundred liras here. You keep them for now." After a slight hesitation, she reached out and plucked the bills from my hand. I bent down, got Nathan's wallet from his jacket, and counted the remaining banknotes before her eyes. "Thirty-two. All right?"

She nodded slowly, frowning, not sure where I was going with all this, the two hundred liras clasped in her hand.

"You got through to the cops?" I asked after I put the wallet back in its place.

"They're on their way. The policeman I spoke with said he'd call an ambulance." She shrugged. "I told him it was no use, but he insisted."

"That's all right," I said. "An ambulance is as good a way as any to haul away a corpse. You okay?"

Greta shuddered. She was still holding my coat in one hand. She thrust it at me. "Here. Put this on. No use catching a cold."

I smiled in relief. Greta's maternal instincts were kicking in. It was a good sign. It meant she was on her way to trusting me again. I slid on the coat. "You better head inside and get your own coat. And put the money away before the cops get here."

She gave me a puzzled look but went inside without comment.

I lit a cigarette and stood puffing away over the corpse of a man whom I had only spoken with for the first time three days ago, but who was in a way as close to me as a brother. From where I was standing, I could no longer see into his dead eyes, but I imagined them still fixed on me. Despite my coat and the warm cigarette smoke in my mouth and lungs, I felt a finger of ice brush along my spine.

Greta emerged from the café and came to stand beside me, now wrapped in a long, gray coat. The coat had a belt looped through it and Greta cinched it tight around her midriff. She hugged herself across her heavy chest.

"Two hundred liras," she said. "That's a great deal of money."

She was right, of course. It was more than what many Israelis earned in six months.

"I wonder how he got it," she said.

"He was a criminal. That's how."

She looked at me. "You know him, Adam?"

I nodded, taking a final drag from my cigarette before dropping it to the pavement and crushing it under my shoe. I stuck my hands in my coat pockets. "His name is Nathan Frankel."

"How do you know him?"

I was about to answer when a pair of headlights swung into view at the corner of Allenby and Balfour. The police car coasted to a stop, its lights washing over Greta and me before settling on the body. Two men climbed out. The younger one, the driver, was in uniform, while the older one was dressed in civilian clothes. The uniformed cop froze at the sight of the body, shedding about a decade off his early-twenties face, looking like a petrified ten-year-old. The older one noticed and said, "If you're going to lose your dinner, Elkin, do it on the other side of the car." He cast a quick glance at Nathan's corpse, sucked on his lower lip for a second, then turned to Greta and me. "I'm Inspector Leibowitz. You the one who called?"

"Yes," Greta said.

Leibowitz shifted his gaze to me. "And who might you be?"

I gave him my name and told him I had helped Greta close up the café and that I had been heading home when I came upon the body.

"Did you touch anything, Mr. Lapid?"

"He was lying facedown when I found him. I turned him over and checked his pulse. That's all."

I could feel Greta's eyes on me. I dared not return her gaze. Leibowitz wouldn't have any reason to assume I was lying, but I knew that his natural suspicion, the weapon of every good detective, was primed and ready. In a murder case it always is. For the moment, Greta and I were the only two people Leibowitz could connect to the body. There was no one he could consider as suspects but the pair of us. I wasn't about to give him any cause to believe that we were colluding to keep something from him.

"You could have spared yourself the trouble," he said in a flat tone, fishing a small notebook and pencil from his coat. He checked his wristwatch, flipped open the notebook, and muttered as he wrote, "January 7, 1951. Eleven thirty-four p.m. Allenby Street, Tel Aviv. One male stiff."

He was a thin man, age forty-three or forty-four, dressed in a black coat and rumpled blue slacks and dark shoes. He stood five seven or eight and had a slightly bent posture. His hair was light brown, with early touches of gray. Beneath the hair was a tall forehead that sloped sharply to a pair of questioning eyebrows that shaded two very dark, slightly bulging eyes. Under the eyes he'd developed bags of the sort that wouldn't go away even if he slept for twenty-four hours straight. An eagle's beak of a nose and a wide, unsentimental mouth completed the picture. His was a weary, hard-bitten face that gave the impression that he'd heard all the jokes there were to hear and had judged them unfunny. He reminded me of other cops I'd known, cops who took a dim view of the world and the people who inhabited it, who expected the worst of their fellow man and were suspicious of anything better.

He turned to Officer Elkin. "Get on the radio and tell them to send over a photographer and a corpse wagon."

"The dispatcher I talked to said he'd call an ambulance," Greta said.

Leibowitz grunted. "Much good would that do."

At that moment we saw the harsh lights of the ambulance glide down from the north. It screeched to an abrupt halt before us, and a man wearing a white doctor's coat and carrying a black bag jumped out. Leibowitz told him he could put his bag away and asked if they would stick around to take the body to the morgue when the police were done with the scene.

The doctor shook his head resolutely. "No way. That's

not our job."

Leibowitz didn't argue. "Fine. You can go."

"You guys shouldn't bother us with this sort of thing. We might be needed elsewhere, you know."

"Yeah, yeah. I'll make sure to educate the boys at the station. Now get lost, will you?"

The doctor said something under his breath that would have made a lady blush, then got in the ambulance. It swung a U-turn and sped away.

"Goddamn quack," said Leibowitz.

He stepped closer to the body and did a methodical circuit around it, checking it from all angles. By the tilt of his head, I could tell he had spotted the blood trail leading north. He didn't follow it. He didn't have to. The sky had cleared in the evening. There would be no rain that night. The blood would last a while longer.

Officer Elkin leaned out of the police car. "Dispatch said they sent someone to roust Sabban out of bed. He'll bring his camera along."

Leibowitz half-smiled. "I'm sure he'll be thrilled about it. They say how long they'll be?"

"Ten minutes, fifteen tops."

Leibowitz nodded and crouched down beside the body, at almost the exact spot where I had done so earlier. He ran his eyes over the corpse, noting aloud for the benefit of Elkin, and maybe for his own as well, the two stab wounds. Then he started poking through Nathan's pockets. He went through them in just about the same order as I had, stopping and rising with the wallet in his hand.

"Nathan Frankel," he said, holding up the ID card from the wallet. "Twenty-five years of age." Then, with his back to Greta and me, he took out the money and counted it silently.

"How much is there?" I asked.

Leibowitz stiffened. He jerked his head around to stare at me. A deep frown etched his forehead. It was obvious my question had caught him completely by surprise.

"Why do you ask? You didn't touch this wallet, did you?"

I shook my head. "Like I told you, I only turned him on his back and checked his neck for a heartbeat. I'm just curious, that's all."

He kept on looking at me with that frown on his face for a minute longer, unsure whether or not to believe me. Gradually the frown smoothed itself out, but not completely.

"Twelve liras," he said, his dark eyes probing my face, trying to read my mind. I would have bet that over the years more than a few suspects had crumbled during interrogation under the pressure of his gaze.

I kept my expression neutral. From the corner of my eye, I could see Greta's face. It was a good thing Leibowitz was giving me his full attention, because she had a stunned look about her. I sent her a silent message, "Don't say a word," and she didn't. Greta was no fool.

Leibowitz waited for me to speak, almost challenging me to. Like all good investigators, he was familiar with the incredible power of silence. Most people find silence disconcerting and feel compelled to break it by opening their mouth to say something, anything. Often a man might hang himself by revealing things he shouldn't, just because he finds the silence in the interrogation room unbearable. Of course, Leibowitz was unaware of the fact that I was no stranger to this technique and therefore immune to it. After all, I had once been a police detective myself.

He finally gave up after about a minute. He slipped the wallet into his coat pocket, closing the flap.

"I'll need your contact information," he said, all formal now. "Addresses and phone numbers, if you got them."

Like nearly all Israelis, I did not have a telephone in my apartment and neither did Greta. She gave him the number of the café, and I said I could be reached there most days. Leibowitz jotted the information in his notebook.

What followed were a few minutes of general questioning. I could have guessed the questions before they came out of Leibowitz's mouth. Hadn't I asked similar questions on multiple occasions years ago? Only when I'd asked them, I had done so mostly in Hungarian and a couple of times in Romanian.

At precisely what time did I stumble upon the body?

About fifteen minutes before Leibowitz and Elkin came on the scene.

Did Greta or I hear any noise beforehand, like a scuffle or a cry for help? The thud of the body smacking onto the sidewalk?

We shook our heads.

Did we see anyone running by the café's front

window? Or a car streaking past much too fast?

Again, the answer was negative.

When did the last customer before me leave?

Ten o'clock. Greta gave Leibowitz the customer's name, and he dutifully entered it in his notebook.

Was the deceased a patron of the café?

I let Greta answer no to that last question while I held my tongue. A nagging voice in my head informed me in no uncertain terms that I was being a damn fool, that I should tell Leibowitz what I knew about Nathan, that I should let the police do their work, that I had no business or cause to interfere.

I ignored that voice, though I recognized its wisdom. For this murder was my business, and I had every intention of interfering.

When he was done with his questions, Leibowitz told us we were free to leave, though he stressed that he might wish to speak to us again later on. I could feel his eyes on my back as Greta and I retreated to the café.

Chapter 2

We stood at the window and watched as another police car pulled up, disgorging a uniformed policeman and a weary-looking man with a camera. The cameraman proceeded to snap a prodigious number of pictures of the body and its surroundings. A dozen or so curious civilians had gathered to see what all the hullabaloo was about. Elkin and the new officer were gesticulating at them to stand well back from the scene, no doubt exhorting them to go home, which they showed no inclination of doing. Leibowitz seemed oblivious to the onlookers. He stood with his hands jammed deep in his pockets, watching the cameraman work.

"How long will they be?" Greta asked.

"A while, but not too long. I doubt they'll find much here." I told her about the blood trail I'd seen. "Inspector Leibowitz noticed it too. He has good eyes."

"And sticky fingers. Is he really going to keep that money?"

"Not all of it. Officer Elkin will likely get his share, maybe one or two other guys."

"You talk as if it's only to be expected. I was of a mind to call him a thief to his face. I still am." Her face was flushed with indignation.

"Resist the urge, Greta. It would serve no purpose."

"You knew this would happen, didn't you, Adam? That's why you removed the money from his wallet."

"I couldn't be certain, of course, but I knew there was a good chance that some of the money would find its way into the pockets of our boys in blue."

She studied my face, and I could tell what she was thinking before she put it into words.

"Was this something you did when you were a policeman in Hungary?"

I looked into her kind eyes and remembered how I'd felt when she saw me take the money from Nathan's wallet. I'd thought I had lost her respect and friendship forever. I felt a similar fear now, but I had always been truthful with Greta. I did not tell her everything; I kept the darkest days of my past and the blackest thoughts of my present to myself. But I was not in the habit of lying to her.

"A few times. Mostly they were cases in which the victims were criminals, but there were a couple of times they weren't. I'm not proud of it, Greta, but I did it. The first time it happened, I was appalled and tried to resist. The other cop, older and case-hardened, had to force the money into my hand and close my fingers around it. It was the way, he told me. You either took the money or no one would work with you. If you acted too pure, other cops would get nervous around you. You'd be shunned. So I took the money. And I spent it. I didn't feel very good about it, but I did it. It was only after I got ahead in the ranks that I passed the word around that I didn't want any part of murder victims' money. I wouldn't stop anyone else from dipping in, but they could count me out. By then, the other cops knew they could trust me, so they let it slide. Does this shock you?"

Greta didn't answer right away. At length she said, "I can't pretend to like it, but I'm sure glad you didn't make a lifetime habit of it."

I smiled faintly. "Almost all cops take money. They have to. With cops' wages being what they are, they wouldn't be able to support a family without a little extra coming in. This doesn't make them bad cops, not if they do it within reason."

"And the cops who never take money?"

I thought of Reuben Tzanani, who belonged to that rare breed of totally honest policemen, and who had a desk job because of it.

"They don't get far in their careers," I said.

We were both quiet for a while. I gazed out the window at the activity outside. A few more spectators had gathered and the cops were showing signs of losing their patience with them. Leibowitz left the scene, walking uptown, no doubt following the trail of blood drops to see where it led him. By this time, a third car had arrived—what Leibowitz had called "the corpse wagon." The driver got out and parked himself on the hood and smoked a cigarette, a bored expression on his face. Soon, Nathan's body would be hoisted into the back of the car and ferried to the morgue. It wouldn't take long for the police to discover he'd made his living on the wrong side of the law. Once that happened, the case would likely fade in significance. It would go from "murder most foul" to "good riddance to bad rubbish." The police would cease to care. If a solution fell in their lap, they would seize it. If it didn't, they wouldn't put in much effort and Nathan's murder would likely go unsolved.

I could help the police, of course. I could step out right now and tell Leibowitz everything I knew. But I wasn't going to. There were a number of reasons. One, doing so would get at least one innocent person in trouble with the law, not to mention myself. And two, this was now a personal matter. I was going to handle this myself because there was a fair chance that I had inadvertently brought about Nathan's death—that, if it wasn't for my stupidity or excessive honesty or my simply being at the wrong place at the wrong time, he wouldn't be lying dead on a cold sidewalk in the middle of Allenby Street with two knife wounds in his torso.

Which meant that this was now my responsibility, this was now my case. I was going to find out who murdered Nathan, and when I did, I did not want the police to get in my way with their regulations and procedures. I wanted free rein to bring his killer to justice. And odds were that it would not be the justice provided by courts and rules of evidence and jail cells.

Greta broke the silence. "I put the two hundred liras on the second shelf in the kitchen, between the third and fourth trays."

"Good. I'll take them before I leave."

"What do you plan on doing with them?"

"Give them to someone he loved."

She looked at me quizzically but didn't ask me to elaborate. That was the thing about Greta, she knew which questions to ask and which not to.

"How come you know this man, Adam?" she said after a few moments.

"If I'm going to tell you," I said, "we'd better sit down. And maybe we should get something hot to drink while we're at it. Death is a cold business. We might as well try to keep warm."

Once we were settled around my table, with a pot of tea and two cups, I began talking.

"I first heard the name Nathan Frankel four days ago, when I paid a visit to Tova Wasserman…"

Chapter 3

The second Tova Wasserman opened her door, I could tell that something was wrong.

"Come in, Mr. Lapid," she ordered in her crisp, heavily accented Hebrew.

She had been born in Poland sixty-five, maybe seventy years ago, and every single day of her life showed on her prune of a face. She stood five foot three and was as thin as a walking stick. That day, as usual, she had on a floor-length dark dress made of thick wool. A gold necklace with a tear-shaped amber pendant hung against her scrawny chest. A gray shawl was draped over her shoulders.

The reason I knew something was wrong was that this was the first time she hadn't commanded me to wipe my feet before crossing her threshold.

She led the way down a narrow hall festooned with pictures of her relatives—both the living and the dead—and into her living room. Neither hall nor living room sported a speck of dust.

"Sit," she ordered, gesturing toward a large, thickly padded three-seater that had been new when the Ottomans still ruled the Land of Israel. The rest of the furniture was of a similar vintage and style—the kind that was built to last the ages, but would never be mistaken for beautiful.

On a low table before the sofa rested a plate stacked with cookies. Mrs. Wasserman lifted it in her bony hand and extended it to me.

"Take one," she said. "I made them yesterday."

Declining was not an option. I selected one of the smaller cookies, set its edge carefully between two molars, and bit down slowly. The cookie, almost vacant of taste and as hard as gravel, crunched under the pressure of my teeth. The first time I had tried one of Mrs. Wasserman's cookies, I nearly chipped an incisor. This time went smoother. I couldn't say why her cookies came out so hard and had never dared to ask.

"Thank you, Mrs. Wasserman," I said, taking another careful bite. "It's very good."

My praise elicited a slight tip of her head but no smile. This wasn't surprising. The only evidence I had that Mrs. Wasserman was capable of smiling was some of the pictures on the walls in her hall, and those had been taken many years ago. She had a narrow, severe face with sunken cheeks, a sharp nose, and a small pinched mouth with lined lips that moved very little when she spoke. Two metallic blue eyes gazed upon the world from beneath a pair of thin arched eyebrows. They were hard, shrewd eyes and the years had narrowed them so only part of her irises showed. Today the eyes were even narrower than usual, wary.

She did not speak until I had finished my cookie. Outside, a January wind wailed down Ben Yehuda Street, rattling the windowpanes. Mrs. Wasserman pulled her shawl tighter around her. Her fingers were long and arthritic, and on her ring finger she still wore her engagement and wedding rings, even though her husband had been dead for at least ten years.

Once the cookie was done and I had carefully rubbed the crumbs off my fingers over the plate, Mrs. Wasserman said, "You wish to make an exchange?"

"Yes," I said, reaching into the inside pocket of my jacket and withdrawing a slim wad of green banknotes. One hundred American dollars in tens and fives. I handed them over to her.

Mrs. Wasserman licked her forefinger and counted the money. Then she set all of the bills but one on the coffee table and began carefully examining the remaining note. She felt it between her fingers, peered at it through squinting eyes, and held it up to the light, seemingly poring over every inch of it. I watched her repeat this process with each of the banknotes with mounting curiosity. On our previous transactions, she had confined herself to a cursory inspection. This was something new.

When she concluded her examination, she gave a small nod to herself. Then she turned her eyes to me and named an exchange rate. It was far lower than the official exchange rate set by the government, but that was to be expected. Black-market transactions tended to benefit the seller, who could demand exorbitant prices. In this case, Mrs. Wasserman was selling me Israeli currency, and she was making a tidy profit.

"That's fine," I said.

Mrs. Wasserman instructed me to wait, rose from her chair, and shuffled out of the living room. She returned a minute later, a sheaf of Israeli currency in her right hand. "Here. Count it."

I did, though I did not for a moment suspect that she would stiff me. It turned out that she had given me thirty liras more than what we agreed on.

"You gave me too much," I said.

"It's for a job I want you to do for me."

"What job?"

She slid a hand into a side pocket, brought out two American banknotes, and laid them on the table. She pointed to the one on the left. "This is one of the notes you gave me. And this—" she shifted her finger to the other bill "—I received two weeks ago. Take a good look at them. See if you can spot the differences."

I did as she instructed, but after a minute's worth of scrutiny could not tell the two banknotes apart. She told me where to look, and it was then that I saw the small imperfections in the second bill. A slight variation in color here, a tiny excess of ink there, an almost undetectable smudge around the intelligent eyes of the man at the center of the bill.

"It's good work," I said.

"Yes," she said. Her pinched mouth crimped even more. "Very good work."

"I take it there is more than this one bill."

"Eight hundred dollars."

I stared at her. While the sum was no fortune, it was more than what many Israelis had to their name. Mrs.

Wasserman met my gaze without a change of expression, but in her eyes I could see the burning anger she felt.

I said, "When did you notice the money was fake?"

"I didn't. A person I do business with spotted the irregularities. He has seen forged money before. He said the forgery was of high quality, though unlikely to fool anyone who had experience in such matters. I got the bad news three days ago."

"Where did the money come from?"

"A young man called Nathan Frankel. He said he got the money from a wealthy uncle in America."

"Was this the first time you've done business with him?"

"Yes."

"Did you know him beforehand?"

"I did not."

I refrained from asking whether she felt it had been imprudent on her part to carry out such a large transaction with a man she did not know. Aside from satisfying my curiosity, it would have served no purpose other than to make her feel bad. What was done was done.

"How did he know to come to you with the dollars? Who gave him your name?"

"He said he got it from Zalman Alphon. Do you know him?"

"No."

"He runs a stationery store on Daniel Street. But aside from pencils and sharpeners and erasers, he also dabbles in the black market. The sugar in these cookies came from him."

I had not detected a trace of sugar in the cookie I'd eaten, but decided not to share this with her.

"Alphon vouched for him?" I asked.

Mrs. Wasserman shifted in her seat. When she spoke next, her eyes were averted.

"I did not check with Alphon prior to making the exchange. I should have, considering the sum involved, but the young man—Frankel—he made a good impression. Clean cut, well-spoken, educated, honest. A nice Polish boy. He seemed trustworthy. I did not for a moment suspect that he would cheat me."

"And what exactly do you want me to do?"

She fixed her hard eyes on mine, and I noticed that her thin fingers had coiled into fists in her lap. "I want you to find Nathan Frankel and get my money back."

I nodded. I'd expected as much, but I needed to hear her say the words. If a client is unable to say what she wants, it means she has not made up her mind yet. But Tova Wasserman had never struck me as a woman prone to indecision, and it was clear she had no doubt in her mind as to what she wanted me to do.

I had first met her in October 1948, two years and three months ago. I arrived in Israel from Europe in September 1947 with a small stash of foreign currency— money I'd taken from Nazis I'd killed in the aftermath of the Second World War as revenge for the death of my family in Auschwitz—and I was told that she could exchange it for me.

She never asked me where the money I brought her

came from, and I never inquired as to what she did with it after I gave it to her. I sometimes wondered how she got into this business, and I imagined that she either had a relative or a business partner in Europe to whom she sent the foreign banknotes. In truth, I didn't much care. I knew very little about her and thought she knew almost nothing about me. She never asked me any personal questions, maintaining a strictly professional attitude, and I never volunteered any information about myself. But apparently she knew more about me than I had believed. Otherwise, she would not have offered to hire me to retrieve her money.

And it had to be me, or someone like me, because the sort of business she and I conducted—the same business she'd conducted with this Nathan Frankel—was against the law. I had never declared any of the foreign money I had brought with me to Israel, and I highly doubted she was paying any taxes on the income she derived from her money changing. Tova Wasserman could not go to the police. She had to go outside the law for restitution.

I said, "Is there any chance that this was an innocent mistake on Frankel's part? That he thought the money he brought you was genuine?"

She shook her head resolutely. "None. When I learned the money was fake, I ran his visit through my mind. Every second of it. He played me from the moment he walked in. A real charmer that one is, a sweet talker. Full of compliments, all of them said with the straightest of faces. He didn't look it, but he was working hard at getting on my good side the whole time he was here. He knew what to say to get me to trust him. He made a fool out of me."

She said all this through gritted teeth, and I got the sense that as much as she hated being swindled out of money, it was the humiliation of being duped that hurt her the most.

"I need you to understand something," I said. "I may need to get rough with him. I need to know that you're okay with that."

Mrs. Wasserman said nothing for a few seconds. Then slowly, as if awakening from hibernation, her thin lips twitched, then started to stretch, then gradually curved upward into a smile that went well with the cold that was seeping in through the windows.

"Adam," she said, using my given name for the first time in our acquaintance and still smiling her cruel, frosty smile, "not only am I okay with it, I hope very much that you hurt him badly."

I looked at her for a long moment and did not like what I saw. There was a predatory edge to the curl of her lips, a bloodthirsty shine to her sharp, brilliant white teeth. Above the smile, her eyes had narrowed to slits of blue steel. The way her face was set reminded me of people I long wanted to forget and knew I never would. Camp guards in uniforms and high boots, with cruel eyes and vicious grins, with a gaping black hole where their heart and conscience and morality should have been. People without pity or mercy, who relished causing pain and death.

I laid the thirty extra liras she had given me on the

table beside the plate of cookies and said, "Find someone else. I'm not interested."

Mrs. Wasserman's icy smile melted off her face. Her eyes turned bigger than I had ever seen them.

"What? Why?"

"Because I'm not in the beating-people-up business. It seems to me like what you're really after is for Nathan Frankel to get a broken arm or a busted kneecap. That's not what I do."

"But you said—"

"I said it may come to that, but it's not certain. If I manage to persuade him to give back what he stole from you, no violence would be necessary. Understand?"

Mrs. Wasserman's eyes contracted back to their normal size. She gave me a long, piercing look. "Is this about money? Would it change your mind if I gave you, say, twenty liras more?"

"No," I said flatly. "It would not."

Mrs. Wasserman pursed her lips, making her mouth look like an old, wrinkly apple. She was still giving me that penetrating look and was giving no indication as to what conclusions she reached.

"Very well," she said at length. "Find Frankel. Get my money back. That's the important thing. If you end up doing more, well—" her smile reappeared, sending the living room temperature plummeting "—make sure you tell me about it. In detail."

Chapter 4

Before I left her apartment, Mrs. Wasserman forced four more cookies on me. Out on the street, I stopped beside a trash can, meaning to throw them away, but halted with my hand poised over the mouth of the can. The number tattooed on my left forearm itched and I found myself unable to uncurl my fingers and let the cookies drop. Eating them would give me no pleasure, but they were still food. And I could not throw away food.

With a sigh of exasperation, I shoved the rock-hard cookies in the side pocket of my coat and stomped south on Ben Yehuda Street. It had rained that morning for two hours straight, and the sidewalks and road were slick and wet. People walked about encased in coats or heavy jackets, furled umbrellas at the ready. The air smelled clean and fresh and damp. The trees lining the street were naked of leaves and had been turned a darker shade of brown by the rain. The cold was persistent, with sharp teeth that tried to gnaw through my clothes.

Feeble sunlight slanted down like an afterthought, and the white stone buildings of Tel Aviv looked gray. The city had been founded just forty-two years earlier, but on that January day it seemed older, worn out.

Starting south, I liberated a cigarette from the pack I carried in my pocket. The wind had not abated, so I ducked into a doorway to light up. The smoke warmed me up some, but I could have done with an extra layer of clothing.

As I smoked, the image of Mrs. Wasserman smiling her icy smile popped up in my head. My skin crawled and I wondered whether I had made a mistake in taking this assignment on. By the time I'd smoked my cigarette down to a nub and flicked the remains into the street, I'd convinced myself that I hadn't. True, Mrs. Wasserman was much too keen on tasting Nathan Frankel's blood, but she'd seemed to accept it when I told her I would only resort to violence if I had to. And it was also true that she had been wronged and deserved to get her money back. Besides, if I turned her down, she would simply find someone else to take my place, and that someone was unlikely to have my scruples. Indeed, he might turn out to be similar to those men Mrs. Wasserman's smile reminded me of—a person who found pleasure in hurting others.

And there was the question of money. I had some socked away, but it wasn't as if I were rolling in it. Paying assignments did not come to me often. I tried hard not to decline those that did.

My mind made up, I caught a bus that ferried me all the way to Carmelit Street, then walked a block north to Daniel Street. Mrs. Wasserman had given me the exact address of Zalman Alphon's store and I found it without trouble, tucked between an insurance agency and a bicycle repair shop.

It was a small square space, with shelves on either side and a counter at the back. The sort of setup that invited petty theft, as it was easy to step inside, grab some pencils or staples off a shelf, and make your escape before the proprietor had time to react. But the layout made sense if where Alphon kept his most lucrative merchandise was not on the shelves but in the back of the shop.

Behind the counter was a closed door and, recalling what Mrs. Wasserman had told me about Alphon's involvement in the black market, I guessed it opened on where he kept his illicit goods. Ever since 1949, when the government enacted the rationing system, hundreds of citizens had become black-market vendors, selling anything that was restricted—meat, fish, butter, eggs, coffee, cooking oil, and even non-edible items such as quality soap. The government tried to crack down on the black market, but it was fighting a losing battle. Too many people were involved in it—as sellers or buyers or both— and among them were politicians, policemen, and the elite of society. Many black-market vendors were small-business owners such as Zalman Alphon, and some of them made more money selling contraband than they did with their legitimate enterprises.

The man behind the counter was bald, forty or thereabouts, and could have stood to lose fifteen pounds. The fringe of hair that he had left was as black as tar, and he wore it long and had combed some of it over his shining pate. He had a well-fed face that was in the beginning stages of acquiring a second chin. A bristly mustache monopolized the space between his flat upper lip and fleshy nose. He had on a buttoned white shirt with suspenders that were drawn too tight atop his shoulders. A brown coat hung from a nail on the wall behind him. He had been filling a fountain pen when I walked in, and now he set it aside and gave me a welcoming smile.

"Good day," he said. "Foul weather, isn't it?"

"I like it," I said. "Washes the dust off the streets."

He nodded a couple of times as if I had voiced a profound wisdom. "Got a point there, I'll give you that."

I got the impression that he would have agreed with almost anything I said. He likely thought it was good for business to make the customer feel that they were of the same mind, regardless of what that mind happened to be.

"If you're looking for notebooks for the kids, I got some new ones on that shelf there. Eighty pages each."

I felt the old familiar pang that came whenever someone mentioned children. My daughters would never go to school. My daughters would never do anything again. I kept the pain from showing on my face. Doing so used to be hard, but after almost seven years of practice, it was becoming second nature.

"I don't have children," I said, grabbing a pocket notebook and a couple of pencils. I laid them on the counter. "Just these. And I understand you may have some sugar as well."

His eyebrows drew closer together as he eyed me with suspicion. He had small eyes the color of pine and he blinked rather rapidly as he took my measure.

"I can spare a spoonful or two, I suppose," he said cautiously.

"According to what I heard, you may be willing to part with a bit more."

"Where did you hear that?"

"Does it matter?"

"It may. It may, indeed."

"Tova Wasserman," I said.

His face relaxed and he let out a chuckle. "I've known the old battle-ax for nearly two years and you're the first person she ever referred to me." He offered his hand. "Zalman Alphon."

I shook it. "Adam Lapid."

"How much sugar do you need, Adam?"

"What's the going rate for a pound?"

He shook his head with grave sadness. "Alas, sugar is hard to come by these days. I'm almost ashamed to say how much I have to charge just to make it worth my while."

I almost smiled. The crafty bastard could have done with acting lessons. The words were right, but they were as transparent as a windowpane. He knew his asking price would likely prove painful and was aiming to make it seem like he shared some of the hurt.

"Times are hard for everyone," I said. "We all have to make sacrifices. I'm sure your prices are fair."

Alphon nodded solemnly and named a price. It was actually not too bad. High, of course, but not over the top. We haggled a bit, and he brought it down a notch. "I doubt I'm even making a profit at this price, but since this is our first business transaction…" He told me it would take a minute and instructed me to give him a shout if anyone happened to walk in the store while he was in the back. Then he opened the door behind the counter and disappeared.

No one came in while he was gone. He reappeared with a small cloth bag in one hand and a teaspoon in the other. He dipped the spoon in the bag and held it out to me. "Want a taste?"

I took the spoon and put it in my mouth. It was sugar all right.

"Very good," I said.

He smiled. "My stuff's the best. All my customers say so. That's why they keep coming back."

He looped a rubber band around the neck of the bag and gestured expansively at the notebook and pencils on the counter. "No charge for these. Call it a nice-to-get-to-know-you present."

I told him he was a very generous man. He beamed.

"Anything else? I got some coffee I could make you a good price on. It's the real stuff, not the chicory crap the government rations out. You drink coffee?"

"Maybe another time. What I would like is some information."

He raised both eyebrows but said nothing.

"I'm looking for Nathan Frankel. I understand you know him."

The eyebrows came down and his eyes filled with apprehension. "You're not a cop, are you? Tell me you're not a cop."

"No," I said.

"Because you sort of look like one, anyone ever tell you that? I thought so the minute you walked in. But Tova Wasserman would not have given my name to a cop. No matter how much they squeezed her."

"I'm not a cop."

"Then what do you want with Nathan?"

"To talk to him."

"What about?" Alphon said, but then he held up a hand and added, "Forget it. I don't want to know." He looked away and then back at me. He was blinking rapidly again. "Listen, I don't want to get in the middle of anything. I mean, what business is it of mine what goes on between you and Nathan? I barely know him, and you I met for the first time today."

"You know him well enough to have given him Tova Wasserman's name."

"Is that what this is about? Did he do something to ruffle the old bird's feathers?"

"I thought you didn't want to know."

"You're right, I don't." He nibbled on his mustache for a few seconds. "Listen, I know Nathan because he buys from me occasionally, and I like him well enough. He's a really nice guy. So when one day he tells me he's got some dollars and asks me if I know anyone who can exchange them, I tell him to go see Tova Wasserman."

"This was when?"

Alphon scratched his naked scalp, flaking off tiny bits of dead skin. "Two, three weeks ago. I don't remember exactly when. What I do remember is once I tell him

33

about Mrs. Wasserman, he starts blasting me with questions: How old is she? Where is she from? What is she like? Etcetera, etcetera. Finally I ask him why the hell he wants to know all this, and he just smiles and says he's a curious guy. I gotta admit I thought it was a bit strange, him asking me all those questions, but I soon forgot about it. With all I got on my mind, it's not surprising."

"Did he say where he got the dollars?"

"An uncle or cousin sent it to him from New York or some place. Not that I asked, he just came out and told me."

"How long have you known him?"

"He first came in…four, five months ago, something like that. Bought some coffee and butter."

"How often does he come in?"

"Every once in a while. Nothing you can set your watch by."

"Know where he lives?"

Alphon thought for a moment, then said he didn't think Frankel had ever mentioned an address.

"How about where he works?"

He hesitated, looking away and rubbing his mustache with a forefinger.

"What is it, Zalman?"

He sighed. "I don't know what he does, okay? But I got the impression that whatever it is, it's not one hundred percent kosher."

"You mean he's a criminal?"

He twisted his lips as though he didn't like the sound of the word. "In this day and age, who isn't? This bag of sugar I sold you makes criminals of you and me both."

"But you think he's involved in something more serious than that, don't you?"

Again Alphon hesitated. Finally he nodded.

"What makes you think that? Something he said, something he did? What, he wears clothes he shouldn't be able to afford? He acts like a tough guy?"

"No. Nothing like that. I told you, Nathan's a nice guy, and I could be all wrong about him. But what happened was that on the same day I told him to go see Mrs. Wasserman, he invited me to join him and some friends of his at a card game. I went, and one of them had a face that looked like it belonged on a most wanted poster. You know the kind I mean?"

I nodded.

"So that's the only time I went." He rubbed his mustache again. "Which was probably smart, since I lost four liras that night."

"So it's a regular thing, the card game?"

"That's what Nathan said. A weekly game. Every Thursday."

Today was Wednesday, January 3, 1951. Tomorrow, then. I had a lead on where Nathan Frankel would be tomorrow.

I asked him where the card game was held and he gave me an address in Jaffa, close to the port. Then I asked him to describe Frankel to me.

What I heard was all good. The man I was after was shorter than me by five or six inches and, according to Alphon, did not possess a formidable physique. Not the sort of person who could punch holes through you, or absorb hit after hit without going down. Of course, these assumptions could prove catastrophically wrong. Experience had taught me that looks could be deceiving and that a small man with a scrapper's attitude and the willingness to fight dirty might prove to be more than a match for someone twice his size. And, of course, put a knife or a gun in the hand of any man and size ceases to matter all that much. But, playing the percentages, I was still gratified to learn I was not about to face off with a giant.

I got some money out of my pocket and handed it to Alphon. "Thank you, Zalman. You've been most helpful."

I took the pencils, notebook, and bag of sugar, and was turning toward the door when he spoke.

"You're not going to tell Nathan I told you where to find him, are you?"

"No, I won't. You have my word."

He let out some air.

"And if he happens to drop by today or tomorrow," I said, "be sure not to mention me."

He smiled a nervous smile. "That you can count on." The smile gave way to a frown. "You sure you're not a cop?"

I nodded with a grin. "Not anymore I'm not."

Chapter 5

The following night, after an uneventful day and dinner at Greta's Café, I went home to prepare for my potential encounter with Nathan Frankel.

My home was a third-floor one-bedroom apartment on Hamaccabi Street that had a kitchen, bathroom, and balcony that were little larger than alcoves. The one room served as bedroom, living room, and dining room. The furniture was well-used and mismatched and had come from diverse sources. One chair I'd found dumped in an alley, the other I bought from a restaurant that was going out of business. The nightstand and reading lamp were given me by a former client in lieu of cash payment.

The bed was in the apartment when I moved in. According to my landlord, four previous tenants had slept and dreamed and perhaps loved in it. The condition of the mattress lent credence to his claim—it was lumpy in places and excessively soft in others—and some of the springs creaked like an old man's joints when I shifted on the sheets. I wasn't complaining, though. Compared to other places I'd slept in, that bed was fit for a king.

I'd purchased the closet from an Arab in Jaffa. He had lugged it all the way to Hamaccabi Street on a donkey cart and together we hauled it up the stairs to the third floor and into my apartment. He'd lost a son fighting against us Jews in Israel's War of Independence, and he asked me where I'd fought in the war. A look of relief passed over his face when he learned I'd not been involved in any fighting in Jaffa. I suppose the money he got from me felt less tainted that way.

Most of the closet was empty. I only made use of two of the five shelves, and the hanging rod had just four hangers dangling from it. Below the rod, on the floor of the closet, lay my spare sheets, pillow cases, and summer blanket. Beneath these, under a false bottom I'd constructed myself, I kept my most valuable possessions.

They lay in a wooden box with a metal clasp and I never brought them out without first closing the shutters across my windows and balcony door so no one would be able to peek inside and see what I had hidden.

I proceeded to do so now, plunging the room into pitch darkness. I flicked on the light switch and the overhead bare bulb came to life, casting its yellowish illumination over the room. I put my linen on the floor, set the false bottom aside, and drew out the box. I placed it on my lap and opened it.

Most of the items the box contained I had brought with me from Germany. These I'd taken from the Nazi officers and officials I killed after I'd recovered from my time in Auschwitz and Buchenwald. Among them were a Luger pistol and ammunition, a finely crafted folding hunting knife with a swastika stamped into its handle, and a slim stack of foreign currency that I had taken as loot.

Since my arrival in Israel in 1947, my original cash

hoard had dwindled considerably. A few months ago, however, while working on a case, I had the occasion to add seven hundred dollars to my stash. Some of the American money had since gone to buy real coffee, butter, sardines, and other rationed items that were sold for steep prices by vendors such as Zalman Alphon. A further hundred I'd taken with me the day before to exchange with Mrs. Wasserman.

I was far from well-off, but I had enough to get by for a while, even if nothing new came in. I lived alone, and I had learned the hard way how to make do with little, so my expenses were low.

The only thing I spent real money on was the food I purchased on the black market. I had a weakness for food—in terms of both quality and quantity. I had known starvation, and I had eaten my share of rotten, rancid, foul food. Experience had taught me that having the latter was better than suffering the former. It also explained why I had trouble discarding anything edible and why I was willing to part with a good deal of money to have something better than the very basic and meager rations the government allotted each citizen. My attitude toward food troubled me at times, but I'd come to accept it as something that was simply part of the man Auschwitz had made of me.

My possessions were few. I owned two pairs of shoes; four shirts; three pairs of pants; enough socks, underwear, and undershirts to fill half a shelf in the closet; two hats; a pair of gloves; two jackets; and one coat. None of the clothes were the sort tailors would be falling over themselves to claim as their handiwork.

My kitchen cupboards housed four plates; two soup bowls; two cups; three glasses, two tall and one short; a frying pan; and a pair of cooking pots, one of which was missing a handle. I also owned a large metal sieve, but I couldn't remember the last time I'd made use of it.

The cutlery in the drawer beneath the sink came from numerous sets of unknown origin and some of it was speckled with stains that I had failed to scrub off. The icebox squatted in a corner of the kitchen like an old, immovable rock; and like the rock that Moses was said to have struck with his staff, it leaked water, though not so much for me to get too bothered about it.

My bedroom walls were adorned by nothing but two empty nails that had been hammered there by some previous lodger. Pictures must have hung on them once, and I sometimes let my imagination paint them in my mind. But I had never bought new pictures of my own, so the nails stood out, small and black and forlorn, like an empty house hoping to be filled.

I looked at the blank walls and asked myself whether it was time to find a picture or two. Truth be told, I never had a problem with the naked white walls, but maybe having a couple of pictures would make the room look a little less like a cell and more like a home.

Shaking my head to banish my foolish thoughts, I lowered my eyes to my box of valuables, my gaze lingering on the Luger. It had sharp, crude lines, and it glistened darkly under the light from the ceiling bulb. All guns are made for inflicting harm, but the Luger looked especially malevolent, like it wasn't simply an inanimate object but one endowed with an evil spirit. Or maybe I was imagining it. Maybe it was the fact that this was a German gun, a favorite among those who had tormented me and murdered my family, that made me see things that weren't there.

Should I take the gun with me tonight? I was not about to go unarmed, that was for sure. Nathan Frankel might end up being as nice a guy as Alphon had said he was, but he was also a criminal. He was unlikely to look kindly on my demanding that he give back the money he'd stolen from Mrs. Wasserman. There was a good chance he would resist with force, in which case Mrs. Wasserman might end up getting her wish, because whether he wanted to or not, he was going to return her money.

Normally, I would have taken the knife and left the Luger behind. The knife was the safer weapon. It was easier to control the sort of damage you did to your opponent with a knife, and it was easier to keep the police out of a knife fight than a shooting. The knife was also lighter, less bulky, and easier to carry than the Luger. On this occasion, though, I decided to bring the Luger along. If what Alphon had told me was true, it was possible Frankel would not be the only criminal in that card game. I could handle myself well enough in a one-on-one fight; going against multiple opponents was another matter. I might need to threaten them off, and the Luger was the perfect tool for that.

Even though I knew the gun was loaded, I rechecked

the magazine. Full and ready to go. I stuck the Luger in the waistband of my pants, put the folding knife in my pocket, returned the box to its hidey-hole, set the false bottom, and stacked my linen on top of it.

I took a drink of water, and then I headed out.

Chapter 6

I took a bus that let me out on Shalma Road and headed west toward the sea. Five minutes later, just as I got to Hashaon Square, with the clock tower at its center, lightning pierced the sky and thunder boomed and rain began falling hard. I turned my collar up, lowered my head to keep water out of my eyes, and quickened my step.

By the time I found the bar where Zalman Alphon had played cards with Nathan Frankel, my hair was matted to my scalp, my pants were drenched, and water had seeped past my collar and was making its way down my back. To add insult to injury, I managed to step into a puddle and turn my left shoe into a pond. In the paper that morning, the forecast had called for no precipitation that night. I wondered how many angry letters the editor would be getting this week. I hoped he would drown in them.

The bar took up the ground floor of a two-story building a stone's throw away from the Port of Jaffa. The upper floor had a boarded-up window facing the street and bullet holes in its facade, remnants of the fighting that had taken place in Jaffa during the War of Independence.

The front door opened on a rectangular space with half a dozen rickety tables and a bar on the left. Two of the tables were taken by stoop-shouldered, grim-faced men who seemed intent on their beers and gloomy thoughts. There were mud tracks on the floor and grime on the window. It was one of those places where the customers didn't care much about aesthetics or hygiene.

The place carried the scents of damp clothes, aged cigarette smoke, and fish in varying degrees of freshness. Probably the haunt of the fishermen who had their boats moored at nearby piers.

Behind the bar stood a tall bearded man with a toothpick in his mouth. He eyed me wordlessly while I scanned the faces of the patrons. All were much too old to be Nathan Frankel.

I took off my swamped shoe, shook water out of it, and put it back on. Still wet, but it would have to do. I wiped my face, crossed over to the bar, and bid the bartender good evening. He nodded in return, shifted the toothpick from one side of his mouth to the other, and said, "Got a little wet there, I see."

"A little," I said. "It'll save me having to wash my clothes."

He nodded again. Maybe he appreciated my ability to see the good side of a bad situation. Or maybe he just liked moving his head up and down.

He said, "First time I see you around here."

"That's right. Heard good things about the place."

His eyebrows shot up. He was clearly shocked by the very notion that someone would lavish praise on his workplace. "Yeah, who from?"

"Nathan Frankel."

"You a friend of Nathan?"

"That's right."

He smiled. His teeth weren't much to look at, but it was still a nice enough smile. "Name's Fyodor."

"Adam."

He asked me what I'd have, and I said a beer would do nicely. He filled up a tall glass and set it on the bar. I let it sit. If I could avoid consuming anything this place served, so much the better.

"Nathan around?" I asked. "He told me there was a card game here tonight."

Fyodor nodded again. "Up the stairs." He gestured with his chin toward a closed door set in the rear wall. I paid for the beer and took it with me.

The door was made of wood that was flaking around the edges. Beyond rose a staircase, down which flowed the sound of male chatter and a wedge of yellow light. I left the beer on the lowest step and started climbing.

I mounted the stairs slowly, shifting the Luger from my waistband to my jacket pocket, my hand locked around the grip. My skin started tingling and I got to thinking that I was playing this all wrong.

I was acting with unwarranted haste. I didn't have to barge in on their game like this. It was asking for trouble. I could head back down, take a table, and pretend to nurse my beer until Frankel and his friends called it a night. Then I might be able to talk to him alone.

Two reasons made me keep climbing those steps, one

infantile and one rational. The infantile one was that the card game might go on for hours, and I was wet and cold. I wanted to get this over with so I could go home and dry off.

The rational reason was that if I stayed below, Fyodor might start wondering why I wasn't heading upstairs to meet my good friend Nathan. He might decide that the prudent thing for him to do was to go warn him, and that was the one thing I wanted least of all. If I had one advantage, it was that Nathan Frankel did not know I was coming.

At the top of the stairs stood an open door and past it stretched a long room with a painted floor in alternating red and green squares. In the middle of the room was a large round table. Three men sat around it on straight-back chairs. On the table were cards, cash, ashtrays, glasses, and four bottles of alcohol in various stages of consumption. Above the table hung a glaring bare bulb on a long cord. Smoke drifted lazily around it like a moving wreath.

It didn't take long for one of the men to notice me. He was stocky with a wide, square face and thick scar tissue over his close-set eyes. His nose had been busted multiple times and had been set inexpertly at least once. He had the look of a brute. Not smart but able and willing to employ his fists.

"Hey," he said—not to me, but to alert the others to my presence.

The other two men turned their heads. One of them said, "You made a wrong turn, pal. This is a private game.

If you're looking for the john, it's down the stairs and out in back."

He had short ginger hair and a mean, pasty face that shone sickly under the light. Freckles dotted his cheeks and nose, and his mouth was a cruel slash of pink. The only part of him that wasn't ugly were his eyes, which were the color of dewy grass. He held a cigarette between two fingers and his raspy voice brought to mind a snake slithering through dry straw.

"I'm here to see Nathan Frankel," I said, looking straight at the third man. Of the three, he was the only one who matched the description given me by Zalman Alphon. He was staring back at me funny, his eyes wide and unblinking.

The ginger-haired man, suddenly on edge, let his cigarette drop to the floor and slowly pushed his chair back from the table. "He's got something, Dov. Something in his pocket."

The brute squinted at me. His shoulders tensed and he slid his hands off the table. I could no longer see them, but they weren't keeping still. They were inching toward something. A gun of his own?

"What've you got there?" said the ginger-haired man. "Take your hand out slowly and show us."

I was ten feet away from the table. Frankel was the closest, the other two farther away and spread out on either side. If more than one of them had a gun, I would have to shoot fast, without aiming, and hope that my instincts proved superior to theirs.

I pressed the Luger into the front of the pocket so its

outline was unmistakable. I pointed the muzzle at Dov. "Don't you move a muscle or you'll get a fist-sized hole in your chest." He froze, his nostrils flaring. His eyes jumped to the ginger-haired man, asking for instructions. Obviously, he was the one calling the shots.

"I don't want trouble," I said, hoping to defuse the situation.

"You already got it," the ginger-haired man said. "More than you can handle. Smartest thing you can do is take out your gun and toss it over here."

I made myself smile, acting all calm and self-assured. "I'll hang on to it, thank you. And you stay still. My finger's on the trigger. Make me nervous and it just might twitch."

He shrugged. "You're making a mistake. A big mistake." He sounded almost sorry for me, but the way his eyes were shooting poisoned arrows at my head belied his tone. I had run into his kind before. Like a wild animal, he was fiercely territorial. I had encroached on his turf, so I had to pay.

Licking his lips, he shifted a little in his chair. His hands hung loosely at his sides, close to his jacket pockets. Did one of them contain a gun? Or maybe it was stuck in his belt, at his hip. Keeping my eyes on the three of them wasn't easy. If one of them moved fast when my attention was focused on another, he would get me.

The ginger-haired man said, "You know this guy, Nathan?"

Frankel didn't answer, didn't even look like he'd heard the question. He sat motionless, an odd expression on his face, like he'd seen something that couldn't possibly be real.

The ginger-haired man frowned. He raised his voice. "Nathan? Nathan, do you—"

"Yes," Frankel said in a faraway voice. "Yes, I know him."

What was he talking about? I had never met him before. I hadn't even heard his name until I was hired to find him. But he sounded both sure and sincere. And awed. But why would that be?

"What the hell does he want?" the ginger-haired man said.

"I don't know," Frankel said. He kept his eyes on my face, his expression still one of disbelief. He was the only person in that room who didn't look nervous or scared. Not one bit.

"Why are you here?" he asked me.

"Tova Wasserman sent me. She wants her money back."

Just like that, Frankel snapped out of his daze, his expression of wonder vanishing, to be replaced by one of abject fear. Only I saw it, as he had his back to his associates, and I would have missed it had I blinked at the wrong time, since it was gone just as fast as it appeared.

Then he threw back his head and laughed. He made it sound natural, and if I hadn't seen that flash of fear, I would have believed he was truly amused. But no, he was still terrified. But of what? Me? Then why the fake laugh?

He turned to his comrades, a broad grin on his face. "A word of advice: don't ever take money from a girl you jilted. You might get a visit from this guy." He jabbed a thumb in my direction.

Dov, the square-faced brute, grinned back. The ginger-haired guy did not show even a hint of a smile. He was watching Nathan Frankel intently, his expression inscrutable.

Frankel raised his hands palms out. "Everyone relax, all right? This is my mess." He turned to me. "You sure know how to make an entrance, I'll give you that. If ever I want to frighten someone to death, I'll be sure to give you a call. Now why don't you and I head downstairs to settle this matter in private?"

Why was he putting on such a show? It wasn't for my benefit, since I knew the truth. It was for his friends. He did not want them to know about Tova Wasserman.

But why? It was obvious these two were no virgins when it came to crime. Why would Frankel wish to hide how he'd tried to cheat Mrs. Wasserman? Maybe he wanted to spare himself the ridicule his buddies were likely to heap on him were they to discover he had failed to hoodwink an old widow.

"Well?" Frankel said. He sounded nonchalant, carefree, but his eyes were sending me a different message. They were pleading with me.

I did a quick mental calculation. I could force the issue right where I stood, but every second I stayed in that room was a second in which I was outnumbered three to one. Besides, I was curious. I wanted to know why Frankel had lied to his friends. I wanted to know why he thought he knew me.

"Fine," I said. "Let's go."

He clapped his hands once. "Great. Dov, Gregor, you guys wait for me. I'll be back shortly. And don't touch my money. I know how much there is." He paused, and in a more serious tone said to Gregor, "It's a personal matter. Let me handle it my way, okay?"

Gregor took his time before answering. He was mulling something over, and I got the distinct feeling I wouldn't like knowing what it was. Finally, he gave a tight-lipped smile and nodded his ginger head. "Okay, Nathan. You do what you have to do."

I went first, walking backwards down the stairs, facing up so Frankel wouldn't be able to attack me from behind, and also so neither of the other two could peek over the edge of the landing and shoot me in the back.

Down in the bar, I shut the door leading to the staircase and said, "What was all that theater for?"

Instead of answering, Frankel asked, "Are you here just for the money, or are you supposed to do more?"

So he'd guessed what Tova Wasserman would like to see done to him. A perceptive man.

"Just the money. Hand it over and I'll be out of your life."

"Not here," he said. "Follow me. There's a place close by where we can talk."

Chapter 7

He might have been stalling, but I didn't think so. I followed him out of the bar and onto the dark street. The rain had died. A chilly wind was blowing in from the sea. I knew I was still wet and cold, but I was feeling neither. Curiosity had overwhelmed all other sensations.

He led the way south, cutting through a number of narrow streets little bigger than alleyways, until he came to a stop outside a nondescript door and pushed it open.

We entered a small café, nearly deserted except for a single customer and a potbellied man in an apron, who broke into a smile at the sight of Frankel.

"Nathan," the aproned man said, "great to see you, boy. How've you been?"

He had a warm, welcoming voice, and his accent was distinctly Polish, indistinguishable from Frankel's.

They clasped hands and smacked each other's shoulders over the bar.

"I'm well, Misha," Frankel said. "Very well. Can I have the key to the back room? This man and I need to speak privately."

The back room contained one table large enough to sit

eight. Frankel gestured for me to sit and took another chair for himself. I watched him closely, my hand still on the gun in my pocket. I had to remind myself that he was a criminal because he looked nothing of the sort.

He had an open, frank face that inspired instant trust, the face of a man incapable of guile or subterfuge. With his fresh, rosy complexion, he could have passed as an innocent eighteen-year-old, though I could tell by his hazel eyes that he was significantly older than that. He was five ten and had a trim, athletic build. His hair was black and dense and wavy, a tad too long for a man, and his cheeks and chin showed not a hint of stubble. His features were masculine but delicate, a mix of the man and the boy, and I wondered whether women found him attractive and decided they probably did. He likely sparked within them not just sexual attraction but also that innate protective instinct that women seem to possess from birth.

While I had been studying him, I realized he had done the same to me. His eyes had traveled the length and breadth of my face. Some of the wonder that had overtaken him when he'd first laid eyes on me that night had returned. He seemed to be in the middle of an internal dialog in which his mind tried to reconcile what it believed with what it was witnessing.

Finally he took a deep breath, gave a tiny shake of his head, and smiled. The smile came easily and naturally and there was a beguiling quality to it, an invitation to intimacy. I could feel its effect on me as a tangible force. Yes, he was probably popular with the ladies, but men would also seek his company. For what Nathan Frankel possessed was that enviable quality of being liked without effort.

"First," he said, "let's dispense with the business at hand, shall we? How about I give you half of what I took from Tova Wasserman and you tell her you couldn't locate me?"

I shook my head. "The money isn't mine to take and it isn't yours to keep."

Oddly, he looked satisfied with my answer, like one of my schoolteachers had looked whenever I had answered a particularly difficult question correctly.

"Very well, then."

He reached inside his coat, and I said, "Slowly now, and no tricks. I have a nine-millimeter pointed at your heart."

"No tricks," he said. When his hand emerged, it was grasping a wallet. He opened it and drew out a thick wad of Israeli bills. He counted out a sum equal to what he'd taken from Tova Wasserman. It was nearly all the cash he had on him. "There it is. That's everything."

I gazed at him, puzzled. He did not seem to mind the fact that I was relieving him of the bulk of his money. This ran contrary to my experience with criminals. Most considered whatever they stole to be their rightful property. Try to get them to return even a small piece of it and they would fly into a rage.

But Frankel was not enraged. He was the picture of tranquility.

I counted the money myself. The sum was right, but

was the money real? I picked up a note and peered at it closely.

"I assure you these are authentic," he said.

I put the note down and inspected another. "Forgive me for not taking you at your word."

He shrugged and waited quietly until I finished my examination. I could find no fault with the banknotes he'd given me.

"You know," he said, "as I was pulling the wool over the old lady's eyes, I was struck by a premonition that this would not end well."

"It might not have," I said, slipping the money into my jacket, "but in the final analysis, you're no worse off than you were beforehand. You may consider yourself fortunate in that regard."

A strange melancholy invaded his eyes. So maybe he did care about losing the money after all.

He said, "In a way I do feel fortunate. It's not every day that one gets to see a miracle."

"What do you mean?"

He cocked his head to the left and smiled faintly. "You don't remember me, do you, Adam?"

"No, I don't. Have we ever met?"

"Not exactly. We've never spoken before tonight. But we have seen each other before. Or maybe I saw you, but you didn't see me."

He was making no sense. "I'm not following you. Where do you think you know me from?"

Instead of replying, he got to his feet and shucked off his coat. Then he undid the button of his left cuff, rolled up his shirtsleeve, and rotated his forearm so I could see it—his number tattoo. Branded in blue ink into his flesh, just like mine.

I gaped at it. He had been there, in Auschwitz. There was the indelible proof marked on his skin, a number more uniquely his own than his name. I raised my gaze to his face and scoured my memory for its likeness.

Face after face flashed through my mind, an endless procession of gaunt features with haunted eyes. How many had I seen during my imprisonment in Auschwitz? Thousands, perhaps tens of thousands of faces. Standing in morning roll call in the freezing Polish winter or marching to begin another day of backbreaking labor. Or shuffling to the barracks as darkness fell, struggling to put one foot ahead of the other, on the one hand longing for sleep, on the other fearing that this time your body would surrender in the night and you'd never wake up.

And there were also the public executions, the mad scramble for the trenches as air-raid sirens wailed, the soul-draining daily disposal of the bodies of those who had passed in the night. I never knew most of their names. With most I never exchanged a word. And no doubt my brain did not record all those I saw in that hell on earth called Auschwitz; there had been too many to remember every single one.

I peered at Frankel's face more closely than I had at the banknotes he'd given me. Despair washed over me. Suddenly, though I could not say why, it became vitally important that I recall him—not the free man sitting with me now in a café in Jaffa, but the prisoner who had been with me in Auschwitz and who remembered me from there.

With my heart pounding in my ears and the phantom scent of bodies being put to the torch clogging my nostrils, I delved in the nether reaches of my mind, where so many unwanted memories lurked. They lay in wait like hunting beasts for the opportunity to pounce with hungry jaws and sharp claws, to tear into me, to flood me with pain and guilt, and, above all else, to punish me for ever having attempted to banish them from my consciousness.

I rummaged through the dark corners of my memory, sifted through images of death and torment, but could not recall ever seeing Nathan Frankel before that night.

I tried to account for changes in his appearance. He would have been wearing a prisoner's uniform, not the well-fitting clothes he had on now. His body would be leaner, verging on skeletal, and the contours of his facial bones would be easy to make out through the paper-thin skin stretched tautly over them. The look in his eyes would also be different—a desolate, distant look filled with anguish and despair. But try as I might, I still could not place him.

Shaking my head, I felt an odd sense of shame and could not meet his eyes. "I'm sorry. I don't remember ever seeing you there."

He offered a comforting smile. "That's all right. I probably wouldn't have remembered you either if it weren't for what happened that day."

"What day?"

All of a sudden he seemed uncomfortable, as though

he regretted ever raising the subject. Then he sighed and made a vague gesture with his hand.

"The day you were whipped by that pockmarked Austrian son of a bitch."

My throat constricted and for a stretch of time no air made it through to my lungs. Blackness started creeping in at the edges of my vision. Light-headed and nauseated, I swallowed a mouthful of air, breaching the blockage in my throat. I did not remember Nathan Frankel, but the image of the Austrian guard who had whipped me was seared into my memory.

Frankel was right. The guard's cheeks had been pocked and pitted by some childhood disease. He had evil blue eyes and pale skin that flamed red in the frigid Polish winter days. He was one of those guards who took great pleasure in their dominance over other men. He enjoyed humiliating prisoners and sought out any opportunity to inflict pain on them. He did not require a reason, really, just to be in the right mood. One day, I had been unfortunate enough to draw his attention.

He ordered me to my knees and commanded me to remove my shirt, leaving my back bare. He had a whip; he carried it wherever he went, slapping it playfully against his thigh, knowing full well the terror it evoked in our hearts.

I remember thinking, as I braced myself for the pain, that I wasn't going to cry out, that I wasn't going to give him the pleasure of hearing me suffer.

That conviction lasted four lashes. Then I did cry out—howls of pain and agony that rose from the depths of me, that left my throat raw for days afterward.

I could not say how many times he lashed me. The memory of those moments was a dark blur. Nor could I tell by the scars on my back. There were so many and they weaved in and out of each other in such a manner that made it impossible to count them. But they numbered in the dozens.

When he grew bored, or when his arm began tiring, the guard cackled out a raucous laugh and called me a stinking Jew and spat at me. Then he walked off, whistling "The Blue Danube" by Strauss, pleased with his day's work. I was helped to my feet by some other prisoners and carried to the barracks. They laid me on my bunk and someone brought water to wash my back. And somehow, I don't know how, I found the strength to get up from my bunk in time for the next meal. If I hadn't, I would have died, as I doubted anyone would have brought me food. Not because the other prisoners were heartless, but simply because I was deemed unlikely to survive having been whipped so severely, so there was no point in wasting food on me.

"Hey." Frankel's voice brought me back to the present. "Adam, are you all right?"

I blinked a couple of times and ran a hand over my face. It came away damp with the sweat that had broken on my forehead. Frankel was peering at me with a worried expression on his face, and it came to me that while I had been mired in dark memories, he could have attacked me and I would not have been able to offer much resistance.

It took me a moment to summon the strength to speak. "You were there? You saw it?"

He nodded. "The whole dreadful thing. He must have whipped you fifty times, the stinking Nazi. You held up quite well at first, which might have prompted him to hit you harder. In the end, you just lay there, facedown in the mud, your back gashed and bleeding. I was sure you were dead. Nobody could survive that. Nobody. No way. And then you moved. It was a small thing, barely noticeable, like you'd been holding your breath till your lungs were fit to burst, and then air started coming out slowly.

"At first I was sure my eyes were playing tricks on me, but then you let out this muffled moan, like a bubble of hurt had just popped inside you. I shouted around, asking for someone who knew you to help me. Two guys came forward and together we hefted you to your bunk. Then I went and fetched some water to wash your back. I didn't think it would change anything—you were going to die that day, the next at the latest, long before any infection set in—but I figured it might ease your suffering a bit. You remember any of that?"

I rubbed my neck, where the small hairs were standing on end. "Partly. I remember being lifted up and how the water cooled my burning wounds. But I can't remember the faces of the men who took me to my bunk." I looked over at Nathan and a wave of warm affection washed over me. "I owe you a great deal. My life. If my wounds had gotten infected, I would have died for sure. Thank you."

He made a don't-mention-it gesture with his hand. "It

was nothing. What I can't understand is how you managed to survive. Your back—I'll never forget how it looked."

I let out a deep sigh. "Basically, it was like any other day in Auschwitz—you got up in the morning and tried to make it through to the next sunrise. You conserved your energy, ate what food they gave you, did what you needed to do to carry on living. That was one of the harder days. Not the hardest, but pretty close."

He didn't ask me what the hardest day had been, though I'm sure he was curious. There was an unspoken etiquette to these conversations. You didn't dig for information. You didn't take a shovel and start mining for nuggets of anguish. You let the other guy share what he wanted when he wanted, and you listened.

We sat in silence for a few minutes, each lost in his own past. Then I remembered the money and asked, "Why didn't you tell me all this before you gave me Mrs. Wasserman's money?"

He shrugged. "Because you'd've felt uncomfortable taking it and uncomfortable not taking it. I knew that when I offered you half to turn your back and walk away and you said no. You're a man of honor. It may be your own kind of honor, but you have it all the same. Besides, what I did for you back then, I didn't do for money or anything else. I'm no saint, as you're well aware—there's a chance to make some cash with little effort, I'll grab it. But I won't take a lira for what I did that day in that camp."

"Well, I owe you, Nathan. If you ever need anything…"

Again he waved me off. "The day after you got whipped, I was transferred to a different sub-camp. Otherwise, I would have sought you out, even though I was sure all I'd learn was that you'd died. What I did learn was your name. I made sure to remember it ever since. I figured there was a good chance that there would be no one else who would."

"I know what you mean. I carry around a few names like that, too."

Another wordless minute passed. I was going over my list of names in my head, and maybe he was doing the same with his own list. Then he said, "You know how I got through Auschwitz? By lying."

"Lying?"

"Yes. I became the best damn liar you ever met. I honed the skill in the ghetto at Dąbrowa Górnicza. What I discovered there was that if you got on the guards' good side, you could get by a bit more easily. So I would butter them up, tell them how good they looked in their uniform, make them feel bigger than they really were. I became their pet Jew, their favorite little animal. I encouraged it, because I figured they wouldn't harm their pet. I did the same thing in Auschwitz. It allowed me to scrounge a little extra food and clothes and it helped me stay alive. You think it was dishonorable, what I did?"

The answer came as automatically as reflex. "No. Anything to survive."

Nathan nodded his agreement to that precept. "The

thing is, I wouldn't be the man I am today if not for the ghetto and Auschwitz. Those places turned me into a criminal, and I've remained one ever since."

I thought of the man I had been before Auschwitz and the man I was today. I often doubted my parents would recognize who I had become. Apart from what time had altered, my face was the same, but my character and values had changed beyond recognition. I heard myself say, "It's not too late to choose another path."

He pondered this for a moment. "I think you're right," he said at length. "Maybe it's time."

Then he grinned, and it was like a ray of sunshine had pierced the dome of gloom that had settled around us.

"You know something? When I saw you tonight, I thought I'd either gone mad or that God had sent an angel with a message for me. Then I learned it was Mrs. Wasserman. Talk about a wrathful God."

I laughed. "She is something, isn't she?"

"One of a kind." He shook his head. "That face of hers. If she ever smiled in her life, it must have been before I was born."

I felt an icicle worm its way up my back, remembering Mrs. Wasserman's frosty smile.

"You should have picked someone else to put one over on, Nathan."

He didn't notice the shift in my mood. "Now you tell me. Before, I figured I'd have no trouble, her being so old. I never would have guessed she'd spot the money was fake, and even if she did, I never expected her to actually hire some muscle to get it back from me."

"She's not a woman who easily gives up what's hers. Not a person you want mad at you."

He grinned, mischief in his eyes. "I played her like a fiddle. I asked around beforehand, learned a bit about her. For instance, I learned she was born in Warsaw. Some Warsaw Jews tend to look down their noses at Jews from more rural parts of Poland, like where I came from. So I passed myself off as a Warsaw boy, listened raptly as she prattled on and on about her childhood, and nodded in all the right places when she groused about the new people swarming into Tel Aviv. I complimented her on her clothes, hair, furniture, just about everything I could think of. I even ate three of her cookies, for goodness' sake. She ever serve you any, Adam?"

"Every time I see her."

"So you know what they're like—rocks with a thin layer of flour around them." He shook his head again, still smiling. "I could barely get them down. But when I was there, I just smiled and told her what a marvelous baker she was, and she actually blushed—God strike me dead right now if she didn't. By then she would have bought anything I said."

"You sound pretty proud of yourself," I said and watched the smile on his lips shrink.

"Don't think badly of me, Adam. Yes, I earn my living outside the law, but I don't make a habit of targeting old people. It was a onetime thing. All right?"

His expression was earnest and the imploring look he gave me amplified the boyish side of his features. He looked incapable of uttering a falsehood. I recalled Mrs.

Wasserman saying what a charmer he was and that by his own admission he was a gifted liar. I told myself that his earnestness might be as fake as the dollars that had brought him and me to this room. But, for all that, I believed he was sincere.

"All right," I said. "If you don't go after old folk, what sort of crime do you do?"

"What have practically all the criminals in Israel got their hands in these days?"

"The black market."

Nathan smiled. "The government makes it easy to turn an illegal profit. It makes criminals of almost everyone."

Zalman Alphon had said a similar thing. Both he and Nathan were right.

"What do you sell?"

"It's best you don't know, Adam."

"Okay. But tell me, how did you come by the counterfeit bills?"

"I'll keep that bit to myself, as well, if it's all the same to you."

I shrugged. "Fine."

"If it sets your mind at ease, that was all the phony money I had and there won't be any more of it, either."

"I hope so. I wouldn't want to see you get in trouble."

He pursed his lips and looked down at his hands. "Don't you worry. I've learned my lesson."

A short while later he said, "I feel like we could talk for hours more, Adam, and I want to know everything that's happened to you since the liberation, but I got to head back or Gregor and Dov might start wondering where I've disappeared to."

"How did you end up friends with those two?"

"When you move in certain circles, you meet certain people."

"Dov looks like a thug."

"He is. He used to box. Don't ever be on the receiving end of his fist."

"And the other guy—Gregor?"

Nathan drew a long breath through his nose. "Gregor is a different breed. And now I must get going."

We left the café together, Nathan pausing midway to exchange a warm goodbye with the potbellied proprietor, and walked back to the bar where Dov and Gregor were waiting. Before we parted, I scribbled the address and phone number of Greta's Café on a page from my notebook, which I tore out and handed to him.

"I'm at this place practically every day. Come by, I'll buy you a cup of the best coffee in all of Tel Aviv and we'll talk some more."

He said he would, folded the paper, and put it in his pocket. He said goodbye and made to go, but then he stopped and turned back to me. "Could you do me a favor, Adam?"

"Didn't I say I owe you, Nathan? Whatever you need."

From his inside pocket he took out a small black box. "Could you hold on to this for me? Just for a few days."

He put it in my hand. I knew the sort of box it was. It had come from a jeweler.

"What is it?"

"A ring. An engagement ring."

"You're getting married?"

He smiled self-consciously. "If she'll have me. I haven't worked up the courage to ask yet."

"Who's the girl?"

"Her name is Tamara Granot. The loveliest, smartest, most adorable girl I've ever met."

"Why give this to me?"

His smile faded. "I have my reasons, all right? Let's leave it at that."

"Okay. Whatever you say."

"Give me that notebook, will you? And that pencil too."

He found an empty page and scrawled a few words on it. Then he returned the notebook to me.

"It's her address," he said. "If I don't see you in, let's say, a week's time, go there and give her the ring. Will you do that for me?"

I studied his face. He'd slipped on a mask of calm composure, but I could see something behind it. Despair? Fear?

"Are you in trouble, Nathan?" I asked.

"Don't you worry about me. I can take care of myself. Just say you'll do this favor for me."

"Of course I will. But what should I say to her when I give her the ring?"

"Just tell her I love her, though I suppose the ring says that already. But tell her all the same, and that I'm working on something and will come see her as soon as I can."

"Very well. But, Nathan, if you need help with

anything—and I do mean anything—you call me, you hear?"

"Didn't I tell you not to worry about me?" He grinned his boyish grin and the night around us turned a lot brighter. "I was in Auschwitz and made it out alive. I can handle anything."

He shook my hand, his left hand gripping my forearm. "See you soon, Adam."

"See you," I said, and watched him walk away and disappear into the bar where his colleagues waited.

Chapter 8

"And...?" Mrs. Wasserman asked me.

A minute before, I'd handed her the money Nathan had given me the previous night and she'd proceeded to count it, carefully checking each bill. She was still clutching the money in her gnarled fingers, much like a bird of prey holding its squirming dinner in its talons, as she looked at me expectantly.

"And nothing," I said. "All the money's there, isn't it?"

A muscle in her jaw twitched. "What I mean is, did you have to apply any pressure on Frankel in order to get it?"

As during our previous meeting, I was sitting on her bulky sofa, while she perched her gaunt frame on an uncomfortable-looking chair. At the center of the coffee table between us was a plate brimming with her rock-hard cookies, but so far she had not offered me any.

She was leaning a bit forward in her seat, her narrow eyes latched on my face. Her lined lips were parted slightly. She radiated an intense aura of eager anticipation.

I could have lied and told her what she wanted to hear. I doubt she would have checked up on me. It would have been the easier choice, I suppose, and the smarter one. It certainly would have made her happy. Perhaps she even would have offered me a bonus, and it wasn't like I couldn't use the extra cash. But something in her face made me opt for a different path. It was that bloodthirstiness again, that hunger to see Nathan hurt. It irritated me.

I put a smile on my face and said, "Fortunately, Mrs. Wasserman, I didn't have to lay a finger on him. Once I explained the situation, Frankel willingly handed your money back." I paused, then added, "He even asked me to tell you he apologizes for trying to trick you."

The instant that last bit came out of my mouth, I knew it was a mistake. It wasn't only untrue, it was also childish. I had said it because I knew it would get under her skin, and I could tell by the set of her mouth that it did. She sat perfectly still for a moment, her body held rigid with repressed fury, the bulging blue veins on the back of her hands pulsing erratically. The only sound was the crumpling of the banknotes as she tightened her grip on them.

Finally, she drew in a hissing breath and let it out through her sharp nose. Suddenly aware of her clenched fist, she unclasped her fingers and laid the money on the table between us and attempted to smooth the wrinkled bills with the palm of her hand. Then she raised her eyes back to me. The anger in them was torch hot, and I wasn't sure that all of it was directed at Nathan.

"It's not right, you know," she said, her tone carrying a keen edge of bitter accusation.

"What isn't?"

"He got off easy. Much too easy. He wasn't punished

at all for stealing from me."

"You got your money back, Mrs. Wasserman, isn't that what you wanted?"

Instead of answering my question, she said, "How much?"

"How much what?"

"How much for you to go back and finish the job, teach him a proper lesson? Something he isn't likely to ever forget. You must have a price. Everyone has a price. Fifty liras?"

I shook my head. "No."

"Hundred. Hundred and fifty. Two hundred."

She sounded desperate and seemed to be aware of it, as she clamped her lips together and made a visible effort to compose herself. She leaned back in her chair, loosening her tight shoulders, trying to appear casual.

"Well?" she demanded once she had regained control of herself.

I didn't answer straight away. Instead I took a few seconds to try to come up with something that would convince her to set aside her pride, to ignore the humiliation she felt, to let go of her rage.

A number of things came to mind, but none of them felt likely to have an effect on her. Finally, I settled on what I should have done to begin with—lie to her.

"Mrs. Wasserman, I know a thing or two about anger. And also about revenge. Believe me when I say that the latter doesn't make the former go away. It doesn't even make you feel any better about yourself or what was done to you. I understand that you're hurt and you wish to see

Nathan Frankel pay, but it would serve no purpose. You got your money back. Isn't that enough? When all is said and done, he failed in trying to steal from you. Let that be the end of it."

She kept her eyes fixed on mine all through this little speech and it was abundantly clear that not a single word I'd said had made any impact on her. There remained that hard, unyielding, simmering outrage within her. I could see its poisonous steam roiling in those slitted eyes of hers.

Her anger, I realized, was valuable to her. To give it up so soon would, in her mind, belittle what had been done to her.

Feeling an unexplained prickle of anxiety, I made another stab at mollifying her. Reaching into my pocket, I said, "Tell you what, Mrs. Wasserman, let me give you back the money you paid me to find Frankel. That way, it'll be as if you and he had never met."

Now I was the one who sounded desperate. I had my money in my palm, ready to count off thirty liras, when she gave a slashing wave of her hand.

"Put your money away, Mr. Lapid. You did a job for me, exactly as we agreed that you would. You've earned your payment."

Her tone left no room for discussion, so I did as she asked. Looking at her, I was glad to see that her expression had softened a bit—as far as her severe features would allow it to, anyway. Perhaps my offer at refunding her had taken the sting out of her rage. Or maybe my little speech had had a delayed effect on her.

Either way, I felt a relief that was as bewildering as the anxiety that had preceded it.

I doubted that her hatred of Nathan had been completely extinguished, but perhaps the worst of it was over and now it would cool with time till nothing but lukewarm coals of distant resentment were left.

And why shouldn't it be so? Mrs. Wasserman had lost nothing but a little money and pride. She could easily make more of the first and replenishing the second was a matter of personal decision more than anything else. I had not been so lucky. What I had lost, what had been taken from me, could never be returned or made up for. Tova Wasserman had no true need for revenge. For me, there had been no other choice.

"Thank you, Mrs. Wasserman," I said.

She gave a curt nod of acknowledgment and said in an even tone, "I appreciate you doing this service for me, Mr. Lapid. Now, unless you have some money to exchange, I do believe our business for the day is concluded."

I rose to my feet and neither of us said a word as she followed me to the door. We bid each other a perfunctory goodbye, and it was only after I had descended the stairs and stepped out onto the windswept sidewalk of Ben Yehuda Street that it occurred to me that this was the first visit I paid her in which Tova Wasserman had not offered me any of her cookies.

Two days later, I found Nathan dead in the street.

Chapter 9

"You think she killed him, Adam?" Greta asked when I finished my story.

"Not herself," I said.

"But she might have hired someone to do it."

"It's possible. I'd say it's even likely. After all, she did try to get me to physically hurt Nathan."

"Not to kill him, though."

"No, and maybe she never intended for things to go this far. Maybe she paid some goon to break Nathan's arm or put him in the hospital and things got out of hand. Maybe Nathan resisted and whoever she hired panicked and sliced him up."

Before me I could see Nathan's dead eyes and I recalled him saying how he could handle anything after surviving Auschwitz. The poor sap. I heaved a sigh and put both hands over my face.

When I took them down, Greta reached over and clasped my hand. "It's not your fault, Adam."

I said nothing.

"You don't even know that Mrs. Wasserman had anything to do with it. And even if she did, it would still not make it your fault."

She was right about the first part, but I wasn't too sure

about the second. If Mrs. Wasserman was indeed behind Nathan's murder, I couldn't see any way to avoid facing the fact that I might have prevented his death had I simply told her I had beat him up, or if I hadn't succumbed to the infantile urge of needling her by claiming he had sent his apologies to her.

I turned my head to stare out the window. Two cops hoisted a stretcher with Nathan's body on it and stashed it in the back of the "corpse wagon". A minute later it was gone, heading south to the morgue. The crowd started to drift off, but not before Inspector Leibowitz had a chat with each of them, his notebook at the ready. By the brevity of each conversation and by how little use Leibowitz made of his pen, I could tell that all of the spectators claimed to have seen nothing, heard nothing, and to know nothing. Maybe the police would have better luck when they canvassed the street, but I doubted it. If anyone did witness Nathan's murder or saw him fall in the street, wouldn't they have called the police before Greta and I did? Allenby Street was not a high-crime area. People here did not fear or hate the cops.

Outside, Leibowitz was walking to his police car. He opened the passenger door, but instead of sliding in, he turned and looked right at the window of Greta's Café. I couldn't make out his expression—not at that distance and at night—and I was glad he couldn't make out mine either. He got into the car and shut the door. Officer Elkin was already in the driver's seat. He pulled a U-turn and ten seconds later their headlights disappeared around a corner.

Greta was still working hard to persuade me I bore no guilt for Nathan's murder.

"Someone else might have killed him. He was a criminal. It's a professional risk, isn't it?"

She was right. It was.

"And you hardly knew the man," she went on saying. "He probably had other enemies. Someone he stole from, someone he cheated—there could be any number of such persons."

Again, she had a point, but the guilt that now gripped me did not abate.

What Greta was missing, purposely or not, was the fact that on the night he and I had spoken, Nathan had known he was in danger. Otherwise, why would he entrust me with the engagement ring? He had belittled the risk he was facing, saying he could handle anything that came his way, and he likely believed that he could. But, just to play it safe, he had given me the ring for safekeeping and instructed me as to what I should do with it if he did not come to reclaim it.

Had this danger been present before I barged in on that card game? Or did my unexpected presence somehow give birth to it?

I couldn't shake off the conviction that it was the latter that was true. Otherwise, wouldn't Nathan have found someone else to deposit the ring with?

It was possible that he knew no one he could trust with such a treasure—I hadn't opened the box, so I could not estimate how much the ring was worth, but it did carry a hefty emotional value if nothing else—so he had carried it with him for a while, until I came along. He didn't really know me either, but, due to our history, the connection between us was as powerful as that between siblings. And he had also tested me by offering half of Mrs. Wasserman's money for me to look the other way. So I might have entered his life at just the right moment.

But if he knew he was in danger, would he keep the ring in his pocket for any stretch of time? Wouldn't he have stashed it somewhere or simply gotten on with the business of proposing marriage?

Too many questions. No answers.

"Maybe one of his partners turned on him," I heard Greta say. "That's a common occurrence in the underworld, isn't it?"

It was. And I remembered that flash of fear I had detected in Nathan's eyes when I mentioned Tova Wasserman's name in the presence of Gregor and Dov. And he had reacted by lying about who she was and how he had come by her money. Was he afraid that they would do something worse than ridicule him?

Both Gregor and Dov were criminals. Dov was obviously prone to violence and Gregor was—how had Nathan put it?—a different breed. Whatever that meant, it was bad. Gregor had killed before, of that I was sure. I couldn't shake the certainty that if Gregor and Dov had found Nathan fit for killing, the seed of that decision had been planted by my barging in on their card game.

A bitter taste coated my tongue. Whichever way I looked at it, there was every chance that I was to blame for Nathan's death. I was not the one who had plunged the knife into his torso, but if I had done things differently, he would be alive at that moment.

He had saved my life and I had brought about his death.

Greta was saying, "However it happened, whoever killed him, you're not responsible, Adam. You mustn't torment yourself."

I squeezed her hand. "You're wonderful, Greta, do you know that? Absolutely wonderful."

She notched her head to one side, smiling tenderly. "I'm wasting my breath, aren't I?"

I returned her smile. "It doesn't matter."

"It doesn't? Why not?"

"Because whether he died because of me or not, it doesn't change what I have to do."

"Which is?"

"I'm going to find out who killed him, and I'm going to make sure they pay."

After Greta and I parted, I walked up Allenby Street, my eyes tracing the tiny drops of blood that dotted the sidewalk. I followed them all the way to the corner of Allenby and King George, where they petered out.

A dead end. Nathan might have come down King George Street, or from somewhere farther up on Allenby. He might have been stabbed on Sheinkin Street, which intersected Allenby less than twenty meters away, or on any other of a number of nearby side streets. Wherever it happened, his blood took its time soaking through his clothes before it began to drip, drip onto the pavement.

I wondered what went through Leibowitz's mind

when he saw that the blood trail gave him nothing. He probably expected nothing better.

I also asked myself why Nathan had not received help in the time between his stabbing and his collapse. Had he cried out for help and was ignored? Had he hammered on doors he passed by, but none was opened?

Back in my apartment, I walked over to the nightstand where the box Nathan had given me sat. I picked it up in my hand. It weighed next to nothing. Rings usually do. The wedding band I'd given my wife, Deborah, was as light as air. But it was worth my weight in gold to me and her.

What had happened to that ring?

Most likely, she was ordered to remove it before entering the gas chamber. Or maybe the ring was yanked off her finger after she lay naked and dead, my two daughters beside her. Then the ring, along with all the other valuables robbed from that week's bounty of dead Jews, would have been shipped back to Germany, into the coffers of the Third Reich.

It was also possible some guard or soldier fancied it and took it for himself. If so, at that very moment, it adorned the finger of some German housewife. Either way, it was lost to me forever. Just like my wife was. I stared at the box in my palm, hesitating. Finally, I set it back on the nightstand, unopened.

I stood at the open window, a cigarette burning between my lips. A cold wind from the north whisked away the smoke into the inky night sky. I watched it blow away and recalled thicker smoke rising from the chimney stacks of the crematoriums. All of a sudden, the taste of the cigarette became unbearable. I mashed it out against the windowsill.

I got undressed and turned on the shower. I let the warm jet pummel my head and back for several minutes. Despite being bone tired, I dreaded sleep. The nightmares tonight would be especially bad. I had roused too many bad memories and it would take time to bury them again in my subconscious.

But there was no escaping it. Sleep, like food, was imperative. Whether it gave you pleasure or not, you needed it to sustain life. It was very cold in my room with the winter air flowing in, but that would soon change. I shut the window and the balcony door so that no neighbor would be awakened by my nightmare-induced screams.

I lay on my back, staring at darkness, and began to recite my list of names. The names of dead men I remembered from Auschwitz. It wasn't a short list, but I always felt guilty that it wasn't longer. When I got to the end, I added one new name.

Nathan Frankel.

Then I closed my eyes and waited for the nightmares to come.

Chapter 10

I woke, shivering and sweating, on the wrong side of dawn. I groaned to my feet, staggered to the window, threw it open, and breathed in the frosty morning air. Goosebumps prickled my arms and chest. My head ached and my stomach roiled. Hugging myself against the chill, I continued breathing deeply, and, bit by murky bit, the black foggy remnants of my nightmares lifted.

It had been a bad night, worse than I had predicted. The dreams came in waves, without respite, scenes of pain and torment that I had long fought to consign to the farthest reaches of my subconscious.

The predawn cold felt good, refreshing. I rubbed my face and arms, feeling the blood course under my skin. I checked my watch. A little past four thirty. I couldn't dawdle. I had work to do. Work that, in retrospect, I should have seen to last night. Now I would have to hurry and hope I wasn't too late.

I grabbed two pieces of dark bread, slathered them with an uneven layer of butter, and took them with me as I left the apartment, walking briskly down the stairs and onto Hamaccabi Street.

Chewing as I walked, I headed uptown through the dark streets. This was the quietest time of day, both in the good parts of town and in the bad. These were the hours just before law-abiding citizens began their day and just after criminals ended theirs. When I was a policeman, I used to love these hours.

The air was still and cold. It nipped at my nostrils with each inhalation. I walked quickly and ate quickly, and by the time I crossed Dizengoff Square, the bread was all gone and the first cigarette of the day had taken its place.

From Dizengoff I took a right to Arlozorov Street, walking east. The fact that I was going to the home of a murder victim who had lived on a street named after a murder victim did not escape me. Haim Arlozorov, the prominent Zionist leader, was shot to death on the beach of Tel Aviv in 1933. His killers had never been identified. I swore to myself that this would not be the case with Nathan Frankel's murderer.

He lived on the fourth floor of a building just east of the corner of Arlozorov and Manger. On the ground floor was a photography studio, which specialized in wedding pictures. Before entering the building, I did a quick scan of the street. No one was out and about. Not a soul appeared to be watching me.

The lobby was small and clean. Each of the mailboxes was neatly labeled. Nathan had lived in apartment six. I peeked through the flap of his mailbox but could see nothing inside.

I climbed the stairs, sliding on a pair of woolen gloves. Around me, the building was quiet. No stirring feet, no baby crying, no kettle whistling, no dog barking a warning after catching my scent.

The fourth floor housed two apartments, one on either side of the staircase. I soft-toed to the door of apartment five and pressed my ear to it. All was silent within. The Zilbers—as the name on their door identified them—were likely still ensconced in their beds.

I crossed the landing to Nathan's apartment. Not everyone in Tel Aviv bothered locking their doors, and those who did placed too much confidence in them. Most doors could be gotten through, either by forcing the door itself or by picking or popping the lock. To do the latter, I had brought my knife along.

It was in my hand, my finger on the button, when I noticed that someone had beaten me to it. Up close, I could see the door was not quite shut. It hung with its latch only partly engaged, a filament of light showing in the paper-thin crack. Around the lock the wood was scored and gouged.

Who had forced the lock? The cops? I doubted it. They would likely have sought out the landlord and gotten his spare key. But maybe they couldn't locate him and felt it was urgent that they get a look at Nathan's apartment.

Or maybe it was someone else. Gregor and Dov or some other criminals. I didn't know all the criminals Nathan knew or associated with.

The biggest question was whether they were still in the apartment.

Holding my breath, I leaned toward that sliver of space between door and frame.

Not a rustle or a whisper.

Still, I pressed the release button on my knife. The blade twanged as it jumped and locked into place. Gripping the knife tightly in my right hand, I reached over with my left and pushed the door open.

A short hall lay beyond. A door on the left, two on the right, and another straight ahead. The latter was the only one that was closed. By the front door stood a naked coat hanger. Two jackets and a dark-gray fedora lay in a mess on the floor. Someone had stepped on the hat. It was crushed out of shape.

I closed the front door as softly as I could and silently counted to sixty. No one challenged me. When I got to sixty-one, I stepped over the clothes and made a quick tour of the apartment. First room on the right was the kitchen. Empty. Second room—bathroom, empty. Living room. Empty. By the final door I paused, suddenly jittery. I inhaled and exhaled, put my left hand on the handle, and burst inside, knife at the ready.

No one was there.

I hissed out a breath of relief, folded the knife, and deposited it in my pocket. Then I returned to the kitchen.

Someone had done a thorough job on it. All the drawers and cupboards hung open. So was the icebox. They'd left the ice compartment open, and much of the ice had melted into a pool of water on the floor.

Plates, pots, bowls, and pans stood on the counter, more orderly than I would have expected. Whoever had searched the room had done so with patience and caution. They did not want to make noise by breaking dishes.

The icebox contained an assortment of quality food. Meat, fish, cheese, eggs, and butter in larger quantities than any one man was supposed to have. Contraband. Black-market goods. I was surprised to see it here. Some of this stuff was as good as cash. A half-full bottle of milk stood on the bottom shelf. I twisted off the cap and took a whiff. It hadn't gone bad. In this weather it wouldn't have happened fast, but it was still an indication that whoever had tossed the place had done so recently. Right after Nathan was killed? Probably.

I swore quietly. If I had come here last night instead of going home to sleep, I might have caught the killer then and there. Now I would have to do it the hard way.

I checked each cupboard and drawer, even knelt to make sure nothing had been taped to the underside of anything. If Nathan had hidden something in the kitchen, the people who'd tossed the room now had it.

The bathroom was next. It was small. No tub, just a shower stall, a toilet, and a tiny sink with a mirror over it. A tin cup stood beside the faucet. A toothbrush would have looked at home in it, but the cup was empty. There was also no tube of toothpaste, no razor, no shaving cream. I doubted any intruder would have taken them. Had Nathan spent the night before his death somewhere else? Or perhaps more than one night? If so, where? With his would-be fiancée, Tamara Granot?

The bathroom window was shut, the air in the small room stale and lifeless. I left the window closed; the less noise seeped out the better. I crouched down, examined the underside of the sink, felt around the pipes, then took the mirror off its nail and checked behind it. Nothing.

The shower stall was dry. Empty apart from a much-used bar of soap.

Last came the toilet. I peered into the tank, found nothing, then ran my hand along the small space between the wall and toilet. No luck.

I crossed the hall and entered the living room. It had received a rougher treatment than the kitchen and bathroom. The sofa cushions were eviscerated. The back padding hung in slices. The rug was turned over and left in a crumpled roll. The grille cloth of the Philco radio was ripped to shreds. A large painting leaned against the wall under an empty nail, the canvas torn. Was all this damage done to facilitate the search or in order to vent some pent-up rage? If it were the latter, it had been done in a controlled manner. None of the furniture was busted or broken. Nothing was done that might make a racket.

I ran a meticulous search of the living room and found nothing of interest. No personal papers, no money or other valuables. An empty wineglass stood solitary watch on the dining table by the south window. There was no sign of the bottle.

What remained was the bedroom. There was barely enough space to move with the queen-sized bed and the closet crowding the cramped room. The pillow and blanket were slashed and gutted, down feathers littering the sheets and floor. The mattress had undergone a similar mistreatment. It lay crooked on the bed frame, parts of it hanging over the floor. Someone had lifted it to check underneath. It was probably pointless, but I did the same and came up empty.

Clothes were strewn on the bed and the little vacant floor space. More clothes than I owned, and pricier. The furniture was in better shape, too. Nathan hadn't been throwing money around, but he hadn't been hoarding it all either.

I peered under the bed. Nothing taped to the bottom, a little dust where the frame met the wall, where it was hard to reach with a broom or a mop. Otherwise, Nathan had kept his home clean.

The closet had been dragged away from the wall and no one had bothered pushing it back. I glanced anyway and saw nothing. I tapped the closet walls and bottom, listening closely for hollow sounds. Zilch.

The bedside table drawer had been yanked out and upended over the bed. Someone had rifled through the contents, leaving them spread out over the sheets. A box of matches, a pencil with its end chewed up, sleeping pills, a bus ticket to Ramat Gan, and four photographs.

The first showed two teenage boys with their arms around each other's shoulders. Both were grinning at the camera with the ignorant naiveté of youth. The older boy was Nathan Frankel, thirteen or fourteen years old; the other was a few years younger and looked so much like Nathan that he had to be his brother. How had Nathan managed to hold onto this photograph through his years in the camps? Or had he returned to his prewar home and found it there? I had no doubt as to what had become of the brother. Turning the picture over, I hoped to see the brother's name scribbled on the back, as I doubted there was now a living soul on this earth who remembered him. There was no name, just a date. August 18, 1939. Two weeks before the Germans invaded Poland and the world ended for Polish Jews.

I considered how much this photo must have meant to Nathan. It was probably more valuable than all his other worldly possessions combined. I knew I would gladly part with all I owned for just one picture of my family. All that remained of them were my memories.

The second photograph showed Nathan standing at the railing of a ship. He was older now, about twenty, and was thinner than he'd been when I met him. The smile on his face was as bright as the sun, but in his eyes I could detect the dark imprint of Auschwitz. Was this the ship that had brought him to Israel? Had he ever imagined his life might end as it did?

The remaining two pictures showed Nathan with a woman at his side. Only it wasn't the same woman. In fact, the two were nothing alike. The first was petite and pretty in an unassuming way. She had long mousy hair, unblemished skin, and brown eyes that gazed shyly at the camera. She and Nathan were sitting at a wooden table in a café. I didn't recognize the place. Nathan had an arm wrapped around her narrow shoulders and was beaming his usual grin.

The second woman was a different story. She was nearly Nathan's height, with a strong oval face, high cheekbones, and large liquid blue eyes. Her black hair curled seductively at the nape of her long neck. The stare she gave the camera was direct, unabashed, challenging.

Her smile was confident and relaxed. A striking woman, not classically beautiful, but definitely alluring. While she was looking at the camera, Nathan's eyes were directed at her. His adoration of her was unmistakable.

One of these women had to be Tamara Granot, the soon-to-be recipient of Nathan's ring. But who was the other one? The backs of the pictures provided no clues. Both were blank.

I took both photos, feeling a twinge of internal resistance as I slipped them into my pocket, well aware that I was crossing a line. Before, I had been guilty of nothing more than withholding information from the police. Now I had swiped evidence that might aid in their investigation. The first might be explained or excused. The second could not.

There was no helping it. While I could certainly memorize how each of the two women looked, a picture might come in handy if I needed someone else to identify them.

I pawed through the clothes on the floor. No money. Just a little lint in the pockets. Whoever had been to the apartment had taken all the cash—both real and counterfeit.

It was when I was going through the last shirt in the heap that I came upon the cap.

It had been rolled up inside the shirt and fell to the floor as I spread the shirt wide. Roughly circular in shape. Made up of rough, scratchy fabric. Blue and white stripes, smudged and stained in places. Ugly to behold and uglier still to remember.

An Auschwitz prisoner's cap.

For a long, breathless moment I simply stared at it, dumbfounded. Here was this artifact of another world, another planet, lying rumpled on a dead man's floor in Tel Aviv.

Why had he kept it? For what purpose? I had gotten rid of my prisoner's uniform the first chance I had, and I never wanted to lay eyes on it again. But Nathan had held on to his cap through six years of freedom. He had kept it close by, where he could at any moment gaze on it, feel it, and use it to arouse his memory.

I reached down a trembling hand and picked it up. My scalp tingled, a circle of prickling skin where my own cap had used to sit.

Against all reason, I brought the cap to my nose and sniffed. It had not been washed in a long time, perhaps not since Nathan had been liberated. It held an awful mix of smells, some of which might have been drawn from my imagination. Sweat, smoke, dust, fear. The stench of tens of thousands of dirty, lice-ridden men. The smells filled my nose and mouth and blocked my throat as if a sock had been stuffed down it.

I gagged, gasping for air, the cap slipping from my fingers. Staggering to my feet, I bumped into the bed, groped out a hand, found a wall, and just barely managed to stay upright. I wobbled out of the bedroom, coughing and sputtering, no air coming in, my face hot, scorching. Retching, I tottered down the hall to the bathroom, darkness closing in, and scrabbled for the toilet.

My shins thudded into the seat. I crumpled beside it,

pulled myself to my knees, face over the hole, and shoved two fingers down my throat.

Everything I'd eaten the day before came out in one violent spew. My throat burned, but I could breathe again. Sweat running down my face, I gulped air like a man saved from drowning. Leaning against the wall, wrung out, my nose picked up the stench of my own discharge, and I went into a series of painful dry heaves, my stomach emptied out.

After a minute or so, I pushed myself to my feet, flushed the toilet, and shuffled to the sink. I stripped off my gloves, splashed water on my face, rinsed, gargled, spat, then drank a few mouthfuls. The water was very cold and wonderful.

The stink in the small bathroom was overpowering. I pushed the window open. Crisp morning air wafted in, but it wasn't enough. I stuck my head out into the dawning sky, eyes shut, and sucked in clean air, purifying my airways.

The faint growling sound of a motor made me open my eyes. It was a police car, at the corner of Arlozorov and Ibn Gabirol, a couple of hundred meters away. It was approaching slowly, as if the driver was searching for a specific address. I had no doubt who was in the car or where it was heading. It was Inspector Leibowitz, and he was coming to Nathan's apartment.

Heart hammering, I ran out of the bathroom, down the hall, and out onto the fourth-floor landing. There was nowhere to hide. No nooks or crannies of any kind, and the trapdoor to the roof was secured with a padlock.

Knocking on doors, hoping to be admitted, was out of the question. I had to get out of the building or Leibowitz would see me.

Throwing caution to the wind, I bounded down the stairs. With my feet pounding on the steps, I couldn't hear whether anyone else was in the stairwell. Leibowitz might have already gained access to the building. If he caught me, he would doubtless subject me to a search and find the pictures. Then he would arrest me for breaking into Nathan's apartment and tossing the place. He would demand to know why I'd done so and why I'd taken the pictures. I doubted he would believe me.

Faster! I told myself, though any increase in speed would have likely resulted in my performing a rather painful somersault down a flight or two of stone stairs.

As it was, I just barely managed to sidestep a woman on the staircase between the first and second floors.

She was short, wide-hipped, and gray-haired, about sixty-five years old, and clutching a small white poodle to her bosom. The dog was yapping in agitation, trying to wriggle free of her grasp. Her expression was a blend of outrage and terror as I fought to slow my headlong descent and avoid colliding with her and her pet.

"Watch it, you fool!" she barked at me, her eyes shooting daggers as she squeezed herself against the banister, making as small a target of herself as she could. Without thinking, I said, "I'm sorry," but did not pause until I reached the ground floor.

The street door was made of wood with a glass panel running down its center. Beyond it, parked at the curb directly in front of the building, was the police car. The passenger door swung open. A trousered leg lowered itself from the car to the pavement.

I didn't wait to see more. I sprinted toward the rear of the lobby, hoping to find a back door. There it was. Two long strides and I was at it, reaching for the handle with my right hand.

My right, gloveless hand.

Damn it!

In my haste, I'd left my gloves behind on the bathroom sink. I'd removed them after I had thrown up in order to wash my face. And they'd been off when I opened the window to let in some air, possibly leaving my prints behind.

Spectacularly stupid and careless. The sort of mindless mistake that puts more criminals in jail than any amount of brilliant police work. But it was too late now. With my hand on the back-door handle, I offered a quick prayer that the door would not be locked.

It wasn't. I burst through the door into the backyard, scaring a couple of cats out of their naps. Glancing over my shoulder, I could see two shadows outside the street door. Then I was scaling a low fence and running from one backyard to another, adrenaline pumping, legs pounding, hoping against hope that I'd managed to dodge a bullet and not just postpone my downfall.

Chapter 11

When I put some distance between myself and Nathan's apartment, I slowed to a walk and started thinking. Leibowitz—if that was really him and not some other cop—had not seen me. If he had, he would have shouted for me to stop and given chase. It was close, much too close, but I had managed to slip away.

This, however, did not mean I was out of the woods. Fortune had smiled on me by getting me to stick my head out of that bathroom window at just the right moment to spot the police car approaching, but it had balanced the books by allowing me to leave my gloves and possible fingerprints behind, and by arranging my near collision with that dog-owner lady.

Had Leibowitz seen me wearing the gloves the night before? If I remembered correctly, my hands had been tucked safely out of sight in my pockets throughout our conversation. I was pretty sure he never caught a glimpse of them. In that regard, at least, I had nothing to worry about.

The lady in the stairway, however, was another matter.

How good a look had she gotten at me? Our encounter had lasted for no more than a second and a half. I had been barreling down the stairs at such speed that it was likely that what she saw of me was little more than a blur. Likely, but not a certainty. She had been looking right at me, at my face. I knew from experience with eyewitnesses that the human memory is a fickle and unreliable instrument. Often, a witness will provide a description that will end up being as dissimilar from the suspect as night from day.

There are occasions, however, in which you come across a witness with a quick eye and crystal clear recollection, as good as any photograph. When I was a policeman investigating a crime, I would pray for such a witness. Now, I fervently hoped that the gray-haired lady on the stairs was nothing of the kind.

Since I did not put much stock in either hoping or praying, I decided to take a measure of precaution.

I headed south toward home, knowing that I should have ample time, but nonetheless feeling a mounting sense of urgency that spurred me to walk briskly.

In my apartment, I stopped only to hastily brush the taste of bile out of my mouth before closing the shutters on all the windows and taking out the box I'd hidden in the closet. I had planned on taking it and everything in it with me, but now I was having second thoughts.

If what I feared came to pass and the police searched my apartment, there was a chance that they would discover the false bottom I had installed in my closet. If the space beneath it were empty, they would know that I had removed something from it and would want to know what it was. I could disassemble it, but I wasn't sure I could do it without leaving a trace. And besides, there was a benefit to having my secret compartment discovered in a search. It might lead the police to assume that there was nothing else to find and that I had not expected to be searched at all.

To accomplish that, however, I would need to leave something behind. I winced at the thought, knowing that whatever it was might be lost forever.

But it could not be helped. A sacrifice had to be made. I opened the box and examined its contents.

The gun and knife were coming with me. I might have need of them. And there were other souvenirs from my Nazi-hunting days that were emotionally dear to me. All these stayed safely in the box.

What remained was the money. It included what was left of the foreign currency I had brought with me to Israel, the dollars I had not yet exchanged, and a small sum of Israeli liras. I hated parting with any of it, having gone to a good deal of trouble to earn it, but, unlike the other items in the box, the money held no emotional value whatsoever.

I considered leaving nothing but Israeli money behind, but that might look suspicious. I had too little domestic currency to justify having built a hidden compartment. I could just as easily have deposited the money in the bank. And I needed to have local cash on me, as I doubted I would be able to exchange any more foreign currency in the foreseeable future. I did have the two hundred liras I had taken from Nathan's wallet, but that money wasn't mine to spend.

Riffling through the bills, I selected a few French

notes in various denominations, added a small portion of my Israeli currency, and counted off a hundred and fifty-five dollars, thinking that a large, un-round sum would seem more natural. All these I dropped into the hidden compartment.

Rubbing the back of my neck, I looked at the money for a long moment. It was enough to feed myself on for a good stretch of time. I had a powerful urge to snatch it all and leave nothing behind. With a curse, I quickly repositioned the false bottom and heaped my linen over it.

There. Out of sight, out of mind. But better if I left now, before I had a change of heart.

I took out all the Israeli liras I had left and shoved them in my pocket. My fingers brushed against the top edge of my notebook and I remembered something. Nathan had scribbled the address of Tamara Granot— the girl he'd planned on proposing to—on one of the pages. I found it, memorized the address, and tore out the page. In the kitchen I lit a match and burned the torn page in the sink. Back in the living room, I raised the shutters, found a small shopping bag, and put the box inside it. Then I grabbed Nathan's ring and his two hundred liras and was heading to the door when I stopped. What about the pictures of Nathan and the two women? I wanted to have them on me, in case I needed to show them to someone. But if Leibowitz found them in my possession, I would have some difficult explaining to do.

There was no choice. I slipped the two pictures in the

box, then grabbed the shopping bag and exited the apartment.

I needed someplace to stash the box. Somewhere safe, where I could get to in a hurry, with someone I trusted.

Greta was not an option. Leibowitz had seen us together. It would take him no time to learn that I was a regular at her café. Reuben Tzanani was out of the question, too. It was no secret that he and I had served together in Israel's War of Independence and were still friends. There was also the fact that Reuben was a policeman. I did not want him to risk his livelihood for me.

That left only one person I could think of.

Chapter 12

She owned an apartment on a quiet, tree-lined street in the modern northern section of Tel Aviv. It was where well-to-do people lived, those with respectable careers—doctors, lawyers, city officials, journalists—people who had money and positions of influence or were closely associated with those who did.

She also associated with those of means and influence, but her line of work was far from respectable. She was a prostitute. The sort that doesn't ply her trade in dark alleys or in a john's automobile or in a smelly room in some fleabag hotel. She belonged to that exclusive club of the high-end call girl, the kind who charges an arm and a leg before one is permitted to lay a finger on her.

I could have called first—she was also rare in the fact that she had a phone in her apartment—but for some reason I chose not to. I just went to her building and knocked on her door.

I waited an interminable minute, my heart bouncing in my chest in anticipation of her. Then I heard her approach the door on the other side, followed by the snick of the lock being turned, and there she was.

Sima Vaaknin.

She said, "My, my, Adam. You're up bright and early."

I gawked at her and had difficulty finding my voice. "Tell me you used that peephole before opening your door looking like that," I finally said.

All she had on was a large towel that covered her from her chest to the tops of her thighs, leaving her shoulders and most of her legs exposed. The towel was the color of cream and contrasted alluringly with her caramel skin. It hung loosely about her, but only partially obscured the perfect contours of her body—the fullness of her breasts, the swell of her hips, the tautness of her thighs. She was barefoot, one foot set solidly on the floor, the other en pointe, like a dancer about to perform a twirl. Her ankles were slender, her calves shapely and firm.

Unbidden, my eyes traveled the length of her, feasting on her, while other parts of my anatomy wailed in hunger for her. My fingers started tingling, eager to touch her flawless skin.

Reveling in my admiration, she smiled a mischievous, knowing smile, and I had the irrational thought that she'd planned this, knew I was coming and had hopped in the shower at just the right time to answer my knock looking as she did.

She said, "Rest assured, I have not survived this long in this life by being a reckless fool."

Which reminded me how much of a careless fool I had been earlier that day and why I had come to see her.

"Can I come in, Sima?"

"Sure. Follow me."

With that, she drew the door fully open and turned on

her heel, hip-swaying her way to the living room. I shut the door and followed, my nose picking up the scent she'd left in her wake—lilac and bananas.

In the living room she stopped and spun to face me. Her thick black hair hung wet and straight and shiny past her shoulders and down her back, framing that gorgeous face that made men ache in desire and women simmer in envy. A few damp strands clung to her cheeks and forehead, and I felt a powerful urge to brush them into place. Her eyes were large, widely spaced, and the color of irrigated earth ready for sowing. Between them and her delicate chin was a pert nose and a pair of plush lips, slightly parted as if in a gasp. No scars or moles or marks marred her face. If you didn't know her, if you never had the occasion to peer closely into the deep wells of her eyes and spot the dark sediment at their bottom, left there by trauma and loss and abuse, you might mistake her for an innocent teenager. In truth, she was twenty-eight years old.

Cocking her head slightly to the left, it was now her turn to peruse me. Her eyes took in the bag I was holding, but she didn't comment on it. Instead she said, "You're not sick, are you?"

"Do I look sick?"

"Yes," she said simply. "Your complexion is sallow, your face is drawn, and your lovely green eyes are bloodshot. I would guess that you haven't had a good night's sleep in weeks. It's a good thing you don't earn your living as a prostitute. Looking as you do, you'd starve to death."

She plopped on the sofa, her eyes locked on mine, running her hand along her upper chest, her fingertips slipping beneath her towel, brushing the tops of her breasts. This she did for my benefit, of course. Sima, the consummate seductress, was almost never at rest. Every turn of her hands, every flick of her eyelashes, every twist of her feet or legs or hips was designed to snare the eye, to arouse and entice.

It was as innate and automatic for her as breathing. I was aware of what she was doing but remained defenseless in the face of it. Heat spread from my center to my extremities.

"Come," she said, patting the sofa next to her. "Sit beside me."

I remained standing. "Perhaps you should go put something on first."

"What for? Won't I be taking it off shortly?"

I inhaled slowly. "Not for my benefit, you won't."

She stared at me as if I were an alien creature, a thing beyond comprehension.

"You are a strange man, Adam," she said at length. "A very strange man."

The very idea that any man would decline a clear invitation to share her bed was unfathomable to her. She was the ultimate temptation, a woman no man should be able to resist. I only did so with the utmost difficulty. Even now I could feel my body yearning for her.

She rose from the sofa in one smooth motion, as fluid as a panther, and padded toward me. Her skin glistened, and between her lips I saw her tongue waiting like a promise. She stopped three inches from me, close enough so I could feel the warmth of her body, and tilted back her head to stare into my face. Stretching herself up, she pressed her mouth to mine. Her tongue slipped past my lips, sending a jolt through me. Her hand reached into my hair, kneading my scalp with deft fingers.

Her mouth tasted like honey and biscuits, and her lips were as soft as a fluffed pillow. She moaned into my mouth and I felt a slight dizziness wash over me. When she finally broke the kiss, I could feel her like a sweet memory on my lips.

She gazed at me, and in her eyes I thought I detected a hint of something like desperate vulnerability.

"I thought you'd come sooner," she said in a silky voice. "You haven't been to see me in a long time."

Four months, I thought. *I managed to stay away for four months.*

The first time we met, a little over a year before, I was investigating the murder of a young Arab woman whom Sima had known. We made love, and afterward, I felt an overwhelming sense of guilt, as though I had betrayed my wife, Deborah, despite her being dead since the day we arrived in Auschwitz in 1944.

I wanted Sima like I'd wanted no other woman before her, but I feared that seeing her again would lead to a severing of the emotional ties that bound me to my late wife and the love we'd shared. I couldn't bear that thought, so I resolved never to see Sima again.

I succeeded more than most men would have, but I did succumb a smattering of times over the succeeding year. Each time we met, I paid her for her company, but less than other clients did. And often, unlike other clients, I stayed the night.

And after each encounter I would see my wife's face hovering before me like a silent accusation. It didn't help that I knew it was me who was conjuring up Deborah's face, that the real Deborah would have wanted me to let go, to live my life fully. I still felt that I owed her my faithfulness. The fear that the more I saw of Sima, the more tenuous my connection with my past would become kept me away from her.

Four months ago, on the Jewish New Year, we met for the holiday meal and pretended to be each other's family. We both had no real family of our own, I having lost mine in Auschwitz, she having been orphaned by an Arab mob in Hebron in 1929 when she was but seven years old. A few days later, on Yom Kippur, was the last time I saw her before today. Then, feeling lonely and out of sorts on that holiest of days, when no traffic moved in the streets and all the shops and cafés were closed, I came here, to her. She surprised me by informing me that she observed the fast. She'd shown no sign of faith or religious observance before that day. When I asked her about it, she said, "I fast each year. It's good for the soul, repenting your sins. Don't you have things to repent?"

I did, but I did not believe fasting would help. I did not believe anything would help with my sins.

When I told her I did not fast, Sima cooked me a meal—a spectacular one, rich with black-market delicacies her well-heeled clients had brought her as gifts.

Then she sat with me and watched me eat, and if she derived any pleasure from my enjoyment of her food, she didn't show it. It was a strange domestic scene, as if neither she nor I knew precisely what our roles were.

Later that night I discovered that her fast did not extend to other hungers.

When I left her apartment the next morning, it was with an odd feeling. The image of Deborah that I saw in my mind's eye had turned hazy, and the guilt I felt had waned. I realized that, like Mrs. Wasserman and her anger, I did not wish to relinquish my guilt, that it was part of who I was.

So I did not return to visit Sima. We'd made no specific plans, but I knew she expected me to join her on the *Sukkot* holiday five days after Yom Kippur. I didn't show, nor did I call. On her part, she never sought me out. It wasn't her way. I was a man, and men were supposed to come to her, not the other way around.

"I can feel you," Sima now said, her fingers still in my hair, her voice husky and tantalizing. "Come to bed."

I wanted to obey, every inch of me screaming in desire, but I steeled my resolve and took a step back, breaking contact with her body. "Not right now, Sima. I've got things to take care of."

A flash of annoyance crossed her face. "I will not be kept waiting, Adam. And I have clients coming later today."

She must have guessed that would hurt me, and it did. For her clients were men who would pay to share her bed and body, and I resented the existence of such men. I struggled to resist Sima Vaaknin's pull on me, but at the same time I wanted no other man to have her.

I owed her no explanation, yet felt compelled to give her one. "I'm working on a murder case. A man I knew, a man who saved my life in Auschwitz, was killed yesterday. I owe it to him to try to find out who killed him. The more time passes, the muddier the trail becomes."

She knew all about owing someone her life and about paying off her debts. She let out a breath of what might have been frustration and said, "Give me a moment," and disappeared down the hall to her bedroom.

When she returned, she had on a white robe and the towel was coiled around her hair. She reminded me of a picture I'd once seen of a statue of an Egyptian goddess that was on display at a museum in Britain.

"What's in the bag?" she asked.

I set it on the coffee table and took out the box. "I need to hide this somewhere safe, someplace the police aren't likely to come looking."

"The police? Are you in trouble with them? And why don't you let them investigate this murder?"

"The less you know, the better, Sima. Which is why I advise you not to open this box. In the unlikely event the police do knock on your door, you can honestly claim ignorance of what's in it. Just say you were doing me a favor by keeping it."

She didn't hesitate before saying, "All right. I'll do as you say. How long do you expect me to have it here?"

"A few days, a week. Not much longer than that, I think."

"Are there things in it you're likely to need in that time frame?"

I thought of the gun and the knife. I didn't want any weapons on me right now, not when I ran the risk of using them in anger at the next place I visited. In addition, if that lady on the stairs provided him with a good description, Leibowitz might come looking for me today. But I felt it in my bones that there would be violence before this case was done.

"Yes," I said. "Almost certainly."

"So you'll be back here? We shall see each other again soon?"

The question hung in the air between us like a wish yet unfulfilled.

"Yes," I said again. "Almost certainly."

She flashed me a smile that brought out the seven-year-old girl she'd once been, the last time she was truly, fully happy. Then she picked up the box and told me to follow her.

She led me to the smaller of two bedrooms, where she kept her clothes and her linen. She opened her closet and I half-expected her to lift a false bottom just like mine, but all she did was stash the box behind a tall stack of folded sheets.

"Not much of a hiding place, is it?" she said.

"It will do fine. Thank you, Sima."

She looked at me and was about to say something. Then, as though driven to it by an irresistible force, she curled a hand around the back of my neck and pulled my face down toward hers. She kissed me hungrily, with more animation than she usually displayed outside of her bed. There was a desperation to that kiss and I started to feel it, too. My hands went around her, over her robe, and pulled her tightly into me, her breasts mashing against my chest.

At five foot five, she was much shorter than me, and I discovered, when we broke off our kiss, that I had lifted her off her feet. Our breaths mingled as we stared at each other, our faces inches apart.

I lowered her to the floor and took a step back, holding her at arm's length. "I have to go," I said, and a voice inside me shrieked in protest. Yet my mind was set, for I knew that I had been on the brink of falling into her, on the verge of snipping one more of the slender threads that bound me to the dead wife I still loved.

Sima didn't protest. On her threshold she said, "If you plan on coming tonight, you should know I'm occupied until ten o'clock."

And with that final jab she shut the door, leaving me with my desire unfulfilled on the landing.

Chapter 13

I headed west to the beach and watched waves crest and crash. The sun peeked through the cloud cover, casting wild colors on the shifting water, and a black bird was pecking at the carcass of a fish the sea had deposited on the sand. A middle-aged couple, wrapped in warm clothes, sauntered along the water's edge, holding hands with the instinctive ease of those who'd been happy together for many years. I thought of Deborah and felt a twinge at my core.

At eight it started raining, and I ran for cover under the awning of a dress shop. By eight thirty the rain had ceased, and the clouds began scattering. The sun seemed sharper through the rain-cleaned air. Puddles sparkled on the road.

I ambled south along Hayarkon Street and spied a man cleaning the window of his café. Inside it was empty. My stomach grumbled loudly. Throwing up, making a last-second escape, and trying to cover up for it had left me famished.

"Are you open?"

"Sure. Hop on inside and I'll get to you in a couple of minutes."

He was true to his word. I ordered a large breakfast

and a pot of tea. He served the food along with a steady patter of conversation. He was one of those people who found nearly everything worth chattering about and assumed that everyone else shared their passion. I was grateful when another customer ventured in and the proprietor shifted his verbal barrage his way.

At nine, the proprietor turned on the radio and we listened to the news together. Toward the end came a short report about last night's murder. The announcer identified Nathan by name and said that the police were asking those with pertinent information to come forward. So far, it seemed, the police were pursuing the case. I doubted their zeal would last for more than a few days once they learned how Nathan had made his living, unless an easy solution presented itself.

At nine thirty, after browsing through yesterday's edition of *Davar* that someone had left behind on a nearby chair, I rose, paid for the meal, and left.

I made my way to Ben Yehuda Street, thinking of Sima Vaaknin and asking myself whether I'd made a mistake by going to her. I failed to come to a conclusion by the time I reached Tova Wasserman's building.

***

Tova Wasserman was looking positively chipper. Her thin lips dug a hundred creases up and down her sunken cheeks as they stretched to a smile. It was not the icy, hungry smile she had given me the day she hired me to retrieve her money from Nathan, but the satisfied, sated grin of a full-bellied predator. Watching her, I came to the conclusion that, after seeing Tova Wasserman smile twice, I could quite happily pass the rest of my life without seeing her smile again.

Arching an eyebrow, she cocked her head at what might have been construed as a coquettish angle and said, "Why, Mr. Lapid, this is a surprise."

I was on the verge of bursting at her, but doing so on the landing, where her neighbors might hear me, would not do. I reined in my anger.

"Can I come in, Mrs. Wasserman?"

"Certainly. Just wipe your feet first."

There was a bounce to her step as she led the way to the living room. I found her cheerfulness grotesque and out of place. Like watching a corpse trying to wiggle its toes.

"Sit there." She gestured toward the sofa. Then she disappeared into the kitchen, returning a minute later with a plate heaped with her atrocious cookies, carrying it with both hands like a pagan priestess holding an offering to a ravenous deity.

She set the plate on the coffee table and herself on her regular chair. She sat with her knees pressed together, one hand toying with her tear-shaped pendant. Her cheeks glowed. The fiendish woman was happier than I'd ever seen her.

I said, "You've heard, haven't you?"

"If you're referring to the unfortunate death of Mr. Frankel, the answer is yes. It was on the radio earlier. I heard it while I was eating my breakfast." She paused and gave me a sly look. "Was that where you heard about it, Mr. Lapid?"

"No. I happen to be the one who discovered his body."

Her eyes twinkled. She could barely contain her glee. It threatened to spill out of her like sewage from an overflowing grate. "Did you now? How dreadful. Sometimes I wonder what this city is coming to. Have a cookie, Mr. Lapid. I baked them this morning."

Clenching my jaw, I stifled the impulse to swat the plate of cookies off the table. I gave her a long hard look, knowing that I was procrastinating, that I did not want to ask the question because I feared hearing the answer.

"Was it you?"

She frowned. "Was I what?"

"Did you have Nathan Frankel killed? Did you hire anyone to kill him?"

She laughed. A high-pitched, braying cackle. It was a moment before she was able to speak. "I wasn't expecting that, Mr. Lapid, I can tell you that."

"I know you wanted him hurt. You had cause. He stole from you and humiliated you. I can understand your desire to get back at him. Believe me, I do. Who did you hire after I refused to harm him? Did he go too far, or did your rage mount to the point where nothing less than a man's death would do?"

Her lips were still smiling. Her teeth gleamed like a faraway snowy range of sharp mountain peaks. Then she said, "Come now, you've had your little fun. Let's cease with the jokes, shall we?"

"Why would I joke about something as grave as a man's untimely death?"

She shrugged her bony shoulders. "How should I know? I've only met you a handful of times, Mr. Lapid, and from what I've heard, you're not above twisting an arm here and there if someone is willing to pay you for it. When I saw you at my door, I was certain you were here for a bonus."

"A bonus?"

"Of course. Why else would you be here? You just exchanged money with me a few days ago. What other reason could you have for visiting me other than that you finally came to your senses and realized that a vermin like Nathan Frankel deserved no mercy or leniency. His kind need to be stomped. Granted, I said nothing of killing him—I just wanted him roughed up—but I must say that I was overjoyed when I learned of his demise. That being the case, Mr. Lapid, I am willing to make an exception to my usual business practices on your behalf. Normally, I would consider you entitled to nothing. I did, after all, offer to hire you to give the late Mr. Frankel his just deserts, and you turned me down. The time to seal a bargain is when an offer is made, not at some later date and time. If you're now ready to quit playacting and stand behind your actions, you may consider this lesson a part of your compensation. Also know that while I am happy with the outcome, I will not pay you as much as I offered on our previous meeting. I'm willing to match the original payment of thirty liras. I hope that meets with your expectations."

I sat absolutely still for several moments, but inside I was seething. She sat before me as if she were a queen on a throne and I was one of her minions. She was either as cold-blooded and conceited as they come or she was putting on an act, trying to divert my suspicions away from her.

I said, "You can keep your money, Mrs. Wasserman. I did not want it before and I want it now even less. I would not have laid a finger on Nathan if you'd paid me a million liras. What I want to know is this: Did you hire anyone else to go after him after I refused to do so?"

"I don't see how it is any of your business whether I did or did not."

"I'm making it my business," I said, raising my voice. "Now answer the damn question."

For the first time there was a hint of fear in her eyes. She leaned back as far as her chair allowed, tugging her shawl tightly around her. Her tongue, quick and furtive, slid across her lips and back inside her mouth. "I did not hire anyone in your place, Mr. Lapid."

I studied her closely. She showed none of the common tells for lying. But her usual expression was hard to read. If she put in a little effort at dissembling and had experience at it, she could be a formidable liar.

"You simply gave up your desire for vengeance? I find that hard to believe."

"You would be wise not to, because I did no such thing. I had every intention of making Mr. Frankel pay for his crimes. Someone simply beat me to the punch." Her confidence had reemerged. The hint of fear was gone. She was enjoying herself. "As the rabbis say, 'The work of the righteous is done by others.'"

A part of me I did not much like wanted to wrap my hands around her scrawny, wrinkled neck and strangle her. Instead, I said, "I would advise against lying to me, Mrs. Wasserman. You will regret it."

She answered in a mocking tone. "I appreciate the warning, Mr. Lapid. Allow me to reciprocate. I would advise you not to threaten me. I do not take kindly to threats. Am I making myself clear?"

I leaned forward, one finger pointing at her face. "Let me tell you something, just so we both know where we stand. I'm going to find out who killed Nathan. If I find that you had anything to do with it, you're going to be in more trouble than you ever thought possible. Do you understand me?"

That last bit came out in a growl, and I was happy to see her flinch.

I got to my feet, rummaging in my pocket. "Oh, and one more thing. I've been meaning to tell you this for a long time and now seems like the perfect moment. Your cookies are the worst I've ever eaten. They're so hard, hurl them at a Tiger tank and they'd pierce right through the armor. They're not fit for human or animal consumption. I wouldn't feed them to a pig."

With that, I held out the four stale cookies in my fist for her to see and let go of them. They clattered onto the table like a quartet of grenades.

Then came the detonation.

"Get out!" she screamed. "Get out and don't come

back. Why you…you—"

She could not find the perfect killing word. Her eyes blazed like a funeral pyre. Her hands gripped the cloth of her dress so hard, her nails looked about to tear through to her skin. Between her bared lips I could see her small white teeth pressed hard together.

"I'm leaving," I said, "but like I told you, if you're behind this murder, I'll be back for you."

With that I stomped toward the door while she shrieked curses at me. I could still hear her as I made my way down the stairs and out of her building.

Chapter 14

The good weather held. The air was crisp and fresh. The sun rode high in a crystal-blue sky, and were it not for the chilly temperature, you might mistake the season for summer. It was the sort of day to lift your spirits, but inside me a storm was raging.

That wicked old woman might not have been behind Nathan's murder, but she relished his death. Her pleasure made my stomach turn and my hands itch with repressed rage. I'd not experienced a similar enjoyment even while standing over the bodies of the Nazi officers I'd slain.

I leaned against the side of a building and lit a cigarette and tried to calm myself down. I focused on the smoke burning its way down my throat and slowly the storm abated. Good. Anger clouds the mind, and I needed to remain clearheaded. I'd make Tova Wasserman pay, I decided, one way or another.

It was a nice day for walking, so I trekked downtown into Neve Tzedek, one of the oldest neighborhoods in Tel Aviv. In fact, these streets first paved and inhabited by Jews toward the end of the nineteenth century, before Tel Aviv was formally founded in 1909, and were only later incorporated into the city. Here the houses were less modern in design than in the northern parts of the city, and many were showing their age. Some of the facades were smudged by weather and dirt; others were flaking. But there were those, like the house where Tamara Granot lived, that were well kept.

It was a two-story house with a peaked roof and a small balcony facing the street. A ceramic planter brimming with vibrant red and violet flowers hung on the balcony railing. More flowers and plants grew in pots along the edges of the balcony's floor. As with its neighbors, the house did not sport a front yard or steps leading to its entrance. The door was a dark brown and came equipped with a brass knocker. I made use of it and waited.

A moment passed before a timorous female voice sounded from within.

"Who is it?"

"Tamara Granot?"

"Yes," she answered, her pitch climbing at the end of the word, making it sound as though she were posing a question.

"My name is Adam Lapid. Can I talk to you for a few minutes?"

A short pause. "My father will be home soon."

I wasn't sure what to make of that piece of information. "I'm not here to see your father, Ms. Granot. I'm here to see you. I have something for you from Nathan Frankel."

When next she spoke, she sounded closer, as if she'd pressed her face to the other side of the door. "What is it?"

"A present he told me to give you. Can you please open the door?" I paused, searching for the right thing to say, then added, "I'm a friend of his, Ms. Granot."

Another stretch of silence. Then I heard the sound of a bolt being pulled and a key revolving in the lock, and then the door swung open, and one of the questions I had was answered. I had identified one of the two women in the photographs I had lifted from Nathan's apartment.

I might have guessed which one of the two Tamara Granot would be. Her appearance matched her voice and tone. Five foot four and slender, the manner in which she held herself gave the impression of an even shorter woman. It was the way her chin was tilted toward her chest and how her shoulders curved inward, as though a pair of powerful hands were squeezing them closer together.

She wore a simple housedress, navy blue with white trim, that covered her from her neck to her ankles. A fine silver chain encircled her throat. She wore her long brown hair in a braid, which she'd pulled forward over her left shoulder and was now worrying with both hands as she nervously peered up at me.

Seeing her, I was struck by doubt. Was this shy, timid girl really the woman the gregarious, outgoing Nathan had planned on marrying? They seemed an odd match. Yet I had seen them together in that picture, and this was the address Nathan had given me.

Holding the door open, she murmured that I should come inside. As I entered, she pressed herself back against the wall so I would have ample room to pass by her without running the risk of our bodies touching. She locked the door behind me and showed me to a spacious, well-aired living room. There was fine furniture, a radio, and a gramophone. There were leather-bound books in a floor-to-ceiling bookcase. A dozen colorful flowers in a vase on a side table scented the air. A thick rug covered much of the floor. Lacey white curtains fluttered by each window. Everything was neat and tasteful and of good quality. This was an affluent house.

I took a chair while she remained standing, shifting her feet, her eyes going from the sofa to a thickly padded armchair. She finally chose the sofa. It was closer to where I sat than the armchair, but it had the advantage of having the coffee table between us. She sat on the edge of the sofa, her knees close together, one hand still fingering her braid, the end of which had frayed under her constant assault.

I examined her more closely and could see where the attraction might have sprung from. Tamara Granot was a rather pretty girl, in an unassuming way—the sort who is not always fully aware of her own charms and does little to enhance or display them. She had a heart-shaped face, finely drawn lips, smooth pale skin, and large innocent brown eyes that a man might spend some time gazing into. The eyes were now rimmed in red. She'd been crying.

"You've heard the news, I take it," I said.

Tamara nodded shakily, fresh tears trickling from the corners of her eyes. "It was on the radio," she said, drawing a handkerchief from the pocket of her dress and dabbing her eyes. "That's how I learned Nathan was killed."

"That must have been a shock. I know you were close."

"I loved him. I—" Her voice broke and she shook her head and once again had to dry her eyes.

I waited for her tears to stop, then fished out the box Nathan had given me and set it on the table between us. "He asked me to give this to you."

She frowned, her gaze going from the box to my face and back again. Then she reached out a hesitant hand and picked it up. When she opened it and held up the diamond ring between thumb and forefinger, her whole body started shaking.

"I-I don't understand," she said, her eyes begging me to enlighten her, but I could tell she knew well enough what the ring was and what it signified.

I put it into words as simply as I could. "Nathan loved you very much, Tamara. He wanted to marry you."

She did not seem to hear me. Her entire focus was centered on the ring. Her face rippled with a range of emotions before settling on an expression of such unmitigated agony that it was a struggle not to avert my eyes. She slipped the ring on her ring finger and looked at it again. It seemed the perfect fit. A low moan wafted from her mouth, a somber note that sounded as though it had bubbled up from somewhere close to her shattered heart.

A long soundless moment passed before she was able to speak. "Why didn't Nathan give me this himself?"

"I don't know."

"How did you get it?"

"He gave it to me three days before he died. He asked me to give it to you in case I didn't hear from him in a week's time."

"Why would he do something like that?"

"He may have feared for his life."

Her eyes turned to saucers. "Did he say that?"

"Not in so many words. In retrospect, that's what I think he might have felt."

She took a moment to absorb this revelation. Then she said, "Why would anyone want to kill Nathan?"

"I don't know," I lied, discomfort crawling across my skin. "That's what I'm trying to find out."

"I don't understand. Are you a policeman?"

"No. But I used to be one. In Europe, before the World War. That's where Nathan's and my paths first crossed. Then we stumbled into each other four days ago in Jaffa."

"And he just gave you this ring?" she asked, dubious.

I could appreciate her doubtfulness. I had no eye for jewelry, but even I could tell that the ring on her finger had cost a pretty penny. It beggared belief that Nathan would simply hand such an item to a man he barely knew.

"Yes. It's difficult to explain, Ms. Granot, but Nathan and I shared a history and this history made it easier for him to trust me than most other people. It is also why I'm looking into his death. Did you happen to see him over the past four days?"

She shook her head.

"Are you sure?"

Her eyebrows drew closer together. "You sound like you doubt my word."

I smiled faintly, attempting to reassure her that I was on her side. "It's just that Nathan did not sleep in his apartment last night and perhaps not the one before that. I thought he might have spent those nights with you."

Her pale cheeks turned a flaming red. "Nathan and I weren't married yet, Mr. Lapid."

I almost smiled. She sounded truly astounded that I would even raise the possibility that she would sleep with a man before her wedding night. But I got the sense that she wasn't nearly as shocked as her cheeks suggested. She had likely given the idea some thought and found pleasure in the fantasy, even if she was too prudish to have acted on it.

Again, it struck me as strange that Nathan, with his good looks and natural charm, would fall in love with this straitlaced girl. But weirder things have happened, and love is, after all, the most unpredictable of all human emotions.

"Do you have any idea where he might have spent the last few nights?"

She shook her head. "He had no family. They all died in Europe."

"What about friends?"

She thought about it and shrugged helplessly. "When we were out together, he would occasionally run across people he knew. Sometimes he would introduce them to me, but I don't remember their names. I'm terrible with names, I'm afraid."

"Surely you remember at least one person who seemed close to him."

She took a deep breath and closed her eyes. The fingers of her right hand fidgeted with the new ring on her left. When she opened her eyes, I could tell that she remembered something. "He did take me one time to a place in Jaffa. He and the owner were friendly. Nathan said they came from the same town in Poland."

I asked her whether the man's name was Fyodor, and she said she didn't think so. I suggested Misha. She nodded and said that was it. "You know him?"

I said that I'd met him once and asked if there was anyone else she could think of. She said there wasn't.

"Did he ever introduce you to a ginger-haired man? Average in height and build, green eyes, has a raspy voice?"

Again she shook her head. "Was he a friend of Nathan?"

"More of an acquaintance, perhaps," I said.

I considered describing the woman from the other picture and asking whether Tamara knew who she was, but decided to hold off on that. Tamara would likely have questions of her own, and I worried that she would see through any lie I told. The poor girl was going through enough already. Making her suspect that Nathan was going behind her back might break her.

She was looking at her ring and her mouth trembled. "I wish he would have given this to me himself before he died." She raised her glistening eyes to mine. "I would have said yes. Without hesitation I would have said yes."

Her voice broke on that last word and now the tears flowed like a river. She mumbled something unintelligible and fled to the bathroom. Witnessing her heartrending anguish, I was awash with sadness.

Nathan had been on the cusp of achieving what I had not, what I believed I never would—a new life. Had he not been slain, he would have had a wife and, in the near future, children. He would have built a home. But like Moses had been denied entrance to the Promised Land, so had Nathan fallen short of achieving his goal. The Nazis had destroyed the old life he'd once had; the killer, the new life he was to create. A burning-white hatred for the killer ignited within me, incinerating the sadness. For at that moment I became utterly and irrationally convinced that by preventing Nathan from building a new life, the killer had also deprived me of ever having one of my own.

When Tamara returned a minute later, her cheeks were wet and a fresh handkerchief was clutched in her hand. She looked haggard, her face ashen. Losing the love of your life could have that effect.

"I'm sorry, Mr. Lapid, but I'm very tired. I'm expecting my father shortly. He is taking me to the police station. I will probably be asked a million questions, and I'm not looking forward to it. Thank you for coming and for doing the right thing by Nathan, but I would like to rest a bit before I go. So…"

"Just one more minute, Ms. Granot," I said. "I have something more for you."

I held out the two hundred liras I'd taken from Nathan's wallet.

She stared at the money in utter bafflement. "What is this?"

"It belonged to Nathan." I was about to add that he'd told me to give it to her, but ended up saying, "He would want you to have it."

She took the wad of bills, dropped back onto the sofa, and spread the money open like a partially unfurled fan. "How much is it?"

"Two hundred."

She lowered the money to her knees and frowned in bewilderment. "I don't understand. How would Nathan come up with this kind of money?"

Now it was my turn to frown. "Don't you know what he did for a living?"

"He clerked for an accountant. He planned to become one in the future, so clerking was good experience. He never told me what his salary was, but it couldn't have been much."

I scratched my cheek, adjusting myself in my seat. I did not know for sure why Nathan had hidden his true vocation from the woman he intended to marry, but I could venture a guess. Tamara Granot was the embodiment of naive propriety, and her stringent morality likely extended beyond sexual matters. Perhaps Nathan had been afraid of what she might think of him if she knew the truth. It was also possible that he had lied to her on their initial meeting and did not know how to extricate himself from his lie as their relationship deepened.

"Ever visit him at his office?" I said.

"No. Nathan said his boss wouldn't like that, that he was a very strict man." She looked down again at the money. "Perhaps he'd been saving this for a long time. To start a new life after we were married."

I licked my lips, trying to come up with the right words, and finally settled on telling it to her straight. "Ms. Granot, Nathan did not clerk for an accountant. He was a black marketeer."

She lifted her gaze and in her eyes I saw astonishment mingled with righteous fury. So this girl did have some fire in her after all.

"You lie," she spat. "How dare you say such a thing about Nathan."

I stared at her, momentarily silenced by her vehemence. Apparently, Tamara Granot was one of those rare souls who not only did not partake of the black market, but actually abhorred it.

I said, "The police will tell you the same thing when you see them, Ms. Granot. Count on it."

She gave me a probing look, searching for the lie in my face. Giving up, she averted her eyes and I could see her wheels turning. Small questions about Nathan that had cropped up during their courtship, questions she'd ignored till now, suddenly had answers.

"Are you involved in the black market?" she asked.

"No."

"So how do you know Nathan was?"

"He told me so himself."

Her mouth twitched, and I could guess the thought going through her mind: Why did he not tell *me?*

She put the money aside on the sofa and buried her face in her hands. "This is a nightmare. I didn't even know him, not really."

She was right, of course, so I didn't argue with the core of her statement. What I said was, "You knew him better than most. Well enough to love him. And he loved you back."

She lowered her hands. "Did he tell you this as well?"

"He wouldn't have made sure you got his ring if he didn't."

Her chin trembled. "If he loved me, he wouldn't have kept things from me. He would have been honest with me."

I remembered Nathan remarking that soon it might be time for him to change the course of his life. "I think he would have come clean in the near future. I believe he was thinking about turning a new leaf, shifting direction. Marrying you was just one of the big changes he had in mind. The most important one."

I thought she was about to burst into tears again, but she surprised me. Instead of weeping, she appeared to dive deep into her own thoughts. By the fluctuation of emotions on her face, I could tell some of those thoughts were good and some not so much. I couldn't let her go wandering off on me. Not when she was supposed to head out soon.

"It would be best, Ms. Granot, if you didn't mention

our talk to the police."

Her eyes leapt to mine. "Why not?"

"For one thing, I'd prefer they were not made aware that I knew Nathan. I don't want to be questioned myself. For another, it would be easier for you to feign ignorance of his means of livelihood. And don't tell them about the money or the ring, or they might take them from you."

Her breath hitched. "No. Why would they?"

"They might believe them to be stolen property."

"You think he stole this ring?"

"No. I'm pretty sure he did not, but the police might say otherwise."

Her lips twisted. "If he was a black marketeer, then why not a thief?"

"Something like that."

She stared at her ring again, and for the first time it wasn't with forlorn affection. "It's logical, isn't it? Why wouldn't it be true?"

The bitterness was beginning to seep deeper into her. Soon it would poison her memory of Nathan. That would be a shame, as I did not doubt his feelings for her were real.

"Because there are things a man like Nathan would never steal. A wedding ring is one of them. To do so would diminish how he viewed himself."

She pondered my words and her eyes turned wet again. She opened her mouth to speak, but had to swallow hard before she was able to say, "That's good to know."

I was about to ask her what sort of things she and

Nathan liked to do together, when I heard the front door being opened and closed. Then came loud, decisive footsteps down the hall toward where Tamara and I sat.

Tamara just about jumped in her seat, startled. Frantically, she gathered the bills, which lay by her side on the sofa, and stuffed them into her pocket. Then she fumbled at her ring, trying desperately to remove it from her finger, but for some reason, her nerves probably, she couldn't seem to get a grip on it.

She gave up just as the sound of footsteps died down and settled on covering her left hand with her right. She gave me a beseeching look, and I turned to see a man standing at the entrance to the living room, glowering at me.

Chapter 15

The man had eyes the color of dry cement and bristling salt-and-pepper eyebrows. He was five foot nine and thickset, with about twenty extra pounds packed unevenly around his belly, chest, and shoulders, giving him a top-heavy look. He had a ruddy, slightly bloated face, but so far his chin had managed to refrain from doubling. His hair had receded halfway up his dome of a head, and he had made no effort to disguise his baldness. The hair matched his eyebrows in color and was cut very short. His hard gaze moved from me to Tamara, demanding an explanation.

Tamara's cheeks were flushed and this time it wasn't due to embarrassment. In a tiny voice she said, "Father, this is Mr. Lapid. He is...he was a friend of Nathan."

Mr. Granot's glower deepened, carving deep canals in his forehead. His broad mouth tightened in unmistakable disapproval as he weighed me with his eyes. He made no effort to hide the fact that I was an unwelcome presence in his house.

"Are you ready, Tamara?" he said in a gruff, disciplinarian voice, eyes still fixed on me. "We need to get going."

She stood, careful to keep her left hand hidden. "I just need a few minutes," she said apologetically, but made no move to leave the room.

He huffed. "Hurry up, then."

Permission granted, Tamara fled from the room, and I heard her light footsteps clicking rapidly up the stairs to the second floor.

Her father waited until we heard a door close upstairs before saying, "You say your name is Lapid?"

I had risen when he entered the room and now offered him my hand. "Your daughter said it, not I, but that is my name."

He ignored my hand, making a show of clasping both of his behind his back, his posture rigid. He wore a tailored black suit, a conservative gray tie, and square-toed shoes that were polished to a high gloss. His breath carried the acrid, smoky scent of burnt cigars. "Why have you come here today? What's your purpose?"

I lowered my hand. "As Ms. Granot said, I was Nathan Frankel's friend."

"So you're here to offer your condolences, is that it?"

His tone was mocking. I had a feeling it was a tone he used almost as often as he glowered, which I would have bet was pretty much all the time.

"My condolences and my respects."

"You wasted your time, then. My daughter and that man weren't married. They weren't even engaged."

That man, I thought. So Nathan's charm did have its limits. He had failed to win over Mr. Granot.

"If he hadn't died, perhaps they soon would've been,"

I said, skating much closer to the truth than I should have done, but making the decision to provoke him just a little. For here was a man who clearly detested Nathan, making him an obvious suspect of his murder, and I wanted to keep him talking for as long as I could.

Granot huffed again. He had a bulging nose with tunnels for nostrils and his huffing sounded like a fast wind whooshing down a narrow canyon.

"Did he tell you that? If so, the man was suffering from delusions."

"You didn't approve of him, I take it."

"No, I did not. Oh, he tried to present himself as an upstanding young man, a man of substance and potential, but he didn't fool me, not for long." He brought his right hand from behind his back and jabbed a finger in my face. "I saw through him, and I see through you as well. You didn't come here to condole with anyone. What are you really here for? Money?"

"I don't want a single lira from you."

He cracked out a laugh. "And you won't get one, I guarantee it. But you did not have me in mind as your target anyway. You were hoping to get something from my daughter. No doubt your friend Frankel told you that she's a tenderhearted girl. Naive and sweet, the way a proper lady of her age should be, easy to manipulate."

"I'm surprised you allowed her to see him, considering how little you thought of him."

Granot stepped away from me, crossed the room, and came to stand behind the armchair. He placed both hands on top of the tall backrest. Leaning forward, he glared at me, and I realized that I had touched upon a sore spot. And I had a suspicion as to what it was.

I said, "You didn't allow it, did you? Or maybe at first you did, but then you changed your mind and forbade Tamara to see him. But she disobeyed you. That must have been a first. I bet it stunned you. Like a king or a tyrant, you expect obedience at all times."

The ruddiness in his face deepened like a gathering pool of blood under his skin. So this was what Tamara had gotten from her father, the ability to turn red at the blink of an eye. Other than that, I could see no resemblance between them. She must have favored her mother, but there were no pictures of her in the living room to allow me to verify that. In general, I got the distinct impression that, apart from Tamara and her father, no one lived in that house. The mother was probably dead, which allowed this domineering autocrat to rule his daughter as he saw fit. And by the unmerciful, relentless force of his strictness and harsh discipline, he had reared a fearful young woman. But he hadn't stamped all the spirit out of her. Given the right motivation—her desire to be with Nathan—she had managed to overcome what to her must have seemed an insurmountable emotional hurdle and go against his wishes. How it must have infuriated him. Enough to kill?

Judging by the look he was giving me, the answer was a resounding yes.

"You permit yourself too much," he said in a menacing, somewhat shocked voice. He was obviously not accustomed to being addressed this way. "And in my home."

He was on the verge of throwing me out. I needed to ease up, to cool him down, so he would continue talking.

I decided to appeal to his vanity. "How did you see through him? That's quite remarkable. Not a lot of men would have been able to. Nathan was very good at putting up an impressive front."

By the satisfied, tight-lipped smile that spread across Granot's face, I could tell my gambit had worked. He straightened, his hands disappearing once more behind his back. It was the posture of a lecturer, one afflicted with inordinate self-importance, the sort students quickly learn to despise.

"You're right. He could. Your dead friend had his sordid talents, I'll give him that. But—" he tapped a finger half an inch below his right eye "—once I truly set my eye on him, I could sense that something was amiss. I soon found out about his true vocation."

"What vocation?" I said.

"Don't play dumb with me. You know what I mean. I learned that he didn't make his living working for an accountant or in any other legitimate profession. He was a crook, a criminal, a black-market vendor. God knows what else he had his hand in."

"How did you find out?"

He shrugged and said nothing, his eyes flicking down before coming back up. For the first time in our conversation, he was acting cagey, and I was curious to know why.

I said, "You weren't just hit by a sudden suspicion that Nathan wasn't who he said he was. You discovered something specific—that he sold goods on the black market. How did you do that?"

"What does it matter? The important thing is that I did find out."

"Which was when you forbade your daughter to see him again."

"You have no children of your own, do you?"

I blinked, taken off guard by the question. Inside, I felt the stabbing pain that came whenever I thought of my two daughters killed in the gas chambers. This bastard didn't need to know about them, so I simply said, "No."

"I thought as much." He smiled his tight-lipped smile again. He enjoyed being right about people, especially those whom he felt were beneath him. He drew himself up, puffing out his chest, the lecturer once more. "I have invested a tremendous amount of time, effort, money, and, I'm not embarrassed to admit it, also love, in raising my daughter. Of all I've achieved in my life, which is quite a bit, she is my most cherished possession. Since infancy, I have raised her to be the finest of ladies, one who could walk into any upscale European parlor and be at home there. She was instructed by the best tutors, inculcated with the most refined social skills, and molded to be a model of rectitude. In short, she is a young woman of the highest quality. Naturally, the husband I envision for her would have to be of an appropriate caliber. A man who has either made something of himself or is destined to."

He paused to draw breath. The small hairs that peeked from his nostrils vibrated like wind chimes.

"I am partly to blame. I was engrossed in my business and did not pay enough attention to the deepening connection between my daughter and that man. I let myself be dazzled by him. I made the mistake of listening to my heart and not my brain. His family came from Gdansk, the same as mine, and, knowing what the Germans did to his family, I allowed myself to feel pity for him."

He gave a small shake of his head, as though berating himself for his foolish error. But what he was really doing was preening himself on having a big heart, with me acting as audience.

I smiled, but not in appreciation of his generous nature. It was because Gdansk was a Polish city on the Baltic coast. Nathan had told me he came from a rural area of Poland, so he was certainly not from Gdansk. He had told a similar lie to Mrs. Wasserman, saying he was from Warsaw. Apparently, passing himself off as a native of the same locale as whoever he was trying to win over was a tactic he had employed often.

"In addition," Granot said, "Frankel seemed to be doing well for himself. His clothes were well made, he spoke like an educated man, he showed great promise. So I permitted my daughter to see him. Over the course of a lengthy courtship, I planned to see what became of the promise he showed. If he failed to live up to my expectations, or if a better prospect for my daughter emerged, I would sever their connection like that." He chopped his hand down like a guillotine. "Which is what I did once I learned the truth about him. I protected my daughter."

"But she chose to reject your wise guidance," I said.

He did not notice my sarcasm. His lips curled in bitterness. "She fell completely under his spell."

"That must have put a scare in you."

His forehead furrowed and he fixed his gray eyes on me. "Why should it?"

"Impressionable young girls have been known to act foolishly and impetuously, especially in matters of love. They might have eloped."

He smiled, and this time his teeth showed. Tobacco stains browned the lines where his teeth connected to his gums. I liked his closed-mouth smiles much better.

"I would never have allowed that to happen," he said. "Never."

I nodded, rubbing my jaw as a fresh question popped into my brain. "I'm wondering why you simply didn't tell your daughter about Nathan's line of work. It might have completely altered her view of him."

He brought his hands from behind his back and folded his arms across his chest. "Don't presume to know anything about my daughter, understand?"

His tone was threatening, but his posture was defensive. I was onto something.

"I know that Nathan hid the fact that he was a black marketeer from her precisely because he feared it might bring about the end of their relationship. The same must have occurred to you as well. It could have been an easy solution to your problem. So why didn't you simply tell her what you knew?"

I watched him, saw his facial muscles flex and jitter under that crimson, distended skin, noted the engorged vein throbbing at his temple. And then, in a flash, I knew the reason.

"You learned about it in the course of doing business. Either you bought some contraband or you were otherwise involved in some illicit transaction. And you saw Nathan and were determined that your daughter would have nothing more to do with him. It's okay to do the occasional business with his sort, but marrying one of them is out of the question. Did you order him to stay away?"

At the end of his folded arms, both hands were bunched into fists. Rage had robbed him of control of his voice. It soared in pitch, turning shrill, like the screech of chalk on a blackboard. "It's none of your goddamn business. Now get out. And don't you dare set foot in this house ever again, or, God help me, I'll make you wish you hadn't."

I didn't move. "But he wouldn't stay away. He wanted to be with Tamara. So you forbade her to see him. But she disobeyed you. And now you had a problem: if you told her about Nathan's black-market activities, she would want to know how *you* knew about them. You could have made something up, but all those tutors must have done something right—Tamara's a bright girl. You were worried that she would see through your lies. Then her opinion of you might worsen drastically. She would no longer look up to you. And that is what you want most of all, isn't it? To be revered by her."

His face was hard, taut, like a red balloon about to pop. Even his ears were flushed.

"I said get out!" he squealed.

"After all those years, all that work, and here comes Nathan Frankel and he endangers it all. This criminal might just steal your daughter away from you. Your most cherished possession. How you must have hated him. I wouldn't let the police know that, if I were you. They might put you at the top of their list of suspects."

He unfolded his arms and started toward me, fists clenched, spittle on his lips, murder in his eyes. He was capable of it, I could see it in his face. For some people murder requires a giant leap; for Mr. Granot it would have been but a step.

We might have come to blows then and there if the sound of a door closing upstairs did not filter its way down into the living room. Granot stopped in his tracks, hands still fisted, fuming, as Tamara's light footsteps sounded on the stairs.

"I'm sorry for taking so long, Father," she said, entering the room. "I—"

She stopped in mid sentence, shifting her eyes from her father to me and back, over and over, like a tennis spectator. She'd redone her braid and had put on a becoming light gray coat. Her mouth hung open and she began nervously fumbling with her braid again.

If I didn't leave now, she would have to redo it once more. Which would probably cause her father to unleash his fury on her.

"Thank you for your hospitality," I said to Mr. Granot, not bothering to mask my contempt. "And for yours, Ms. Granot," I added in a softer tone. "I'm sorry for your loss. I'll see myself out."

Which I did, an empty silence following me to the door and out into the street.

Chapter 16

I lit a cigarette and hiked north. The sun was still out in force, and birds chirped from trees and rooftops. The day reminded me of summertime in Hungary, when my sisters and I would rush to a meadow near our home to play in the balmy sunshine. Those were good days, when you forgot about the snowy winter that had passed and gave not a thought to the ones you knew were yet to come. When we lay in the warm grass with our eyes closed, basking in the sun, none of us could have imagined the storm that would one day swoop in from the west, from Germany, and tear our entire world asunder.

I mashed my burnt cigarette against the side of a building and flung the crushed stub onto the pavement. I continued north, massaging the back of my neck, working out some of the tension the memory of those happy days had brought. I wanted something to eat, and I wanted to get off my feet for a while. I could have stopped at a number of restaurants along the way, but I held off on satiating my hunger until I made it to Allenby Street and Greta's Café.

Greta was perched on a stool in her usual spot behind the serving counter by the large front window. She liked watching people walk by. "Most of the time, they don't notice I'm watching," she once told me, "and then their faces are without the masks most of us wear when in company. They show their worries, thoughts, concerns, and mood. And I start to imagine where they're going and what their day will be like, and whether they're looking forward to it or not."

"So you let your imagination roam and make up wild stuff?" I asked.

"Oh, no. Nothing like that. I imagine the small things, the mundane, ordinary things. That's where the really interesting things happen, Adam. In real life."

And, I thought to myself, *it is also where all the truly horrible things happen. In real life.*

There were eight patrons inside the café, clustered around three tables. The air carried the mingled scents of coffee, toast, and margarine. A pair of worry lines appeared between Greta's eyebrows as I approached her.

She said, "Go sit down, Adam, and I'll bring you some coffee. You look like you really need it." She went to fetch the pot. As I walked to my table at the rear, I thought about Sima Vaaknin telling me how worn-out I looked. Was it really that obvious?

"Bad night?" Greta asked a minute later, setting a steaming cup before me.

"I didn't get much sleep," I said, lifting the cup and blowing on it before taking a cautious sip. The coffee slid smoothly down my throat, warming up my chest and face and stomach. As always, it tasted terrific. I had no idea how Greta made such good coffee. The one time I'd asked her, she said there were some secrets she planned on taking to her grave. "Besides," she added with a grin, "if I told you how to make it yourself, you might stop coming by so often."

She drew a chair for herself and sat down opposite me. "I slept poorly too. I dreamed terrible dreams."

"About the dead body?"

"No. Oddly enough, I dreamed about the policeman. Leibowitz."

"Oh?"

She nodded. "In my dream he was much taller than in real life. Everything about him was bigger. That nose of his, his hands, his head, his eyes. There was another strange thing about his eyes—they glowed like there were two tiny fires roaring behind his pupils. The scene was that moment when you asked him about the amount of money in that poor man's wallet. When he whipped around to face you, his face was that of a monster, sharp fangs and all." She shuddered. "That's when I woke up. Thank heavens."

"That's some dream. But the real monster is whoever stabbed Nathan."

"I know. I know. The reason I think I had the dream is that I'm sure Leibowitz knew that you had gone through that wallet."

"He certainly suspected something," I said. "Most people wouldn't have asked how much money there was."

"I keep worrying that he'll come back here."

My heart lifted. So Leibowitz hadn't been around to

ask about me. This might be an indication that I had gotten away unidentified from my visit to Nathan's apartment.

Greta was frowning at me. "Why are you smiling?"

I raised the cup to my lips. "Just some random thought. It's nothing important. About Leibowitz, there's a good chance he'll stop by. If he does, you have nothing to worry about. It's routine. He'll want to question other customers, to see if anyone saw or heard anything. Just be polite and helpful and he'll soon go on his merry way."

"I don't know. I have a bad feeling about him."

Now I no longer felt like smiling, because I suddenly had a similar premonition. I shook it off. "Well, don't. You did nothing wrong."

"And if he shows up and asks about you, what should I tell him?"

"The truth. Part of it anyway. Tell him everything that happened, but leave out the part about the money. And don't let on that I knew Nathan."

"What if he found that out himself?"

"Then you'll plead ignorance. Tell him I never said anything about knowing the deceased. You'll be fine."

Greta did not seem entirely convinced, but she gave a solid nod.

"What about you? Have you done any poking around?"

"Some. Do you really want to know about it?"

She considered the question. "I do, but I don't think I should. Not just yet. I'll wait to see if Inspector Leibowitz stops by first."

I asked her to bring me some lunch and, while I waited, finished my coffee and smoked another cigarette.

She served me a hot chicken broth that actually tasted like real chicken, fresh bread, and a plate of rice and vegetables. Staring at the mass of food on the table before me, I couldn't help but think that this would have been considered the stuff of dreams in Auschwitz. Five men would have feasted on this and counted themselves lucky for having done so.

I ate slowly and methodically, chewing each bite rigorously, making the food last. It was a trick I'd picked up at the camp, a way to fool the mind into believing you ate far more than you actually did.

As I finished my meal, I was overcome by a deep sense of guilt, remembering the starving men with whom I had been imprisoned in Auschwitz, those walking skeletons who would shuffle by, detached from the world around them, as hunger consumed their minds just as it depleted their bodies.

I also felt stuffed, as if I had gorged myself, though, in truth, what I'd eaten was an ordinary lunch. I pushed the empty dishes away and shut my eyes and took a couple of deep breaths. I wanted the memories to be gone, but they did not wish to relinquish their hold on me. They were alive, with a will of their own, and their utmost desire was to torment me with their gruesome presence. Because if I did not dwell on them, their very existence was threatened, and this they feared most of all. Like the human beings in which they dwelt, dark memories did not wish to die.

I stuck another cigarette between my lips, piled up the dirty dishes, and took them to the serving counter. Greta asked me if I wanted anything else and I said I could do with another cup of coffee. While she poured, I reached over the counter and got my chessboard and pieces.

Back at my table, I set the coffee aside to cool and set up the pieces on the board. As I did so, I was aware of the funny looks a couple of the other patrons were giving me. I was used to it. It comes with the territory when you play chess without an opponent.

Well, that wasn't exactly true. I was my own opponent.

White went first. I moved the king's pawn two squares forward and immediately responded by vaulting one of the black knights over the line of black pawns. And so it went—lightning-quick moves, with no time for calculation or planning, playing by instinct alone.

Soon, as often happened, my head cleared. For a blessed while, there were no bad memories, no gloomy thoughts, no dark past or hazy future, no guilt and none of the deep-seated pain that comes from missing your dead loved ones.

I played four or five quick games, taking a few sips of coffee each time I reset the pieces. And when the last game was done with black vanquishing white, I leaned back in my chair and smiled with satisfaction at the board.

Then I slouched a little further, stretching my legs before me and lacing my hands behind my head. Staring at the ceiling, I started thinking.

I thought about Mr. Granot. His rabid hatred of Nathan was enough to drive him to kill. Under no circumstances would he have allowed Nathan to marry his daughter. But had he known that Nathan was about to pop the question? Maybe Nathan had been foolish enough to ask Mr. Granot for Tamara's hand. He had not struck me as a man given to tradition, but I supposed it was possible. Perhaps he had been certain he could charm his way into Mr. Granot's good graces, thereby inadvertently goading Granot into stabbing him.

I had to admit that I liked the idea of Granot being the killer. In fact, I liked it just a bit too much. Perhaps enough to cloud my judgment.

The first reason was that I utterly detested Granot. Not only had he looked down his nose at me, but he also considered it his privilege to deprive his daughter of the love of her life. He had already inflicted untold damage on her in the way he had raised her. Now he wanted to maintain his control over her, to determine who she should or shouldn't marry. I suspected that a part of him did not want to let her go at all, to anyone. Once she stopped living under his roof, she would no longer be under his thumb.

Having lost both of my daughters, I could not stand any father who would treat his daughter that way. It was a betrayal of the most basic responsibility of any man—to love and cherish his children, to treat them well, and to raise them right.

The second reason, the main one, was that if Granot were the killer, I would not be to blame for Nathan's death. Up until now, the likely suspects had been Tova Wasserman and Nathan's associates, Gregor and Dov. If any of them were the culprits, I would have to live with the fact that my actions had contributed to their decision to murder Nathan. I had enough guilt in my life as it was. I dreaded adding to it.

All this made Granot an enticing prospect, but that was hardly proof of his guilt. I turned my thoughts to the other suspects.

Tova Wasserman. She had a burning desire to punish Nathan. She had tried to hire me to carry out the punishment. I had refused. Had she hired a replacement? If so, who? I had to figure out what steps I needed to take in order to answer these questions.

The same went for Gregor and Dov. I did not know whether they indeed had a motive to murder Nathan. What I did know was that he had feared their reaction were they to learn the truth about him and Tova Wasserman.

And there was the possibility that none of them was guilty, that the killer was a person I had yet to meet.

I had just finished formulating this last thought when Inspector Leibowitz stepped into the café.

Chapter 17

Leibowitz was not alone.

Officer Elkin came on his heels. Elkin was in uniform, and he removed his cap and nodded to Greta as he crossed the threshold.

Leibowitz also nodded to her. Then his eyes did a sweep around the café before coming to rest on me.

He wore the same black coat as on the previous night, the same dark shoes. The pants were different—a light gray—the same color of the pant leg I'd seen emerging from the police car outside Nathan's building earlier that day.

His expression gave no clue as to what he was thinking.

He wasted no time but came straight to my table, his right hand dipping into his coat pocket. As he and Elkin approached, I became aware that all conversation in the café had ceased and that all eyes were now directed at me. It occurred to me that this might require some explaining later, but that the exact form that later would take was not yet known.

Leibowitz drew out a chair with his left hand and lowered himself onto it. Elkin took up position a foot or so behind him.

As soon as he was seated, Leibowitz brought out his right hand and dumped a pair of gloves on the table. I recognized them, of course. They were the gloves I had left behind in Nathan's apartment.

"You forgot these," Leibowitz said in an even tone.

He was good, giving me no time to steel myself before coming straight at me like a battering ram. And it worked, at least partly. My stomach muscles spasmed in sudden anxiety and my heart stuttered against my breastbone. I tried to maintain a straight face, to show no hint of my roiling emotions. I wasn't sure I pulled it off. I might have let something slip in the instant I saw the gloves. A lump had formed in my throat and it took a conscious effort to refrain from gulping.

I raised both eyebrows and was gratified to hear my voice did not quaver. "What's this?"

Leibowitz said nothing, his eyes not leaving my face. I wondered if he disliked his eyes, the way they bulged. They'd probably earned him much ridicule during his childhood. I noticed he had nicked himself shaving that morning. A small patch of coagulated blood colored his chin. The nick had taken on a purplish tinge, similar to the color of the bags under his eyes. In the light of day he looked even more tired than he had the previous night. He couldn't have slept much, considering how early he had gone to Nathan's apartment.

I knew from experience that there were a couple of ways I could get the next move wrong. I could fidget in my seat or avoid meeting his gaze, thereby suggesting that

I could not bear his scrutiny. Or I could maintain rigid eye contact, unnaturally so, which would indicate that I was actively trying to hide my emotional state and frame of mind. Either would be suspicious. An out-of-the-ordinary approach was best.

I leaned forward and snapped my fingers under his nose. "Hey, did you hear me?"

It was impertinent as hell and it got a reaction, but not from Leibowitz. Officer Elkin drew ramrod straight, took a step forward, pointed at me over the shoulder of his superior, and in a sharp voice said, "You better watch it."

Leibowitz appeared unruffled. Up close I noticed that the brown of his eyes was flecked with what looked like dull metallic dust. No trace of a fire behind those intelligent pupils, though, and his face was not that of a monster.

Behind the two cops, I could see Greta standing at her regular spot, hands on the bar, her face tight with worry. I caught her eye and angled my head down an inch, signaling her not to interfere, that I had this under control.

Leibowitz said, "These are your gloves. I thought you might like to have them back."

I leaned back, spreading my hands, putting on a bewildered expression. "I got no idea what you're talking about."

One corner of his mouth pulled itself up into a cynical half smile that seemed to say that he had heard that particular line a thousand times before and had not once believed it.

He idly massaged the side of his nose with a forefinger. "Mr. Lapid is being difficult, wouldn't you say so, Elkin?"

"I would," Elkin said gruffly, still mad at me, his hand resting on the hilt of the nightstick hanging at his hip. "I would indeed."

"Put your gloves on, Mr. Lapid," Leibowitz said.

"What for? I tell you they're not mine."

"Indulge me."

I blew air out of my nose in mock exasperation, gave an elaborate shrug, grabbed the gloves, and pulled them on. I gazed at them as if this was the first time I'd seen them on my hands, flexing my fingers like I was getting used to their feel.

"There. Happy?"

"A perfect fit," Leibowitz said without a hint of triumph.

I shook my head, yanking the gloves off and tossing them back on the table. "They're a bit tight. But like I said, they're not mine. You mind telling me what this is about?"

Now it was Leibowitz's turn to exhale loudly. His mouth settled into a weary line that was at home on his worn-out, seen-it-all face. I could guess what was going through his mind. It was the detective's lament. One of them, anyway.

Why did they always have to be difficult? Why couldn't they just come clean and save everyone the trouble?

"You'd better come with us, Mr. Lapid."

"Where to?" I asked, though I knew the answer.

"To the station. We'd like to ask you a few questions."

"What about?"

"I'm sure you know." He pushed himself to his feet. "Let's go."

I stayed in my seat, feigning incredulity. "Are you arresting me?"

Leibowitz did not raise his voice, and his tone remained mild. Many cops used volume and harsh tones to strike fear into suspects and witnesses. Others, the better ones, used more sophisticated methods.

He said, "You have two seconds to get up and come with us quietly to the door. If you don't, Elkin will cuff your hands behind your back and force-walk you out like the common criminal I suspect you are. If you resist, he will whip out his nightstick and let you have a taste of it. I got a feeling he would enjoy that."

Elkin grinned. "You're right. I would."

"What will it be, Mr. Lapid? I got very little patience for the likes of you."

I needed no further encouragement. I rose. Elkin looked disappointed.

"You're making a mistake," I said.

"Yeah, yeah," said Leibowitz. "Thanks for the warning. Now pipe down and come along."

We walked to the door, Elkin on my left, Leibowitz bringing up the rear. The other patrons followed our little procession with inquiring eyes. I wasn't friends with any of them, but I'd given none of them reason to dislike or resent me. So I detected no glee as I was led out. They were simply curious, as most people would be in their place.

Outside, the sun shone so bright that it dazzled my eyes. Elkin ordered me to stand still while he opened the rear door of the police car. Then he half steered, half shoved me inside. "Don't move an inch," he said and slammed the door.

I looked out the side window and saw Leibowitz and Greta talking inside the café. He said something; she answered, periodically nodding or shaking her head. This went on for about two minutes. Then Leibowitz came out. Elkin got in the driver's seat; Leibowitz settled in beside me in the back. As Elkin started the car, I could see Greta standing with one palm flat against the large window, staring right at me. I couldn't read her face with how the sunlight reflected off the glass.

Then Elkin swung the wheel and we were off.

Neither of them said a word to me during the drive, but a few times I caught Elkin giving me the nasty-eye in the rearview mirror. He was still mad. It was something he would learn to overcome as he gained experience on the job. You had to keep your emotions in check, to not let every minor insult or display of insolence get to you. Leibowitz could have told him that. He'd already mastered the skill.

They took me to the station on Hayarkon Street and ushered me inside and into a musty, windowless room with a metal table and three chairs.

"Sit down," Elkin told me, pointing to a chair on the side of the table facing the door. Then he left the room.

Leibowitz remained. He held my gloves in his right hand and was slapping them idly onto his left palm—smack, smack, smack. The movement conjured the bleak memory of one of the camp officers at Auschwitz who used to do the exact same thing as he gazed upon us prisoners as though at a column of ants he was about to stomp.

I clamped my eyes shut as a powerful tremor shook me. I felt chilled to my bones, as if I were once more dressed in a tattered camp uniform with the Polish winter raging around me. *You're in Tel Aviv*, I told myself. *You're in Israel. You've left Poland behind, never to return.*

When I opened my eyes, Leibowitz was peering at me as though I was unhinged.

"What the hell's wrong with you?"

I glanced at the gloves. He was holding them motionless by his side. I raised my eyes to his face. He looked nothing like that officer. He looked nothing like a monster either.

I was damned if I was going to explain myself to him. "It's nothing," I said, the tremor gone from my body but still evident in my voice. "I'm fine."

I could tell he didn't believe me, but just then Elkin came into the room, carrying a fingerprinting kit. He set it up on the table and told me to extend my left hand.

"Why do you need my fingerprints?"

"You know why," Leibowitz said, still eying me curiously.

Elkin inked each of my fingers and then pressed them one at a time onto a piece of paper with dedicated squares for each finger.

When he was through, he left the room, the fingerprinting kit in hand. He returned a minute later, empty-handed, and gave Leibowitz a quick nod.

Leibowitz tossed the gloves on the table. "In case you get cold."

And then they were gone.

I had a look around the room. There wasn't much to see. Unadorned, depressing gray walls. At one spot to the left, a former interviewee had gouged his name into the wall.

I was likely in for a long wait. It was a common interrogation technique. You brought in a suspect, isolated him, and let him stew for a while. Allowed his fear to build. Gave him time to wonder what you had on him. Let him ponder what else you might be getting on him at that exact moment. What you might end up with was a guy who was ready to spill the beans in the hope that you'd spare him the worst-case scenario churning through his mind.

I wasn't worried about becoming that guy. What did worry me was the fact that as long as I was here, I could not keep digging into Nathan's murder.

Glancing at my watch, I saw it was a little past one thirty. I dug out my pack of cigarettes and lit one. I sat blowing smoke at the ceiling. There was no ashtray, so I stubbed out my cigarette on the tabletop and left the crushed butt lying there.

I considered my position. I was not formally under arrest, which might have meant that Leibowitz did not have unshakable proof that I had been in Nathan's building. This made me think that there was a chance I might wriggle out of this predicament if I played it right. And if I was damn lucky.

After thirty minutes, Elkin came in with a cup of coffee. By the smell of it, I knew it wasn't the real thing but the chicory kind that was rationed out to each citizen.

Elkin no longer looked mad. He sounded downright polite, saying, "Here you go," as he set the cup on the table before me.

I studied him. Average height, slim build, black hair cut short. A youthful, unmemorable face. Light brown eyes and a tiny bump on the bridge of his nose. Not a trace of stubble on his chin or cheeks. Ironed uniform. A clean-cut, run-of-the-mill young officer. The job had not had time to wear him down as it had Leibowitz. Give him three or four years and the wear and tear would start showing.

I wondered what his cut of the twenty liras Leibowitz had taken from Nathan's wallet was and decided there was a chance he'd gotten nothing. Perhaps Leibowitz hadn't even told him about the money. But he'd learn. It was only a matter of time and the number of corpses he came across.

I thanked him for the coffee and he nodded and left.

It was ninety minutes later when Leibowitz came in to interrogate me.

Chapter 18

He entered without a word and positioned himself on the edge of his chair, hunched forward, hands clasped on the table. Elkin stood behind him, leaning against the door, arms folded across his chest.

Leibowitz allowed the silence to stretch, staring at me with those protruding eyes, giving the impression that he already knew everything, that lying was futile, that what we were about to do here was merely a formality. I studied his face but couldn't read him. He was good. Damn good.

"Do you know what the penalty is for breaking and entering?" he asked after a full minute had elapsed.

"Not off the top of my head," I said.

"Imprisonment for a number of years. Depending on how much was stolen. Five years is not unheard of."

"Thank you for letting me know. I'll be sure to remember that."

"Have you ever served time in prison?"

Yes, I thought, *in one much worse than anything you could possibly imagine.*

"No," I said.

"You won't like it much."

"Then I'll make it my business to never set foot in one."

"That's one business that is likely to go belly up before nightfall," he said dryly before changing tacks. "Where were you at six o'clock this morning?"

"At home."

"Can anyone confirm that?"

"I live alone."

"So that's a no?"

"I suppose it is."

"What were you doing at that time?"

"Sleeping, probably."

"You don't know?"

"I didn't check the time when I woke up. I was either asleep or in bed reading."

"And you left your apartment when?"

I pretended to think. "Eight o'clock or thereabouts."

"Where did you go?"

I knew what he was trying to do. He knew I was lying to him, so he wanted to keep me talking. The more I talked, the more lies I told. He only needed to catch me at a single lie to shred my entire story. I needed to stick to the truth as closely as possible.

"The weather was nice, so I walked around. I went to the beach, to look at the sea. Then I found a place to eat breakfast."

He asked me the name of the place and I gave it to him. He wrote it down in his notebook and tapped his pencil twice on the table as he repeated the address.

"That's not very close to your apartment on

Hamaccabi Street. But it's a short walk from Arlozorov."

"So?"

His lips twitched in what might have become a smile if he had allowed it to blossom. He tapped the pencil again on the table before setting it down on his open notebook. He leaned closer, forearms on the table, his sloping forehead leading the way like the prow of a ship.

"Here's what we know," he said. "Here's what really happened. You were not in your apartment at six o'clock this morning. You were not reading in bed. You were in Arlozorov Street, in the apartment where the late Nathan Frankel used to reside."

I feigned surprise. "Nathan Frankel? The man who was killed last night?"

I was betting that neither Tamara Granot nor her father, each for their own separate reasons, had spoken about me to Leibowitz. If they had, I would learn about it now.

It turned out that I had bet correctly.

"You knew the apartment would be empty, so you burglarized it," Leibowitz said. "What did you take? How much?"

Behind Leibowitz, Elkin adjusted his stance, no longer leaning against the door. He was listening closely. This was the interesting bit, after all.

"I was never there," I said.

"To avoid leaving fingerprints, you brought your gloves along. But for some reason, you took them off and left them on the kitchen counter."

He'd said this so matter-of-factly that my mouth had

already opened to correct him before my brain caught on to the neat trap he'd laid for me. I had to bite back the words I was about to instinctively blurt out—"In the bathroom, you mean"—and shut my mouth with a dull smack, so for a moment there was nothing but silence again. Only this time I could feel its weight.

Leibowitz allowed himself a small smile. His eyes glinted in triumph.

But in truth, it was a partial victory at best. While he had cause to pat himself on the back for talking me onto the edge of the precipice, I had managed to dig in my heels and avoid falling. I had said nothing to incriminate myself. My facial expressions could not be used against me in a court of law. But he had shaken me, and good interrogators always like to keep their suspects off balance.

"Actually, as you very well know, you left them in the bathroom. That was incredibly careless of you. What did you do, use the bathroom and wash your hands? Hygiene and burglary don't mix. What did you touch? The tap, the sink, the walls? It doesn't matter what. We went over the entire bathroom. We recorded every print. At this moment, they're being compared to the ones Elkin took of you in this room. Once we find a match, you're headed straight to jail."

He let the threat hang in the air like the Sword of Damocles over my head. He looked at me dispassionately, as though my doom was a foregone conclusion and he cared not one whit what became of me. I knew what he was doing but still felt a prickle of panic at the base of my skull. He was an adept interrogator. A natural. I couldn't help but admire his skill, even though he was my adversary.

Then, as I'd expected, came the promise of relief. "But if you come clean now and save us a bit of work, we'll go easy on you."

"You won't find any of my prints in that apartment," I said.

Which might end up being true. I had only touched a couple of surfaces and my hands had been wet. There was a good chance I hadn't left any usable prints. This happened quite often—more than any policeman would care to admit. You found prints that were smudged, partial, or unusable in some other way. When I was a policeman, I investigated cases where I knew the suspect had touched a weapon with his bare hands and had not wiped it off afterward, but nonetheless hadn't left any prints I could use against him.

Leibowitz shook his head as though saddened by my stupidity in rejecting his offer of help. "You went through the apartment, searched everywhere. You even slashed the pillows. You took all the money there was to take. How much was there?"

I sighed. "You're barking up the wrong tree."

"And then something happened that spooked you. I think I know what it was. You opened the window in the bathroom for some reason—maybe you needed some air—and you saw a police car coming down the street. So you ran. You ran out of the apartment and down the stairs, but someone was there. One of the residents back from walking her dog. Remember her?"

I didn't answer. A giant fist had closed around my heart, lungs, and kidneys and was slowly squeezing them, crushing them. I knew that the old lady had seen me. Otherwise, Leibowitz would not have guessed that I had been in that apartment. What I did not know was how good a look she'd got of me. How sharp was her memory? Had she simply given the police a general description of the man she'd seen on the stairs and Leibowitz had deduced it was me? Or could she identify my face? If it were the latter, I was done for.

And with that realization, that fist eased up, and my insides no longer felt like they were about to burst under its pressure.

Because if that old lady could identify my face, why hadn't Leibowitz simply marched her into the room to get a second look at me? Why did he waste time with all these questions?

"You need to understand something, Mr. Lapid. Once that woman formally identifies you, there is only so much I will be able to do for you. My hands will be tied. But if you make a full confession and tell me everything you stole from that apartment and where I can find it, I promise to use all my power to see that your punishment is as light as possible."

There was just one thing I could do. I gambled. "Go fetch this woman. She'll tell you it was some other guy she saw."

Leibowitz gave me a long look. He drummed his fingers on the table and said, "Go get her, Elkin."

When Elkin had gone, Leibowitz said, "Empty your pockets on the table."

I complied. He pushed aside my keys and lighter and notebook, emptied my pack of cigarettes and peeked inside it, read my ID card, and finally counted the money I had on me.

"Twenty-seven liras," he said, eyes fixed on the money in his hand. He sounded a trifle disappointed, like he'd hoped there'd be more.

"Are you sure?" I said, uncertain whether I was about to make a big mistake, and forging ahead nonetheless, "I thought there were only seven."

His eyes shot up to my face. The implication of what I'd said was not lost on him. The difference was twenty liras. The same difference between the amount he said he'd found in Nathan's wallet and what had truly been there.

He laid my money on the table and leaned back in his chair. A slight frown dug serpentine lines across his forehead. Crow's-feet appeared at the corners of his eyes as he squinted at me. What I'd said had surprised him, but not all that much. I had merely confirmed a suspicion of his. What he hadn't expected was that I would come out and do so.

As he weighed me anew with his gaze, he sucked on his lower lip. A shiver went through me. He had done the exact same thing when he stood over Nathan's body.

"You like playing games, Mr. Lapid?" he asked softly. "Dangerous, reckless games?"

"Not particularly. But I don't like being called a burglar either."

"I may call you much worse before I'm through with you."

"What's that supposed to mean?"

Before he could answer, the door to the interrogation room opened and inside stepped Elkin and the woman from Nathan's building.

Chapter 19

She did not have her dog with her. Instead she carried a brown handbag large enough to fit a head in. I just hoped she wasn't about to take mine off in the next few minutes.

She wore a conservative gray dress, sensible shoes, and a pair of thick black stockings. Her gray hair was pulled into a bun. Elkin held her coat for her.

Leibowitz rose from his seat. "Thank you for coming, Mrs. Kuperman."

She gave him an uncharitable look. "You've kept me waiting for nearly an hour, Inspector."

The seamless way Leibowitz's expression morphed into a show of heartfelt contrition might have made me laugh were the circumstances different. "I'm very sorry, Mrs. Kuperman. Please accept my apology."

She did so with a curt nod, obviously pleased by the deference Leibowitz was showing her. Her eyes went from him to the tabletop strewn with the contents of my pockets to me. My heartbeat accelerated as I waited for her to point her finger and proclaim my guilt. She did neither. Instead, she shifted her gaze to Leibowitz and waited for him to speak.

"Mrs. Kuperman," he said, "would you be so kind as

to take a close look at this man here and tell me whether he is the man you saw running down the stairs this morning?"

She snorted. "I'd hardly call what he was doing running. It was more like hurtling, like a train coming off the rails."

Leibowitz inclined his head. "Hurtling down the stairs, then. Is this the man?"

She flicked her eyes in my direction. "He needs to stand up."

Leibowitz told me to rise and I did.

She looked at me again. She stood no taller than five three, a foot shorter than me, but she seemed taller, perhaps due to the power she now held over me or the fiercely judgmental expression she wore.

"Say I'm sorry," she instructed.

"What?" Leibowitz asked.

"Tell him to say I'm sorry. That's what the man on the stairs said to me."

"Do it," he told me. "In a normal voice."

I caught her eyes with mine, held them, tried to convey how sincere I was in what I was about to say, that I hoped she'd forgive me for nearly colliding with her on the stairs.

"I'm sorry," I said.

She said nothing for a long moment as she gazed intently at me, and I felt a glimmer of hope as I thought I detected a thawing of her hard features. Then she delivered her verdict.

"As well you should be. You could have killed my

dog." She looked at Leibowitz. "It's him."

"Are you sure?"

Her face tightened in irritation. "Of course I am. Do you think I would have said it was him if I wasn't?"

Leibowitz raised a placating hand. "It's required of me to ask, Mrs. Kuperman."

"Well, I'm sure. He's the man I saw. Is there anything else?"

"No, Mrs. Kuperman. Officer Elkin will see you out. And thank you."

Just the two of us again, Leibowitz flashed a satisfied smile at me. "Checkmate."

"More like a standoff," I said.

Still smiling, he shook his head. He collected my belongings from the table and put them in his pocket. "You're not only a liar and a burglar, but also a fool. Do you really think anyone would believe your little fairy tale?"

"I'm not the only one who knows about the twenty liras."

That wiped the smile off his face. He stared at me, dumbstruck, his expression hostile and calculating, and for a second I could have sworn the metallic dust in his eyes glowed a malevolent red.

Elkin came back into the room. "Well? What do we do with him?"

Leibowitz inhaled loudly and said, "Mr. Lapid is being difficult again. Let's take him for a ride."

"I'll cuff him."

"No," Leibowitz said. "That won't be necessary. Not

yet anyway. You're not going to make a run for it, are you, Mr. Lapid?"

"Where are we going?" I asked.

"To your apartment. Whatever you took from Frankel, I'll find it."

It was a short drive. And a silent one.

We parked outside my building and climbed the stairs single file. I went first followed by Leibowitz and then Elkin. Which was why I saw it first—the busted-up door, wood slivers jutting out of the jamb. I stopped short on the edge of the landing. Leibowitz bumped into my back.

"What is it?"

Instead of answering, I stepped aside, letting him see for himself. Giving me a quizzical look, he came up the rest of the way and glanced at the door.

"Damn," I heard him mutter. To Elkin he said, "Get your gun out. There might still be someone inside."

Elkin unholstered his gun. Leibowitz drew his. He told me not to move an inch, then nudged the door open and went inside. Elkin followed. Disobeying Leibowitz's order, I went in third.

Whoever had broken in had long since gone, but they had left plenty of evidence of their visit. The three of us surveyed the wreckage.

The closet had been emptied. My clothes were strewn on the floor. Some had been torn and shredded. The pillow had been sliced open and rummaged through. White and yellow feathers lay everywhere. Two long, roughly parallel gashes ran the length of the mattress, and its padding stuck out like boulders after an earthquake.

The reading lamp had been knocked to the floor and its bulb was crushed, probably under a shoe.

Two paperback westerns that had been lying on the nightstand would never be read again. The intruders had torn some pages out and mangled what remained. I bent down and picked up a crumpled cover bearing the image of a dusty cowboy with a long-barreled revolver in his hand, stared at it for a second or two, and let it fall to the ruined mattress.

I was surprised by how moved I was by the sight of my wrecked apartment. I had never fully viewed it as my home. It was more a place of shelter, where I could read my books, eat my meals, sleep my tortured sleep. The last place that had felt like home was in Hungary, before my family and I had been transported to Auschwitz.

But perhaps the cramped little apartment had grown on me. For I felt both saddened and angered by what had been done to it. It was, as I recalled a Hungarian once telling me after his home was burglarized, a violation. I had assumed he meant merely a violation of his house, the physical residence. Now I understood that it had been a more personal violation. An act that left one feeling vulnerable and eager for retribution.

"I thought I told you to wait outside," Leibowitz said, slipping his gun back into his coat. Scowling, hands on his hips, he rotated on his heels, taking in the entire space. To Elkin he said, "We should have come here sooner. We might have caught them red-handed."

"We wanted to get the fingerprints first," Elkin said.

Leibowitz's mouth twisted. "Yeah, yeah. You mind

telling me what's going on?"

He was talking to me. "Your guess is as good as mine," I said.

He grunted, then was struck by a sudden suspicion and gave me an appraising look. "This isn't some elaborate trick, is it? You didn't do all this yourself?"

It was an appropriate question, one which I would have likely come up with in his place, but it nevertheless astounded me. "Are you crazy? I had nothing to do with this."

He scrutinized me for a few seconds, then nodded. "Yeah. I don't believe you did. I saw your face when you walked in here. You're not a good liar, Mr. Lapid. And I wouldn't start playing poker, either. You don't hide your thoughts very well."

Sima Vaaknin had once told me the same thing. I wasn't sure I liked being an open book. I had too many secrets.

Leibowitz crossed over to the kitchen. Elkin and I followed. The tiny room was a shambles. A cupboard door hung crookedly off one hinge. Dishes lay haphazardly on the counter. Broken glass littered the floor. Coffee powder had been sprayed in all directions; the empty can had been tossed in the sink. They'd left the icebox open, causing the ice to melt into a puddle, and had swept part of its contents onto the floor. A bottle of milk lay in the center of the puddle like a ship grounded in low tide. A misshaped slab of butter was gradually melting to death. But the worst was yet to come.

Elkin wrinkled his nose. "What's that stink?"

It was unmistakable. That acidic, ammoniac smell could only be caused by one thing.

Leibowitz said, "Son of a bitch took a piss in the icebox. Right on the vegetables."

"God almighty," Elkin said. "That's..." He groped for the right word and finally gave up and retreated into the living room.

Leibowitz was eying me closely, trying to gauge my reaction. It shouldn't have been hard to read. The anger I'd felt earlier had mushroomed to full-blown rage. My arms and hands tingled with the desire for violent retribution. My face felt so hot it was a wonder the skin did not blister or burst into flame.

"No," Leibowitz said evenly. "You did not do this yourself."

The smell might have been worse still if they'd kept the icebox closed. The melted ice had mingled with the urine that had dribbled out of the icebox onto the kitchen floor, diluting it. Which was why the stink hadn't spread to the bedroom.

Walking over to stand by the balcony door, Leibowitz motioned me to follow him. "You slept here last night?"

"Yes."

"And when were you here last?"

"Seven or so."

He smiled a tiny smile, as this was an implicit admission that I had earlier given him a false timeline of my activities that day. But the smile did not last long.

"What were they looking for?"

I shook my head and shrugged.

He gave me a disgusted look.

"If there was anything, they must have found it," Elkin said. "Goddamn, they went through this place like a tornado."

Elkin could be forgiven for thinking that, but he was wrong. I could see they had not disturbed the false bottom in the closet. They had not found the money hidden beneath it.

Leibowitz grunted, went into the bathroom, and emerged a minute later. "The same mess in there." He looked around again. "You don't own much, do you?"

"No."

"Why?"

"I don't need anything more."

He took this in without comment and cast another slow look around. He poked a finger into the mattress, knelt and peered under the bed, and ran a hand under the nightstand. He peeked behind the icebox and inside the cupboards, then went on the balcony and looked there too.

He returned, hands shoved in his coat pockets, his face looking even more cynical and worn-out than usual.

"Nothing, right?" Elkin said.

Leibowitz didn't answer. He sniffed loudly and scratched his chin, thoughtful. He picked up the torn paperbacks, riffled through the remaining pages, and set the books down on the bed more gently than I expected. He lazily nudged my clothes with the toe of his shoe, but there was nothing underneath. Drumming his fingers on his thigh, he began lifting his gaze but stopped midway.

He was still for a second; then his shoulders straightened and his head came the rest of the way up.

"No," he said. "Not nothing."

He was looking right at me, and by the glint in his eyes, I knew what he'd seen. I cursed silently as he crouched down by the closet, reached inside, and lifted the false bottom. He stood up with a fistful of cash.

Off to my right I heard Elkin's sharp intake of breath. "Damn," he whispered.

Leibowitz said, "Let this be a lesson to you, Elkin: You can always find something."

"Are those dollars?" Elkin asked, a trace of awe in his voice.

Leibowitz fanned the bills. "Yes. And some French notes and a few liras sprinkled on top. You want to know how much?" He didn't wait for a response. He thumbed through the notes, mouthing the sums. "Twenty-five francs, fourteen liras, and fifty-five dollars."

We eyed each other as that last bit echoed between the walls of the small bedroom. He had shaved a hundred dollars off the real amount. An outrageous sum. My mouth went dry at his greed. My palms, however, moistened as my hands balled into tight fists at my sides. Even though I had left that money behind knowing that it might soon be gone forever, when the moment of actually parting with it came, I found myself gripped by a powerful desire to pound my fists into Leibowitz's face.

"I suggest you remain calm, Mr. Lapid. Remember your position."

The blood boiled beneath my skin. My face felt on

fire. Too many insults heaped one on top of the other in a single day. The break-in, the destruction of my possessions, the piss in the icebox, and now this theft. It was too much. I was fit to burst with rage. "I suggest you remember yours," I said through gritted teeth.

"Don't delude yourself into thinking you pose me any threat. You are a confirmed burglar. I am the police." He emphasized that last word, making it sound like a gavel pounding home the finality of a lengthy prison sentence. He held up the bills like a small bouquet. "Mind telling me how you got these?"

I took a calming breath. Then another. I had to be smart. Hitting a police officer is the surest way to get your bones broken plus a long stay behind bars. "Some I brought with me when I came to Israel from Europe."

"The French money, perhaps, not the American or Israeli. Where did those come from?"

"I earned them."

"Doing what? Do you even have a job?"

"I perform services for people and they pay me for them."

"What sort of services?" he said, making an out-with-it-already motion with his hand, rustling the banknotes.

"Investigation services."

"What?" Elkin asked. "Like a private detective?"

"Precisely."

Leibowitz's eyebrows rose and his tone turned mocking. "And where did you acquire the qualifications for that kind of work?"

"The same way you did. On the job."

The eyebrows fell. Now he was frowning. "What do you mean?"

I smiled, enjoying his bewilderment far more than I should have. "I was a police detective. That's what I mean."

For a moment there was no sound in that room apart from our breathing. Elkin shifted his gaze from me to his boss and seemed to wish someone would speak, but was not inclined to do so himself. Leibowitz licked his lips and ran a finger slowly down the side of his face.

"Is this a joke?" he said eventually.

I shook my head.

"Where did you serve?"

"In Hungary."

"Hungary?"

"That's right. Before the war in Europe."

"But you were never a policeman in Israel?"

"No."

He exhaled. His bulging eyes peered at me, and I could sense the well-oiled mental machinery behind that sloping forehead processing this new piece of information, combining it with everything else he'd learned about me.

"Are you aware that Nathan Frankel was a criminal, Mr. Lapid?"

"No. What sort of criminal?"

"He probably dabbled in all sorts of mischief. But he was arrested twice, both times on charges related to the black market. The first time he got off with a warning. The second time around, he was facing jail time. Only it didn't turn out that way. Apparently, Frankel was quite the smooth-talker. The officer who arrested him told me Frankel appealed to the emotions of the judge—one of the harshest judges I know—and ended up with a slap on the wrist—small fine, no jail time. The officer was stunned."

I bet he was, I thought, stifling a smile. *Good for you, Nathan.*

"None of this should concern you," said Leibowitz, "only it does. Because you were the one who found Frankel's body, and we both know that you did go to his apartment. And now your apartment has been trashed as well, and not by any run-of-the-mill burglar. A guy like that wouldn't take a leak all over your food. It raises questions. It makes me think you're hiding things from me, and I don't like that one bit. If you know anything, now's the time to spit it out."

I didn't even need to think about it. He was getting nothing from me. "I don't know anything about this."

He nodded a few times as though my intransigence was no more than he'd expected. "You'll need to come with us again, Mr. Lapid. I hope you like jail food."

Chapter 20

They took me back to the station, but this time there was no interrogation. They just shoved me into a holding cell and left me there.

The cell smelled of urine and body odor and an underlying reek of drink-induced vomit. I sat on the cot, leaned against the wall, closed my eyes, and tried to sleep.

There were three cells in total, and only one other detainee—a fat guy who snored like a tank's engine. Still, it was far less noisy than a crowded Auschwitz barracks— and the smell was not as bad either—so I managed to drift off quite quickly.

I awoke to the clanging of metal on metal. Elkin and the duty guard were standing outside my cell. The guard was banging his truncheon between two bars, saying, "Rise and shine. Supper time." Elkin held a tray of food. The smell was not enticing.

After the guard opened the door, Elkin set the tray on the cot beside me and regarded me with his youthful eyes.

"What?" I said.

"I was just wondering where you really got those dollars."

"Exactly where I said."

He grinned. "All right. Have it your way."

I shook my head, knowing I'd never convince either him or Leibowitz. I couldn't blame them. In their place, I wouldn't have believed me either.

He turned to leave. "Holler for the guard when you're done."

"Thank you, Elkin," I said. "You're an okay guy."

He smiled. "Don't mention it."

The food wasn't very good, but I wolfed it down. Something about being imprisoned had ratcheted up my hunger. It kept gnawing at me even when the last morsel was gone. I called for the guard.

"Any chance of getting more?"

He laughed. "Now that's a first. Sorry, no seconds." He took the tray, still chuckling, and went back to his post down the hall.

There was a small chipped sink, where I splashed water on my face and drank a few mouthfuls. Then I sat back on the cot and smoked for a while and thought about Gregor and Dov. I could not be one hundred percent certain that they were the ones who'd trashed my apartment, but that was my working assumption. I had encroached on Gregor's territory that time, and he had responded by invading mine and marking it with his urine like a wild animal.

The question was: Was this just payback, or had they been searching for anything specific? Likely the second, but I had no clue as to what they might have been after. Regardless, I would need to have a chat with Gregor and Dov soon.

I fired up another cigarette and tried hard not to think

how long I might be stuck in a cell.

A little before ten that night I got my answer.

Leibowitz delivered it himself. He said, "I don't quite know what to do with you, Mr. Lapid."

"Yeah, you do."

"I do?"

"Yes. Otherwise you wouldn't have come here. Besides, you've had hours to figure it out."

He allowed himself a brief smile. "I had you checked out. Turns out you were telling the truth about once being a cop."

I said nothing.

"You also helped solve a cold case a couple of years back. A murder." There was grudging respect in his voice. A professional acknowledging a job well done. "And you didn't take any credit for it. I can't help but wonder why."

"It was a high-profile case, and I like my privacy."

He nodded, though I could tell he didn't understand.

"Two of my colleagues vouched for you," he said. "Reuben Tzanani swore by you, said you were in the army together, that you're a war hero, took two bullets fighting the Egyptians. Yossi Talmon wasn't quite so enthusiastic, but he also said you were a good guy. Both wanted to know why I was asking about you. I said it was routine, that you found the body of a murder victim. I did not tell them about your breaking in to Frankel's apartment." He paused. "What were you doing there, Mr. Lapid? What did you take? Those dollars?"

"I didn't take anything," I said. "I was never there, remember?"

He sighed wearily. "Yeah, yeah. I remember. You're a stubborn little bastard, anyone ever tell you that?"

"Too many to count."

"One day that stubbornness will get you into serious trouble."

"It already has. More than once. So what's your decision?"

He tapped the bars with his knuckles, wearing a contemplative expression. Then he drew a breath, straightened his slouched back as far as it would go, and said, "You're free to go. For now. But we're not done yet, you and I. I have you dead to rights on that burglary. I'll decide what to do about that later. So don't take any sudden trips. I want to be able to find you without working up a sweat. Clear?"

"Crystal. Rest assured I've made no traveling plans for the foreseeable future."

Leibowitz did not seem entirely happy to hear that tidbit of news. He called for the guard, who unlocked the cell door.

At the front desk, Leibowitz handed me a paper bag. "Your things." We stood facing each other for a wordless moment. Then he said, "Get the hell outta here before I change my mind."

I did.

Pausing on the sidewalk outside the police station, I raised my face to the night sky, sucking in lungful after lungful of free air, marveling at how cleansing it felt, how good it tasted. There's something stale and polluted and dead about prison air, whether it's in a jail cell or a death camp. It taints your mouth and nostrils and throat and lungs. It always leaves you wanting for oxygen.

I opened the paper bag and transferred my belongings to my pockets. My ID card was there, as were my keys, notebook, and the pencil stub tucked between two of its pages. There was also the money—but not all of it. All the Israeli currency was accounted for. As was the French. But Leibowitz had kept the hundred dollars he'd shaved off when he counted my money. Greedy son of a bitch.

It was almost eleven—too late to go hunting for Gregor and Dov. It would have to wait until tomorrow. I walked north, then cut east, toward my apartment. I wanted to get out of my clothes. I wanted a shower. I wanted to sleep in my bed. Yes, the mattress was ruined, but if I pushed the padding back in, it would serve me well enough for one more night.

Black clouds had moved in, obscuring the stars and moon, and the temperature had plunged. Each exhalation was visible for a second as a puff of white steam before it dissipated into nothingness. I buttoned my jacket and shoved my hands in my pockets. I wished I had my gloves, but Leibowitz had kept them as evidence. A cigarette would have warmed me up, but I was still relishing that tasty outside air.

I kept returning to the question of why Leibowitz had let me go at all. It was true that I had a witness—Greta—who could testify that he had stolen money from a dead man's wallet, but he had been truthful when he said that my position was weaker than his. The police are always more powerful than a regular citizen, especially one who can be placed at the scene of a crime.

So what was his purpose in releasing me? Try as I might, I could not come up with a satisfactory answer.

As I walked, I periodically checked over my shoulder, thinking that Leibowitz might have put a tail on me. I saw no one. The streets were nearly deserted, which would have made shadowing me without being detected a challenge. Still, it would cost me nothing to remain watchful.

I was on King George, two minutes from my apartment, when the attack occurred.

Chapter 21

I only saw one of them at first.

He'd been slouching against a darkened storefront, but now pushed himself off when he saw me approach.

Skinny guy. Five seven. Towheaded. Jutting ears. A thin line of yellow fuzz over his lip.

"You Adam Lapid?" he asked in a nasal voice.

"Yes," I said, and I started asking where he knew me from, but didn't get a chance to complete the question before I was shoved hard from the side by a pair of powerful hands.

They'd timed it perfectly, right when I was passing by a narrow alley between two buildings, and with my attention taken fully by the skinny man. I was shoved so hard I took a few jarring, stumbling steps into the alley, flailing with my arms, trying hard not to fall on my face, before dropping to one knee in a shallow puddle of muck.

I sprang to my feet and whirled around, sure it was Dov who had shoved me and expecting to see Gregor, too. But what I saw were two other guys, the one who had stopped me in the street and a second man, this one burly with muscle-padded shoulders, hands the size of dinner plates, and a blocky head of cropped black hair sitting atop a squat neck. I had never laid eyes on him before either.

The skinny guy moved his head around, checking to see if anyone had spotted them. Satisfied, he took a step into the mouth of the alley, where a triangle of light from a nearby streetlamp painted the pavement a faded yellow. He made a small motion with his hand and a switchblade sprang to life. The burly guy had one too, only his looked smaller in his oversized hand. The burly guy looked serious; his partner was grinning.

"You mind telling me what this is all about?" I asked, cursing the fact that I didn't have a weapon on me and desperately scanning my surroundings for one. All I saw were trash cans, closed, with no garbage on the pavement. No empty bottles, no handy pieces of wood, nothing I could use in a fight.

The two men took another step forward. They left about six inches between them and each wall of the alley. Not that trying to rush past them was an option. I'd get perforated. I could shout for help, but whoever came would probably get here too late to do much good. No, better to wait for them to make their move. It wouldn't be long now.

The skinny guy said, "Tova Wasserman sends her regards. She says you have a problem with your manners," and then he sprang forward, rash and stupid, catching both me and his partner by surprise, waiving his numerical advantage.

He came with his knife held at shoulder level and stabbed with it forward, stretching his arm fully. At the last instant I managed to take a half step back and twist my body and head away so the blade streaked two inches past my jaw. He swung the knife again, this time in a wide arc, and I moved in when the knife whistled past my face and backhanded him across the cheek.

I'd put my entire body behind it and caught him just right, with a solid thunk, and he twirled like a top, crashing headfirst into a wall. His head met the wall at such an angle and with such force that it was pushed sharply sideways and back, and I heard the snap of his neck as clear as a gunshot.

The burly guy heard it too. He stood stunned, gaping at his partner lying half crumpled against the wall, his head drooped against his chest, loose and lifeless. Then he turned his face to me, eyes filled with fury, but not before I'd bent down and picked up his partner's knife.

I showed him the blade. "Whatever she's paying you, it's not worth dying for. Don't be dumb like your friend."

It was the wrong thing to say, apparently, because he let out a roar and charged me. No finesse, no circling each other looking for an opening, just a bull-like charge.

His rage lent him speed. He covered the distance in two long strides and whipped his knife at me, the blade slipping inside my jacket, slicing through my shirt and into my side. I grunted in pain and pushed him off with a forearm, backtracking until I felt a wall behind me.

The burly man's face was twisted into a rictus of manic rage, and he charged me again, going for the same attack as before, only this time I was ready for him. I sidestepped his jab, his blade clanging against the wall at my back, and I brought my knife hand up. I felt that wisp of resistance when blade kisses flesh before the skin gives way and the steel slides through into the muscle and tendon beneath.

He didn't cry out. All that came out of him was a soft surprised gasp. Our faces were close together, his eyes staring bewildered into mine, his breath—tomatoes and onions—hot on my face. Then the strength went out of him and he slid down and back, the blade slipping out of his body as he fell, first to his knees and then flat on his back.

Breathing hard, adrenaline pumping through me so fast my fingers trembled, I examined the knife in my hand. It was a cheap, flimsy thing, the blade five inches long and very thin, not sturdy but strong enough to do the job. Blood coated the length of the blade and some of it was on my hand. Was this the knife that had taken Nathan's life? Or was that the other one, the knife the burly man had cut me with? And were these the guys who had trashed my apartment? And Nathan's?

Turning my gaze to the burly man, I noted how little blood there was on his shirt. Just a monocle-sized circle of red on the left side of his chest, right where the blade had pierced his skin en route to his heart. Damn it. I would have loved to get some answers from him, but he was beyond questioning, and so was his partner.

Two men dead. All because one old woman felt that her honor had been besmirched. I shook my head at the folly of it all, the waste. Then I grimaced at the burning in my side. I slid a hand over the wound and felt wetness on my palm. I would have to take care of the wound soon, but first I had to get out of there before someone saw me with two dead bodies and a knife in my hand.

I closed the blade and used my handkerchief first to wipe my fingerprints off the handle and then to rub the blood off my hand. Then I slipped the folded knife, wrapped in the handkerchief, into my pocket. I scanned the dark pavement as best I could, to make sure I hadn't dropped anything that might lead the police to me, then went to the lip of the alley. Peering left and right, I saw no one. I raised the collar of my jacket, hunched my shoulders, and with my face angled downward, walked off.

I found a sewer grate and dropped the knife into it. Blood had darkened my handkerchief and I chucked it into a nearby trash can. Then, checking again to make sure no one was around, I stopped under a streetlight, untucked my torn shirt from my pants, and examined the wound in my side.

It was a clean cut, ugly and red, but it didn't look deep. It was oozing, though, and would need to be cleaned and stitched.

I didn't want to go to a hospital. They'd make a report of my injury and someone might decide the police should be informed. I could not take care of the wound myself. I had a bottle of iodine and some bandages in my apartment, but no needle or thread.

But I knew who did.

Pressing a hand to my wound and wincing with every step, I made my way to where I hoped to find help.

Chapter 22

Sima Vaaknin had a triumphant grin on her face when she opened the door, but it changed into an expression of mock reproach when she got a look at my face.

"You look even less attractive than last time, Adam. Are you trying to send me a message?"

"I could use some help," I said, each word an effort. The pain in my side had gotten worse, like a pulsing fire. "You still have that first aid kit?"

Sima turned serious. "I'm always prepared for calamity, you know that. Come inside." She reached out to take my arm, but I told her I could manage just fine by myself.

"What's wrong?" she said, running her eyes over me. Then she noticed my hand tucked inside my jacket, and she drew aside the lapel and saw the blood. She didn't flinch or inhale sharply or put a hand to her mouth. Nor did she look concerned. She simply said, "To the bathroom."

Once there, she helped me out of my jacket and shirt, then bent forward to peer at the wound, her expression one of curious fascination. She reached a hand, prodding the skin bordering the cut with her fingers, her lips parted and wet. "Does it hurt bad?" she asked, flicking her eyes to mine.

"Quite a bit," I said, my face screwed tight with pain.

She gave a short nod, drew her hand away, and washed it in the sink. Then she unbuckled my belt, slid my pants and underwear down my legs, and helped me out of them, after removing my shoes. She told me to get into the bathtub and turned the water on hot. Steam started rising.

She drenched a washcloth in the hot spray and began rubbing it gently over my wound. Reddish water sluiced down my legs. She worked with quiet concentration, clearing the blood from the cut, and I watched her, aware that I was seeing a side of her that until now had been hidden from me.

When she had cleaned the wound as best she could, she said, "Come out and get dry."

She took a towel and knelt before me, rubbing my legs and stomach. There was no hiding my arousal, but for once she made no comment about it, did not even show any sign of noticing it.

From a cabinet she took a metal box, unclasped it, and brought out a bottle filled with purplish liquid.

"This will hurt," she said, "but not for long." And she took another washcloth, poured some of the liquid on it, and rubbed it on and into my wound.

It stung like a thousand bumblebees all at once. I closed my hands tight, fingernails biting into the soft flesh of my palms. My teeth were clamped, but still a hiss of pain escaped between my lips. Sima seemed oblivious to it.

She had once told me how, when she started out in her career as a call girl, an older prostitute taught her how to clean and stitch wounds. "It's a dangerous job," the older woman said. "Sometimes, clients can get rough. You need to know how to treat yourself and other girls."

So Sima had learned and made sure to keep a fully stocked first aid kit in her apartment, just in case.

Finished with the disinfectant, she capped the bottle and returned it to its place, then got out a needle and thread. She said, "A doctor would do a better job of this than I would."

"Do you know anyone who can be trusted to keep his mouth shut?"

"I might. Shall I call him?"

A client of hers, I thought. I did not want to meet him. And the less people who knew about my injury, the better.

"No. You do it."

She nodded and got ready. Holding the needle for me to see, she said, "This will hurt far more than the disinfectant. But you've been through worse, haven't you?"

I had and she knew it.

"Hand me my belt," I said, and she frowned but did as I asked.

I folded the belt over twice, till I had a thick coil of leather in my hand. Then I stuck a section of it between my teeth and bit down as hard as I could. I nodded for her to begin.

The pain was fierce and it seemed to last forever, but

as Sima said, I'd suffered worse. Still, by the time she'd tied off the final stitch, my face was drenched in sweat and a tremor had taken over my arms. My jaw muscles had gone so stiff my mouth wouldn't open, and I had to yank the belt from between my teeth. The leather was scored deep with tooth marks, like tiny footprints in clay.

Sima put the needle aside and leaned closer to examine her handiwork. A meandering smile played across her lips. "It will leave a scar, but that's okay. You know how much I love scars. Especially yours."

She more than loved them, she had an unbounded fascination with them. The first time we went to bed together she saw the scars on my torso, left there by two bullet wounds I'd taken in Israel's War of Independence, courtesy of an Egyptian soldier. She displayed an inordinate affection for them, but it paled in comparison to the reverence she showed the scars on my back. These she'd felt before she laid eyes on them, as her hands caressed my back during our lovemaking. When later she saw them, she brushed her fingers along their lines like an archaeologist tracing newly discovered hieroglyphs, striving to decipher their meaning.

Where this fascination with scars came from, I did not know. For some reason I never asked her to explain it. Perhaps I preferred not knowing.

"That's all right," I said. "Thank you."

She leaned back and breathed hard through her nose. "How does it feel?"

I raised my arm slowly, testing my range of motion. "It's a bit tight. It feels like it would tear open if I lift my arm too high."

"I suppose that's natural. It will probably be back to normal in a week or two."

She pursed her lips, turning thoughtful. "It wouldn't be wise for you to go walking back to your apartment. You'll sleep here tonight."

I didn't argue. A heavy exhaustion had settled over me, like a thick down comforter. My body felt drained of energy. Gravity seemed to be exerting more than its usual pull. I yawned loudly, not bothering to cover my mouth.

When Sima offered me her hand this time, I took it.

She led me to her other bedroom, where she plied her trade. The room was dominated by a huge bed. The linen was satin and silver, the pillows gigantic and inviting. Unlit candles stood in saucers on shelves and windowsills. The room smelled faintly of consumed wax. It did not smell of sex or of any of the men who had been there that day. It was part of the illusion Sima sold, that she was exclusive to whichever man was now with her.

She drew back the covers and pushed me down on the bed. The sheet was smooth and cool against my scarred back. The pillow cupped my weary head like a mother cradling a newborn. My body was slack and soft in every place but one. Sima's eyes went to it, and I expected her to give one of her satisfied smiles, but her face took on a serious, almost anxious cast.

She said, "With your stitches, I would need to be gentle, and I don't think I can be. Not tonight. Do you understand?"

I tried nodding my head, but it was too heavy to move.

I breathed out a yes and wasn't sure she caught it. She wasn't looking at my face but down at her hands, on the sheets, close to my hip.

She raised her eyes to me and said, "Sleep, Adam," and drew the blanket over me. As my eyes drifted shut, she placed a warm hand on my shoulder and I heard her asking me something. I answered something back, and then I went under.

Chapter 23

I woke to the sound of rain.

It was coming down hard, pounding the street, splattering against the windows, a barrage of water and noise.

A moment passed before I remembered where I was. In Sima's apartment. In her bed.

A heavy blanket covered my naked body to my collarbones. A plush pillow supported my head. The mattress that held my body was perfect—not too soft and not too firm.

The room was dark and perfumed by the sweet scent of Sima's body. I turned my head, but her side of the bed was empty. I ran a slow hand along the sheets where she'd lain. Cold.

My head was heavy with sleep. A deep, fathomless, dreamless sleep—the kind that I only experienced at the end of days in which I'd shed the blood of others. I winced, remembering the two assailants lying dead in that alley. Had their bodies been discovered yet? Or was the rain pummeling their corpses, drenching their hair and clothes?

Then I remembered my wound and Sima's ministrations. Cautiously, I brushed my fingertips along my flank till I felt the puckered flesh, the knotted stitches Sima had sewn.

I ran a thick tongue over my dry lips. My mouth was devoid of moisture and my throat was parched. I needed water.

From the corner of my eye, I spied a tall glass standing on the side table by the bed, filled with water. Sima must have anticipated how thirsty I would be when I came to.

Remembering my injury, I proceeded with caution, pushing myself up slowly to a sitting position. My side hurt, but not nearly as much as I'd feared. I'd been lucky. An inch or so to the right, and that knife might have cut a hole through a kidney or some other vital organ. I might have been the one lying dead in that alley, soaked by that downpour.

I reached for the glass and drained it in one long, thirsty chug. I held the glass upside down over my outstretched tongue till the last drop trickled out. I felt halfway normal.

I was contemplating the wisdom of lowering my feet to the floor and going to see where Sima was, when I heard the sound of feminine footsteps in the hall. Then the door opened, and there was Sima.

She wore a knee-length dark-red dress that hugged her body in all the right places. Black stockings encased her legs like a second skin. She'd tied her hair back, drawing more attention to her face, making her eyes look bigger. In her hand she held a large carry bag dotted with raindrops.

"You're up. Good. How are you feeling?"

I took stock of myself. My side ached, and I was still very thirsty. But my head was slowly clearing, and I felt myself floating on that pleasant, all-encompassing sensation that only a night of undisturbed sleep could bring.

"Better than I have any right to expect. Thanks to you."

She smiled a glowing smile and curtsied. "I'm just glad I finally got the chance to stitch someone. I was curious how that would be." She sat down at the foot of the bed, reached over, and pulled down the blanket that still covered my legs, hips, and the lower part of my torso. She tilted her beautiful head and examined my wound like an art connoisseur venturing to determine the merits of an abstract painting. Her eyes sparkled. "It hasn't opened. I suppose that's good news. I also have some bad news. Someone broke into your apartment."

I looked at her. "You went to my apartment?"

"Why are you surprised? I told you I'd go just before you fell asleep. I asked if it was all right and you said yes. Don't you remember?"

I ran a hand through my hair. "Vaguely," I admitted.

"It's quite a mess. Though not as bad as what those guys did to my place a year ago."

That I remembered perfectly. It had been my fault. The guys in question—all violent criminals—were after me, and I had inadvertently led them to Sima's apartment. By a stroke of good fortune, I had preceded them there, and together Sima and I escaped before they arrived. But my pursuers had taken out their frustration at having missed me on Sima's belongings—breaking dishes, busting furniture, tearing clothes and linen, destroying whatever they could.

Sima had shrugged off the effects of the devastation. She even rebuffed my offer to recompense her for the damages. She simply declared that it was time to buy new things, which she promptly did. And that was the end of the matter, or nearly the end. The incident had led her to invest in a handgun, which she kept loaded and within reach.

"You don't look shaken by the news," she said, sounding a trifle disappointed.

"I was at the apartment yesterday after it was vandalized."

"Do you know who did it?"

"I have someone in mind."

"Whoever he is, you've certainly made him mad, Adam."

She said this in a lilting, lighthearted tone, as though remarking on the weather. Gone was the concerned, caring Sima of last night. Here was the regular Sima. She was not prone to displays of anxiety, worry or fear. At times, she gave the impression of being unaware of the very existence of such emotions. Nevertheless, she was always prepared for the worst, keeping a packed suitcase under her bed in case she needed to make a sudden getaway.

I had seen her naked, shared her bed, experienced heaven inside her body, and, unlike anyone else, I had even been told some of her darkest secrets. But only occasionally did I get a glimpse of the real Sima, the one hidden behind the protective walls and battlements that she had erected around herself since the day her family was massacred.

"It sure seems that way," I said. "Don't worry, Sima, you won't get involved this time. I'll take my box and leave as soon as I get some clothes on."

"Speaking of which," she said, rising to her feet and brandishing the shopping bag. "The shirt you had on last night is torn and both your jacket and pants are stained with blood. So I went to your apartment and brought you some fresh clothes." She paused, frowning slightly. "Well, the clothes were on the floor, so I don't know how fresh they are, but they certainly smell clean enough."

She set the bag on the bed and from it removed pants, underwear, socks, shirt, hat, coat, and a pair of gloves, all of which she neatly laid on the bed. I recognized all of the clothes—apart from the gloves.

"Where did those come from?" I asked, pointing.

"I couldn't find gloves in your apartment, so I stopped off on the way back and bought you these." She handed them over. "I'm sure the size is right. I have an eye for such things."

The gloves were made of shiny black leather and about them hovered that enticing smell of all things grand and new. Just holding them, without slipping them on, I could feel how luxuriantly soft they were. Far surpassing my previous pair. Much finer than anything I owned.

"Put them on. Let's see how they look."

I did. The gloves exceeded my expectations. My hands

felt as though they'd returned home after a lengthy exile.

Sima clapped her hands like an excited child. "I knew they'd be perfect for you. I just knew it."

"You shouldn't have, Sima," I said, oddly touched, self-conscious, and more than a little proud that this heavenly woman would go out and buy me such an expensive gift. "They look pricey. I'll pay you back."

"You don't need to," she said cheerfully. "I bought them with the money I found in your pants."

I stared at her, my cheeks on fire. What a miserable fool I was. Like an innocent youngster who is sure that the girl he's been dreaming of for months is about to give him her heart, only to see her on the arm of another man the next day.

"You went through my pockets?"

She nodded. "I was searching for your keys. By the way, why do you carry French and American money?"

"It's a long story," I said.

Sima shrugged, satisfied with not knowing. Scooting closer on the bed, she took hold of my right wrist and pulled my gloved hand toward her, pressing it to her cheek before slowly sliding it down her skin to her throat. Tilting her head back, she purred. "Ooh, they feel fabulous. So smooth, almost like bare skin, but drier and not as warm." Her pink tongue darted out, moistening her luscious lips. She gave me a half-lidded look as she tugged my hand toward the neckline of her dress. "Don't you wonder how they'd feel a bit lower?"

The fire in my cheeks spread down my body. Judging by Sima's burst of laughter, I must have turned red. "Oh,

Adam," she said, letting go of my hand. "You must overcome this unfortunate habit of denying yourself so much so often."

She rose, smoothing her dress along her thighs. "Your money—what's left of it—is on top of the dresser in the other room. Put something on and then come to the kitchen. I'll fix you something."

As I dressed carefully so as not to exacerbate the pain in my side, I could hear Sima puttering about in the kitchen. When I emerged from the bedroom, in pants and shirt and socked feet, I found her setting the table. Eggs sizzled in a frying pan on the stove. By the smell, I could tell that she used real butter—an extravagance, some would say unconscionable waste, considering how little butter each citizen was rationed. But Sima was not one to be bothered by such trivialities. She deprived herself of nothing. Her clients could be depended on to supply her with a host of contraband in gratitude for the pleasure she gave them, and her income was such that she could afford to purchase whatever she wanted on the black market.

On the white-clothed table stood a cup of steaming coffee—real coffee—emitting an exotic, unbelievably rich aroma. Alongside the cup squatted a glass bowl filled to the brim with sugar—another rationed commodity. Bread slices lay on a cutting board next to a jar of strawberry jam with French writing on the label. Sardines, glistening with oil, lay on a saucer by a large empty plate. The chair before the plate had been drawn and now stood waiting. Waiting for me.

Mouth watering and stomach grumbling, I dropped onto the chair, eager to get started. Then I noticed that there was just one plate on the table. "Aren't you going to have anything?"

Sima, spatula in hand, said, "I've already eaten a few hours ago."

Frowning, I glanced at my left wrist. My watch was gone. Sima must have removed it while I was sleeping. "What time is it?"

"Eleven thirty. You slept like a log. Hardly moved all night."

So that was the reason I was famished. I hadn't eaten anything since that far-from-satisfying jail supper the previous night.

Sima came over with the pan and deposited what looked like a double-egg omelet on my plate. Two real eggs, what each adult citizen was rationed each month. I frequently bought eggs on the black market, but I couldn't recall the last occasion I'd used two of them at the same time. I stared at the golden omelet on my plate in reverence. It was burned along the edges, just as I liked it, crisp and inviting.

Sima hovered to my right. "A word of advice, Adam. Don't let good things turn cold. When you reheat them, they're never quite the same."

I needed no further encouragement. I grabbed a fork and dug in.

The eggs were perfection itself, and so was the coffee. The jam was unlike anything I'd eaten in years, tangy and sweet. "One of my clients works for the foreign office,"

Sima explained. "He brought that for me from Paris."

She sat on the other side of the table, holding a mug of coffee in both hands, from time to time taking tiny sips from it. She watched me devour my breakfast with a curious expression. Not once did she ask me what I thought of the food. Just like she never inquired whether our lovemaking had satisfied me. It was a foregone conclusion that I had enjoyed whatever she'd served.

I ate quickly and prodigiously. When I finally stopped, I sank a little lower in my chair and looked across the table at her.

"That hit the spot," I said.

She smiled. "I'm glad to hear it. Have some more coffee while I clear the table."

I told her I'd help. We stood side by side at the sink. She soaped and rinsed the dishes. I dried them and put them away in cupboards and drawers. We didn't talk. We didn't need to. I knew where everything went from previous visits.

When we were done, we stood three feet apart, looking at each other in loaded silence. A few strands had worked their way loose from her hair band and now fluttered by her left cheek. I reached over and tucked them gently behind her ear. Then I cupped her cheek in my hand. She pressed her hand over mine, trapping it between warm cheek and palm. Her eyes were fathomless, dark pools, the kind you want to dive into but are afraid of doing so because you can't see the bottom, nor even guess how deep the water goes. It could have been the close of the previous night, or the manifestation of my gratitude and appreciation as flame-hot desire, but at that moment, I wanted Sima Vaaknin without reservation, without a thought as to how I'd feel in the aftermath, with no regard to the guilt that I knew would follow.

I began moving toward her, but stopped at the sight of her shaking her head.

"There's no time, Adam. I have a guest coming by in half an hour."

It took a few seconds for the import of what she'd said to sink in. Then it cut to the bone like a scalpel.

By guest, Sima meant a client. A man who would take what I now wanted with an overwhelming desperation. He would take her.

I took a long breath, a globe of acid in the pit of my stomach. I had the urge to tell her to call it off, to either telephone this client or tell him when he arrived that she was otherwise occupied. Or maybe not answer the door at all when he knocked, let him come to his own conclusions. I didn't care one way or the other how he felt.

But I said none of those things.

I had no right to say them. I had no claim to Sima Vaaknin. Whatever she and I had was undefined and so infrequent that there could be no expectations attached to it. So I took a step back, detaching myself from her palm, and said, "Fine. I'll go. I just need to take some things first."

I put on my coat and shoes. Then, in the smaller bedroom, I retrieved my box from its hiding place and opened it on the bed. One thing was certain, I was not going to be unarmed today. I could have easily been killed last night, and I would likely face danger again before this case was done. I needed to be prepared.

Besides, Leibowitz already had enough to lock me away. It would worsen my situation if he picked me up again and found weapons on me, but not by much. It was a risk I had to take.

First, I grabbed the Luger, checked that it was loaded, tucked it into my waistband, and put the extra magazine in my left coat pocket. Next came the knife. I flicked it open and watched the blade spring to life, hungry and shining, ready for blood-letting. I folded the blade and slipped the knife in my right-hand pocket. The final item I took was the picture of Nathan and the other woman, the striking, self-assured one. What's your name? I asked silently. And where can I find you?

My money, keys, watch, and notebook were on the dresser. I put the francs and dollars in the box and took the Israeli liras and other items with me. Then I returned the box to its place behind the linen.

Realizing that I'd forgotten to take my hat, I stepped over to the main bedroom, where I found Sima dressed in nothing but black lace panties and bra, one foot on the bed as she finished rolling her stocking down her sleek calf.

I stood in the doorway, frozen in place even as my body temperature soared to bonfire heat. A knot had formed in my throat, and in my ears I heard what sounded like galloping horses, which a moment later I realized was just my heartbeat jittering madly.

Sima turned her head toward me and grinned. "Got everything you need, Adam?"

You know damn well I didn't, I thought. But what I said was, "Apart from my hat."

Sima cast her eyes about, spotted the hat where it had fallen to the floor, and, with her back to me, bent to pick it up, giving me a tantalizing view of her backside.

She was in the mode, the seductress mode that came so naturally to her, the one in which she exercised so much power that it was palpable in the air around her. She padded toward me with my hat clasped in both hands, held before her breasts, eyes shooting Cupid arrows from beneath her long eyelashes. She came close enough so I could smell her seductress scent—primal, animalistic, overwhelmingly physical and sexual—close enough so when she stood up on tiptoes to gently place my hat on my head, her breasts brushed my chest. It took every ounce of my self-control to restrain myself from grabbing her.

The reason I didn't was because I knew with a profound bitterness that she was dressed as she was for the benefit of another man. I just happened to be caught in her line of fire.

"Do you plan on coming here tonight?" she said, her voice so low that I had to strain my ears.

I swallowed hard, cleared my throat, and said I didn't know.

"Don't come before ten thirty. And not too late either. It's going to be a busy day. I'll want to be in bed early."

Chapter 24

Outside, the rain was still coming down hard. It pelted my coated shoulders and back, streamed down the brim of my hat like a curtain before my eyes, and gathered in puddles on the road or gurgled its way to the nearest sewer grate.

I felt none of it, not the heavy rain nor the cold wind that blew from the east. I walked with my gloved hands clamped into fists, simmering with nasty thoughts at the nameless man who at any moment would be knocking on Sima Vaaknin's door.

I hiked west to Ben Yehuda Street and followed it south till I found and entered the building. It was only when I began mounting the stairs that I paused to consider what the next few minutes might bring.

I had never killed or even struck a woman. I did not relish the prospect of changing that record. But I couldn't see how this matter could be resolved in any other way.

Calling the police was not an option. I had no proof that Mrs. Wasserman had hired a pair of assassins to kill me. And if I involved the authorities, I would have the deaths of two men to account for.

There was also no evidence that she'd had Nathan murdered. Unless I obtained a confession, I had nothing.

And even if I were to somehow get her to admit her guilt, what was to stop her from withdrawing her confession once she was in the safe custody—safe from me, that is—of the police?

No. This was something I would need to settle myself.

I knocked on her door and waited. There was no answer. I knocked again and got the same result.

Acting on impulse, I pushed down the handle and found that the door was unlocked.

From inside the apartment wafted an ominous silence and with it the faintest of smells. Familiar, but I couldn't place it.

I stepped inside and shut the door behind me.

"Mrs. Wasserman?" I called. "You home? This is Adam Lapid."

The walls of the dimly lit narrow hallway echoed my words back to me.

I treaded down the hall, ears pricked, flanked by the pictures of Mrs. Wasserman's kinfolk. It felt colder in here than it had on the street, so much so that I half expected to see ice forming on the picture frames. Goosebumps sprouted along my forearms, and the skin on my back prickled. Almost without conscious thought, my right hand reached inside my coat to unlimber the Luger. Finger on the trigger, I held the gun by my thigh, muzzle pointed at the floor.

The squeak of my wet shoes on the gray tiles was the only sound that defied the profound silence. Any second now, I'd hear Mrs. Wasserman's angry voice berating me for failing to wipe my feet before entering. But that second passed, as did the next, without a whisper, without a breath, save for my own.

The living room was a mess. A chair had been knocked over. Broken shards of what had once been a ceramic mug lay at the center of a large wet stain on the carpet. The coffee table was busted, and around it were scattered two dozen or so of Mrs. Wasserman's rock-hard cookies, some intact, some in pebble-sized pieces—the result, I supposed, of having been crushed under a heavy shoe.

Mrs. Wasserman was nowhere in sight.

I stood for a moment, letting the apartment speak to me. It didn't. The silence was so thick it seemed to muffle the sound of the rain pouring outside.

Luger pointed straight ahead, I crossed the living room to a closed white sliding door set into the far wall. I had never ventured beyond it on my previous visits, but it was here that Mrs. Wasserman would go with the foreign currency I'd brought her, to return a minute later with Israeli liras.

Grasping the knob with my left hand, I slid open the door, gun aimed at the yawning opening.

The first thing I noticed was her shoe.

It was the left one, an ugly, blocky little thing, brown, with a low square heel. It lay on its side, empty. Past it stretched a large room containing a double bed topped by a thick blue duvet and two pillows set against the headboard. Opposite the bed loomed a mammoth closet with four large doors, two of which hung open, as did a few drawers. Two more drawers lay upside down on the floor, their contents scattered in a wide rough circle.

Socks, underwear, hairpins, earrings, and what appeared to be old letters in envelopes made up most of the discarded items. A foot-long empty metal box lay open near the foot of the closet. A tiny brass key protruded from its lock.

To my right was another door. I nudged it open and peered inside. A bathroom, undisturbed. Empty.

As was the apartment. Whoever had done this was gone. I stuck my gun back in my waistband and allowed myself a moment to calm my breath. And then I noticed it again, that smell, not as faint as before, more invasive. I knew what it was now. I had smelled it before too many times to count.

Following my nose, I crossed the bedroom, and there, on the far side of the bed, was Mrs. Wasserman's other shoe.

It encased her foot; the other was bare, her toenails yellowish and very thick. I followed the line of her feet, up her calves to where the hem of her dress gathered, just above her knees, and further still up her thighs and hips and torso, all the way to her face.

Her lifeless face.

Eyes and mouth both gaped wide and still—the first in abject terror, the second in a silent scream. A red welt covered her left cheek and the skin over her right eye was bloodied. For a moment I was sure the killer had hit her so hard that he'd knocked her teeth halfway out of her mouth. Then I realized that what I was seeing was a set of dentures clinging crookedly to her lips like a man desperately hanging onto the edge of a cliff.

Shifting my gaze downward, I saw the bruises on her neck. She'd been strangled by a pair of powerful hands. Peering more closely, I understood just how powerful. The skin of her throat was sunken in. The killer had squeezed so hard that he'd caved in her windpipe.

My eyes moved to where Mrs. Wasserman's left arm was stretched to the side. A squeeze mark, similar to the ones on her neck, encircled her wrist. But a harsher damage had been inflicted on her fingers. Two of them—her fore and middle fingers—jutted at unnatural angles, having been wrenched violently backward until they'd snapped.

I grimaced as I considered the pain that must have caused her. I felt pity for her, even though she had marked me for death. I'd come to her apartment knowing I might need to end her life, if only to prevent her from sending new assassins after me, but I'd had no intention of torturing her. This she did not deserve.

But why had she been tortured? For some deviant fun? I didn't think so. The man or men who had done this had wanted something from her. Information of some sort. Where she kept her money? Or something else?

With the condition of the apartment firmly in my mind, I envisioned the likely sequence of events.

It probably started innocuously enough. An innocent-sounding knock on the door. Mrs. Wasserman click-clacking her way to open it. A man—or more likely two or more men—stood on the landing. They said they wished to exchange money. Maybe she asked for their names, or who had given them hers. Maybe she invited them in, or maybe they simply barged inside. More than likely, they came armed. One of them might have pointed a gun at her. Or he might have had a knife, which he held close to her face as his forearm encircled her throat.

Now they were in the living room. It was here where things really got rough. Did Mrs. Wasserman put up a struggle? Or were the breaking of the coffee table, the knocking over of the chair, the slap that left a red welt across her cheek nothing more than demonstrations of force and harmful intent? Were they meant to terrify her into submission, into telling what she knew?

Whatever it was, it proved to be inadequate. The men pushed Mrs. Wasserman into the bedroom. One of them began to take apart her closet, searching for something but not finding it. Then they increased the pressure.

They threatened her with grave harm and pain. But she was an obstinate old fool. She wouldn't give in so easily. So one of the men grabbed her wrist with one hand and yanked one of her fingers violently backwards, breaking it.

Did the other man cover her mouth to stifle her screams? Probably. They wouldn't have wanted to alert the neighbors.

The pain had to be excruciating, but it required another broken finger for Mrs. Wasserman to give up. And I know she gave up, or they wouldn't have stopped at two fingers.

After she told them what they wished to know, she

was no longer of any use to them. So one of the assailants grabbed her by the throat and squeezed her life out. And then they left, their pockets full of Mrs. Wasserman's money and their heads holding whatever information she gave them.

All this had happened earlier that day. Otherwise, the familiar smell that I'd detected earlier, the scent of recent death, would have been stronger and instantly recognizable.

Who were the killers? They could have been anyone. Mrs. Wasserman's reputation as a money changer might have attracted the wrong element. But standing over her body, I thought that was unlikely.

In other circumstances, her murder might indeed have been an isolated event. But given all that had happened—Nathan's murder, my apartment being ransacked, and now Mrs. Wasserman lying dead in her bedroom—I did not believe for a moment that this was the case. Her murder was connected to what had transpired before. This meant that she had been truthful when she said she had nothing to do with Nathan's death. She had freely admitted her intention to do him harm, but someone else had gotten to him first. Maybe not by a lot. Maybe the two men she'd hired to kill me were previously engaged to go after Nathan and were diverted onto me after I had threatened and insulted her. That would explain how they were able to mount their attack on me the same day my final conversation with Mrs. Wasserman took place.

But who had killed Mrs. Wasserman? I had a pretty good idea who.

They were experienced criminals, able to get through a locked door, adept at dispensing violence. One of them was angry enough with me to urinate in my kitchen. The other was strong enough to crush a windpipe with his hands.

Gregor and Dov.

Chapter 25

I didn't hang around. At the apartment door, I peeked out of the peephole and determined there was no one on the landing. Then I opened the door and left.

No one met me on the stairs. Outside, the rain persisted, but more moderately than before. The wind had also slackened. It had warmed up some.

I headed downtown, putting some distance between me and the murder scene. I cut a right onto Frishman Street and another right onto Dizengoff. There, I found a café with a telephone at the rear. I ordered a soda and placed a call to the police.

Distorting my voice, I reported the murder and hung up when the dispatcher asked for my name. Then I exited the café and continued south, suddenly gripped by an unsettling sense of urgency. But urgency to do what?

It took a moment before it came to me. Nathan, me, Mrs. Wasserman. We were all connected, links in a chain. But there was one person—one link—unaccounted for.

Now the urgency I felt was no longer merely unsettling. It had ballooned into near panic. I upped my pace, heart hammering. How could I have missed it? Was I already too late?

My eyes scanned the surrounding businesses,

searching for a telephone I could use. But did he even have one installed in his store? Even if he did, I did not have the number. And it would take a while to find out.

I was running now, through the rain, people giving me strange looks as they veered out of my way. My side hurt, the stitched skin protesting, threatening to rip open, but I did not slow down. Arms pumping, legs pounding the wet pavement, breathing hard and fast, I sprinted across Dizengoff Square, angling for the Pinsker Street exit. At the corner of Pinsker and Bograshov, a taxi was disgorging an overweight man in a three-piece suit. He handed the driver some money and had his hand on the door, ready to close it. Charging forward, sweat streaming down my face, I yelled at him to stop. Startled, he jerked his head in my direction, eyebrows shooting up. He quick-stepped away from the taxi and scuttled toward a nearby shop, leaving the back door open.

No one tried to beat me to the taxi. Good. If someone had, I would likely have come to blows with him.

I leapt onto the backseat, grimacing in pain and effort. The driver swiveled his round face toward me. "In a hurry, mister?"

I nodded, gasping, trying to catch my breath. "Daniel Street. Step on it."

The driver looked about to say something; then he shrugged and faced forward and pulled away from the curb.

I pulled up my shirt and peered at my flank. The skin around the wound was red and swollen, but the stitches were holding firm. The pain was intense. I fidgeted on the seat till I found the least painful position. With the sleeve of my coat, I wiped the sweat off my face.

The driver was peering at me in the rearview mirror. "Everything okay, mister?"

"I hope so," I told him. "Push that pedal to the floor. It's urgent."

The drive seemed endless, but it actually took less than seven minutes. Most people in Tel Aviv did not own cars, so the streets were not congested. At the intersection of Ha-Kovshim and Daniel Streets, the driver asked me which way to turn. "Here is fine," I said, tossing him a bill and thrusting open the door. "Keep the change."

I dashed the rest of the way, images of lifeless eyes and bloodied faces flashing before me. Bursting into the store, I shoved the door open so hard that it banged into the display window, rattling the glass in its frame.

He was alone in the store. He stood behind the counter, gripping a pencil in his right hand, staring at me in shock. The sight of him banished the bloody images of death. The panic receded from my body. My breath flowed smoother. Even the pain in my side seemed to diminish.

He was alive. Zalman Alphon was alive.

"Thank God," I said.

Alphon did not look thankful. He looked terrified. Blinking rapidly, he backed away from the counter till his rear end bumped into the back wall of his store. His face, pale to begin with, was now the color of chalk. He had dropped his pencil and was twisting his hands in obvious agitation.

"I-I…" he began, clearly not sure how to continue.

I moved closer. He shrank even further against the wall. I stopped, frowning.

"What's the matter?"

"I told the police nothing," he blurted out, his voice quavering. "And I'm not going to. I swear. On my life." He gulped as his rattled brain absorbed the last three words that had spilled from his mouth.

"What the hell are you talking about, Zalman?"

"I mean you've got nothing to worry about. I'm not going to tell anything to anyone. Why should I care about Nathan? He wasn't my friend. I barely knew the man."

I stared at him. "You think I killed him?"

Alphon's Adam's apple bobbed up and down below his incipient double chin. His blinking accelerated. His mouth was trembling now, making his bristling mustache dance. He spoke fast, words tumbling on top of each other. "I don't care, I tell you. I'm sure you had cause. I just don't give a damn one way or the other. All I'm saying is you don't need to worry on my account."

"I didn't murder Nathan," I said.

It didn't seem like he'd heard me. His eyes twitched this way and that, looking for an escape or a savior.

I took a step forward. "Zalman, listen to me. I didn't kill him."

It was clear he didn't believe me. He started inching his way to the door that led to the back room, where he kept his black-market goods. "Okay, okay," he stammered. "I believe you."

I sighed, bellied up to the counter, and pulled out the

Luger, leveling it at him, waist high.

I regretted it the following instant. His fearful eyes latched onto the gun. The rest of him froze. Like a pillar of salt, he stood rigid, unmoving—even his blinking had ceased. *Good God*, I thought. *He's having a stroke.*

I made the gun disappear, saying, "Zalman."

No reaction.

I banged my fist down hard on the counter, raising my voice. "Zalman!"

He blinked, half-recoiled as though he'd been slapped. He wheezed in a loud, heaving breath. His eyes roved aimlessly for a moment before finding their focus. Me. The fear in them was sharp, overflowing.

"Zalman," I said in my normal tone, "sorry about the business with the gun. I wasn't thinking properly. I just wanted you to see I could have killed you if I wanted. If I were a murderer. I'm not. I did not kill Nathan Frankel."

He didn't answer straightaway, but when he did, the tempo of his speech was almost normal. "I believe you." He paused, running a hand over his bald scalp. "For real this time. God in heaven, when you walked in, I was sure you were here to kill me. I've been dreading it since I heard about Nathan. I'm a loose end, I thought. He'd want to make sure I don't talk."

"If you thought that, why didn't you go to the police?"

"Because I was scared, that's why. If I told them about your visit, I'd have to tell them everything. I'd have to expose myself as a black-market vendor. They'd prosecute me, wouldn't they?"

"It beats dying."

Alphon looked abashed. "I was still weighing the pros and cons of paying the police a visit when you barged in. You scared me half to death, you know."

"I got that impression. I apologize."

He waved a hand and offered a tentative smile, then almost immediately sobered up. "Why are you here, then?"

"To warn you," I said. "Your life might be in danger."

His eyes grew huge. His shoulders shuddered. "What are you trying to do, give me a heart attack? You just said I had nothing to worry about."

"Not from me, you don't. But Nathan's murderers might be coming after you next."

"After me?" He pressed one hand flat to his own chest. He seemed completely flabbergasted by what I'd said, as though he hadn't thought the exact same thing was happening just a minute before. "What makes you think that?"

I considered the wisdom of telling him. As easily shaken as he was, who knew what the news might do to him. But there was no other way to impress upon him the gravity of the situation.

"Because they killed Tova Wasserman."

He gawped at me.

"Sometime earlier today," I continued. "They broke into her apartment and killed her."

He licked his lips. "How do you know this?"

"I went to see her, to ask her some questions about Nathan. I found her body."

His small eyes narrowed. He was reevaluating me and the situation.

"Remember the gun, Zalman," I said. "If I wanted you dead, I would have shot you. Trust me, I didn't kill Mrs. Wasserman. The persons who murdered Nathan did."

"Persons," he echoed. "You think more than one person is involved?"

"Pretty sure, yes."

"You know who they are?"

"I think so. You've probably met them before."

Again, he looked astonished. "Me?"

"You may have met them at that card game you told me about." I described Gregor and Dov.

Alphon nodded shakily. "They were there. The big guy, Dov, he has the look of a thug. A violence-prone thug. But for some reason I found the other one, the one with ginger hair, more frightening."

"That's Gregor. Nathan was scared of him too."

"Why?"

"Because Nathan was afraid Gregor would learn about him exchanging money with Mrs. Wasserman. I'm not sure why, but that's what I think. Something about that deal led Gregor and Dov to murder Nathan and Mrs. Wasserman both."

Alphon was blinking rapidly again. "But why do you think they'll come for me?"

"Because you were the one who connected Nathan to Mrs. Wasserman."

"Yes, but how would they know that?"

Again, I hesitated to tell him the truth but could see no

way not to. "Because they tortured Mrs. Wasserman before they killed her."

"Tortured?" he said in a voice scarcely louder than a whisper.

"I'm afraid so. And don't ask me what they did to her. It's not important for you to know that. What is important is that you understand that she might have told them things about Nathan and whoever else knew he did business with her. Which is where you come in."

Sweat had broken on Alphon's naked scalp. It ran down to his forehead, but he didn't seem to notice.

"If Mrs. Wasserman told the killers about you, it's likely they'll want you dead too. Which means you need to make it difficult for them to find you."

"How?"

"You need to get away. Today, right now. Close the shop, go home and pack, and then get out of Tel Aviv. Take a vacation. Go south to Eilat or north to Haifa, I don't care where. Don't stay with relatives. Choose a place where you're unknown. If you've got someplace in mind, don't tell me. I don't need to know. But go now."

He looked at me, imploring me to amend my recommendation. "Do you really think I'm in danger?"

I was losing patience with him. "Do I need to pull out my gun again to convince you how serious I think the situation is?"

He rubbed a hand over his mouth. "What do I tell my wife?"

I shrugged. "Make up some lie. Tell her one of your clients is upset with you. Or tell her a version of the truth—without sharing any names. Do whatever you need, but get out of Tel Aviv within the next three hours. The longer you take, the more chance you take with your life. And your wife's."

He chewed on his mustache, then gave a nod, and then another, this one more resolute. Sweat trickled off his forehead and into his left eye. He blinked, normally for once, got out a handkerchief and wiped his face and head dry.

"Okay," he said, grabbing his coat. "Okay." Then he thought of something. "But how do I know when it's safe to come back?"

"I'll give you a number to call." I recited the telephone number at Greta's Café. He jotted it on a piece of paper. "I'm there most days. If you call and I happen to be out, don't leave a message with your number or location. Try again later. Give it a week before you call. This whole thing should be done by then."

He put on his coat and was now wrapping a wool scarf around his neck.

"One more thing," I said. "Do you know who this woman is?" I showed him the picture of Nathan and the striking blue-eyed woman.

He shook his head. "Never seen her before in my life." He stuck a brown homburg on his head and grabbed a black umbrella. He gave me an anxious look. "Is there anything else? I should get going."

I shook my head.

Out on the street, I waited until he locked his door. Then we shook hands and he thanked me for coming to warn him.

"I'll call you in a week."

I nodded. "In a week."

Then he went one way and I the other. The rain was coming down harder.

Chapter 26

Chased by the rain, I ducked into a café on Ha-Kovshim Street. The proprietor had a buccaneer's mustache and a gold tooth in the side of his mouth. I half expected him to draw a scimitar, vault over the bar, and charge me with a ferocious grin.

Instead, he asked me what I wanted to drink in a heavy Greek accent. I asked for a beer and hoisted myself onto a stool while he poured it. He filled the glass to the rim and shaved off the excess foam with the flat side of a knife. He asked if I wanted anything to eat, and I started shaking my head, when I realized I was hungry.

He brought me half a loaf of bread on a round cutting board and a serrated slicing knife. Next to the board he placed a bowl, which he filled with olive oil mixed with a pinch of salt and a healthy amount of some green herb I could not name.

And that was it. An odd-looking meal. I raised an eyebrow in question, and he said with a smile, "Try it. It's simple, I know, but it may surprise you."

It turned out he was right. The bread was crisp on the outside, fluffy on the inside. Dipped in the oil, it was both tasty and filling.

I asked him if this was what they ate in Greece. His face took on a melancholic cast.

"This was but an appetizer," he said in a somber voice. "Ah, what feasts we had." He sighed, cleared his throat, and shrugged apologetically. "But that's all the food I have to serve you today. The shortages—you understand."

I wondered what had happened to him, who he'd lost, and if any of his family were still alive. I didn't ask him, though, knowing that this would be an invitation for him to ask me about my family in return.

Two new customers wandered in from the rain and he went to them. They chatted in rapid, incomprehensible Greek while I sipped my beer, contemplating my next move.

I needed to locate Gregor and Dov. There was one place I knew they might be, but I'd have to wait until night to go there. I did not have a home address for either of them. But maybe the police did.

I asked the proprietor whether he had a telephone I could use. He pointed to the end of the bar, where I found a white candlestick telephone, twenty years old at least.

I dialed a number from memory. It rang three times in a second-floor office in the police station on Yehuda Halevi Street before Reuben Tzanani's melodious voice came over the line.

"Hey, Ant, it's me," I said, using his army nickname.

"Adam." He sounded less than his usual enthusiastic

self. "How are you?"

"I've been worse. How about you and Gila and the kids?"

Reuben had four children and a fifth on the way. There was a good chance he and his wife, Gila, would not stop there. Gila was the sort of woman who would not be fazed by a dozen children, let alone six or seven.

"Fine. Everyone's fine. The children were asking about you the other day, wondering when you'd drop by for a visit."

"Soon. I promise."

"They're not the only ones who've been asking about you, Adam."

He could only mean Leibowitz.

"So I've heard."

"Are you in trouble?"

"Nothing I can't handle," I said, my heart skipping a beat when I recalled that Nathan had expressed a similar sentiment to me a few days before his death.

I fumbled in my pocket for a cigarette, lit it, and took a long pull.

"Reason I'm calling is, I need you to look something up for me in the police files."

A long pause. "Does this have anything to do with Inspector Leibowitz's case?"

I tapped some ash loose. "Does it matter?"

"He gave me explicit instructions to report any conversation you and I had. Specifically, he said that if you requested any information, I was to call him and let him know."

That son of a bitch. "I see."

"I'm to tell him exactly what sort of information you wanted." Another pause. "Adam, he said that you've not been forthright with everything you know about a murder case. Is this true?"

I watched smoke curl from the tip of my cigarette. I could have lied, but Reuben Tzanani deserved the truth. "Pretty much."

"May I know why?"

"Maybe it's better that you don't."

Which was true. The less Reuben knew, the less he could be blamed for later. The less chance that action would be taken against him, action that might include him being fired from his job. The job he worked to provide for a wife and four children, with a fifth on the way.

"At least tell me you have a good reason," he said.

"I do." But did I really? Part of it was my desire to see this thing through my way. Another was the fact that the more I told, the more crimes I could be charged with. If I had come clean about everything I knew that first night, things might have been different. It was too late to reverse course now.

"Leibowitz is a good investigator, Adam. Has a good record."

I was about to tell Reuben how Leibowitz padded his pockets with money he lifted from murder victims, but what would be the point? Reuben would be shocked, appalled; he might even change his opinion about Leibowitz. But what actual good would it do? And, as I'd told Greta, as I knew from experience, many good cops padded their pockets. I used to.

Reuben was saying, "If you really need my help…"

"No," I said quickly. "I can manage."

This might or might not be true. But I didn't want Reuben to put his neck on the line for me. I owed him too much for that.

He had saved my life in Israel's War of Independence. When I was shot twice after taking out an Egyptian machine-gun position, Reuben had carried me on his back over a kilometer to the rear, where I received the emergency care that kept me alive.

That was how he had earned his nickname. Reuben was nearly a foot shorter than me and much lighter. But like an ant, he had managed to carry a load much heavier than his own body weight—namely me—and so saved my life.

"Are you sure, Adam?"

Good old Reuben. I could hear the conflict in his voice. On the one hand, he wanted to help me. On the other, he was totally loyal to the department. He believed that police work was noble work. On one previous occasion, he had gone against a superior to help me with a case. But that had been a special case, and it hadn't been easy for him.

"I'm sure. Don't worry about it, Reuben. But do me a favor, and yourself as well—don't tell Leibowitz I called."

"Well, since you haven't actually asked me for anything specific, I have nothing to tell him, have I?"

I smiled, blowing out some smoke. "That's right. That's exactly right."

"Adam," he said, "you watch yourself, okay?"

"You can count on it," I said, ending the call.

Chapter 27

I knew who had killed Nathan, but I still didn't know where he'd spent the last three days of his life. I also didn't know where he had been stabbed or what he'd been doing there.

Heading south into Jaffa, I followed a similar route as on the night I went to find Nathan to get him to return Mrs. Wasserman's money. The night when I had inadvertently marked him for death.

But I steered clear of Fyodor's bar, where the card game with Gregor and Dov had taken place. I planned on returning there that night, when there'd be less chance of being spotted.

Where I now wanted to go was the café where Nathan had taken me, the one run by his friend Misha. Locating it proved to be more difficult than I anticipated. The narrow, crisscrossing Jaffa streets, some of which lacked street signs, all looked very different in daylight. I meandered about like a mouse in a maze for an hour or so, growing gradually more confused and lost and irritated. The few people I stopped to ask for directions had never heard of Misha or his café. I started thinking that I had wandered off into the wrong section of the city by mistake. Thankfully, it had stopped raining and there was virtually no wind.

I'd begun considering the wisdom of heading back north, to start the search anew from some familiar spot, when by sheer luck I ended up finding the place. I was ambling down one street past where it intersected with another when something I saw out of the corner of my eye made me halt and backtrack to the intersection. I peered about, and there, on the far side of the street, was the café.

As I approached, I could see Misha through the front window, stacking glasses on the bar. Inside, it was nearly deserted. Just one grizzled customer hunched over his newspaper and beer mug. A radio played soft, classical music. Not German, thankfully. Something more eastern. Russian, most likely. The scents of barley, yeast, and alcohol wafted pleasantly about.

Misha, seeing me enter, laid down the glass he was holding. He wore the same dark blue apron as the other night. Above it was a chubby face with a fleshy mouth, a round nose, and kind brown eyes. It was a weary, mournful face. It hadn't been the previous time I saw it.

"Remember me?" I asked.

He nodded. "You were here with Nathan. You're Adam."

"You know my name?" I said, surprised, remembering that Nathan had not mentioned it that night.

"Nathan told it to me. He said you might come by."

"When was this?"

He scratched his forehead tiredly. Judging by his face, I would have said he had slept less than six hours total over the past two nights.

"The day after you two came here, I think."

"So you saw him again? What was he like?"

Misha shrugged. "He was in some sort of trouble. He tried to downplay it, but I could tell it bothered him. I think he was scared to be in his apartment."

"He stayed with you?"

Misha motioned up with his head. "Upstairs. He slept up there for two nights. I asked him why he couldn't stay in his apartment, and he said he had a problem with his landlord. I could tell he was lying, but I didn't press the issue. I keep thinking I should have."

So it was guilt that was keeping him up at night. I knew what that was like.

"Don't blame yourself, Misha. You helped him as best you could, as best as he allowed you to."

He sighed wearily. "I guess you're right. In my head, I know you're right. But here—" he laid his palm over his heart "—I feel entirely different. Know what I mean?"

"I do. I know perfectly."

He sniffled, his eyes welled, and a solitary tear rolled down his cheek. He wiped it off with the ball of his thumb.

"You said Nathan told you I might be coming by. Did he say why?"

Misha shook his head. "He just said that you were a good, honorable man. That he trusted you with his life. Where did you know him from?"

"The war. We were both in Auschwitz." And as I said it, I realized it was the truth. Even though the first time I spoke to Nathan was just days ago, I knew him from well before that. I knew him from the camp. This was where his true character was first revealed to me, where we were bonded for life, when he had hoisted my whipped body and carried me to my bunk, thinking that I would die more comfortably there.

"That wretched place. Nathan wouldn't talk about it. I asked him a few times what it was like, but he would always change the subject. I can understand that. It must have been terrible."

He was looking at me as though hoping I'd tell him something, explain what it was like. I didn't want to talk about the horrors of Auschwitz any more than Nathan had.

Misha sighed again. "And now he's dead. The poor boy lived through that, and now he's dead."

He shook his head, sniffling again, and ran his knuckles over his moist eyes. I gave him a moment to gather himself before I spoke.

"Any chance I might see his things?"

He nodded, blowing his nose into a handkerchief. He turned to the sole customer. "Alexios, I'm going upstairs for a minute. Holler if anyone steps in, all right?"

The man raised his weathered face and grunted a yes. Misha bade me to follow him and together we went through a door behind the bar that opened onto a short hallway. There were two doors, one on the right and one on the left, but we walked past them to the far end where a staircase rose into darkness.

Misha flicked a switch and a weak bulb at the top of

the stairs came to life. He plodded up, breathing hard, with me in his wake, and at the top opened a door that revealed a long, narrow, spartanly furnished room.

There was a queen-sized mattress on the floor in one corner, a single chair, a small table, and a battered dresser. A closed suitcase lay at the foot of the mattress. Two small windows let in a meager supply of light, but it was enough to see the smudges of dirt on the blank walls. A moldy, stale smell permeated the room.

"I keep telling myself I should fix up the room," Misha said, "slap some paint on. But there's always something more pressing to do. No one has stayed here since I bought the building. No one before Nathan."

A thin white curtain hung over an opening in the southern wall.

"The bathroom," Misha said sheepishly, and when I pulled back the curtain, I could see why. It was a tiny, airless room, with a sink, a toilet, and nothing else. No bathtub or shower. Nathan would have had to wash himself at the sink.

"I told him he'd be more comfortable at a hotel," Misha said, "even offered to pay for a room, but he wouldn't have it. Kept insisting that this was fine."

"He was telling the truth," I told him. "He'd slept in worse. Listen, Misha, you gave Nathan what he needed— a place to stay where he felt safe. You couldn't have done more than that."

He seemed grateful to hear it. Stood a bit straighter and breathed a little easier. The guilt would return, though. Likely when he turned in later that night. I knew that from experience.

"Nathan was a fine boy," Misha said. "A marvelous boy."

"You knew him long?"

"From birth. We came from the same town. I was close friends with his father, ever since we two were boys. My wife and I lived next door to the Frankels. We would often eat Sabbath meals together.

"In 1934, my wife and I could tell things were going to get bad for us Jews. We decided to leave Poland and come here. I talked to Mendel—Nathan's father—tried to persuade him to take his family and come with us. He wouldn't hear of it. He said I was crazy, that the very idea Jews could rebuild our homeland was crazy. He wouldn't budge. Most of the other Jews wouldn't either, including my three brothers and two sisters. All of them stayed behind. And all of them are no more."

He choked on those last words, and now the tears came in earnest. He buried his face in his hands and wept for a solid minute. I didn't try to console him, not by word nor by touch. Because there was no consolation for his grief. I knew that from experience, too.

When the tears ceased, he dried his face with his apron, then blew his nose into his handkerchief again.

"Why do you want to look at his things?"

"I'm trying to discover who killed him."

"Why?"

"He saved my life in Auschwitz. I owe him."

Misha nodded in understanding.

"Did you talk to the police?" I asked.

He shook his head, lowering his eyes.

"Because of what Nathan did for a living?"

His eyes returned to mine. "So you know."

"Yes. It doesn't change my opinion of him one bit."

"He was never into rough stuff. No violence. Just the black market."

"Any idea what sort of products?"

"He used to sell cooking oil and eggs, but that stopped a while back. I don't know what he was into these days. He did say he was close to making a big score. That's how he put it—a big score."

"Ever meet his partners, Gregor and Dov?"

"No. But he did tell me about them. He said Gregor is a nasty piece of work. I asked him why he did business with such a man, and he said it was temporary, until he made enough money."

"Enough money to do what?"

"He didn't say specifically, but I believe he was thinking about getting married."

"To Tamara Granot?"

His eyebrows rose. "You know her too."

"Nathan told me about her. And you're right, he was hoping to marry her. She told me they came here one time."

"Yes. A nice girl, I think. But very introverted, barely said a word to me. But I could tell by the way she looked at Nathan that she absolutely worshiped him."

"She seemed an odd choice for him," I said.

"I thought so too, but he said she was smart and sensitive and funny in a shy sort of way, and that she made him feel like someday he could once again have a home and a family. For him that was a lot."

Of course it was, I thought. *For people who have lost their home, their family, their entire world, such a feeling could mean everything.*

We were silent for a while, each in his own thoughts. Then he said, "Well, I'll leave you to it. I should be heading back downstairs."

After he was gone, I stood for a minute, moving nothing but my head and eyes. I looked and listened and smelled, trying to imagine Nathan's final nights in this dreary room. They couldn't have been very pleasant.

I started in the bathroom, finding Nathan's toothbrush and shaving kit. Back in the main room, I stepped over to the dresser and discovered that all three drawers had been warped by time and weather to the extent that they were difficult to open. Two of them I managed to wrench free by brute force; the third I failed to open until I used my knife to work it loose. All three drawers contained nothing but dust.

The mattress had been carefully made, the single pillow centered, the duvet's top third folded back neatly on top of itself. I looked underneath the duvet and the pillow, finding nothing. I carried the suitcase over to the table. It wasn't very heavy. Inside I found a jumble of clothes: a comb; a small pouch with a little over fifteen liras in bills and an additional six in coins; two packs of cigarettes; a deck of playing cards; a metal flask about a quarter full of brandy; and, at the bottom of the suitcase, under the clothes, a thin sheaf of paper.

I put the suitcase on the floor, took out the sheaf of paper, and spread it on the table. It contained eight pieces in total, each twelve inches wide and four tall. All were identical. At their center was a colorful drawing of a cow, looking oddly happy with its lot in life. White patches colored its black hide. A glinting bell hung around its neck. The cow was standing on a verdant meadow dotted with sunflowers. Above it shone a warm sun in a blue sky with just a smattering of fluffy clouds.

Below the cow was a line of text in block English letters. It read "BRAMSON BEEF," and below that, in slightly smaller letters, "THE FINEST, TENDEREST CUTS YOU CAN FIND."

There were other writings, mostly extolling the quality of the product Bramson Beef was selling and explaining how, by a unique process developed by the finest food scientists known to man, the meat hereby sold was preserved in salt and other substances, so that even a year after it had been butchered, carved, and canned, it was still as tasty, tender, and juicy as day-old meat. The finishing touch was a small circular mark with the word KOSHER printed underneath it.

These were labels. Labels that would wrap around cans of preserved meat.

Frowning, I turned each label over in my hand, inspecting them closely.

All eight labels were in pristine condition. No tears, creases, or marks. No residue of glue on the back sides either. These had not been removed from cans. These were brand new, never used. Or, perhaps more accurately, ready to *be* used.

Meat, I thought. *One of the most strictly rationed commodities. And one of the most sought after.* Jewish mothers, ceaselessly fretting over their children's nutrition, were willing to shell out inordinate sums of money to get their hands on a little extra meat for their little ones.

You could get away with charging high prices for oil, sugar, coffee, and butter, but these prices paled in comparison to what you could charge for meat. Was this the big score Nathan had mentioned to Misha? Was this what he and Gregor and Dov were selling?

There was a reason why meat came with such a high price tag. It was very difficult to get. The government heavily regulated cattle ranching. A rancher might be able to claim the death of a few cows and calves, then turn around and sell them for more money on the black market, but he would not be able to move a lot of product that way.

Gregor, Dov, and Nathan seemed to have gotten around this problem by getting their hands on American preserved meat. But where did they get it? Where were they storing it now? And how much of it did they have? Enough for a big score, even divided three ways?

And if they did manage to get a supply of canned meat, what were these unused labels doing here in Nathan's suitcase? Any cans from America would already have the labels on them.

I thought it over for a while, but no answers came. I folded the labels and stuck them in my coat pocket. I had a final look around, saw nothing of interest, and was turning toward the stairs when I heard a crinkling sound and felt that I had stepped on something.

Lifting my shoe, I saw a scrap of paper on the floor. It hadn't been there before. It must have fallen out from between the labels when I spread them out on the table.

I bent down, picked it up, and held it to the light. A short message had been written on it in a crabbed hand. Just one sentence long and a name below it. The language was unfamiliar to me. All I could make out was the name. Tadeusz.

I headed down the stairs and into the café. Alexios was still hunched over his newspaper. Misha was behind the bar, fiddling with his cash register.

"Found anything?" he asked.

"Maybe," I said, showing him one of the labels. "Does this mean anything to you?"

He looked at it and shook his head. "I can't read English."

"It looks like a label for a can of preserved meat. It was in Nathan's suitcase. I wondered how he came by it."

"I don't know. Never seen it before."

"Could he and his partners have been selling meat?"

"If they were, he never offered me any. He always did with the other stuff he sold. Never took money for it, either."

I showed him the note.

"This was with the labels. Can you read this?"

He took it from me, held it at almost arm's length, and squinted at it. "Yes. It's Polish. It says, 'What do you think of these? Tadeusz.'" He lowered the note. "What does it mean?"

"I don't know. Do you know who this Tadeusz is?"

"No. Nathan never mentioned a man by that name. I'm sorry."

He handed me the note back. I made it disappear into a pocket and got out the picture of Nathan and the other woman.

"Ever see her?"

Misha nodded, smiling, glad to be of help. "Yes. Nathan brought her over a few times. Her name is Iris, eh—" he closed his eyes in concentration "—Rosenfeld. Yes, Iris Rosenfeld. They were pretty involved for a time."

"But not recently?"

"I don't think so. The last time I saw her was probably five, six weeks ago."

"Did Nathan stop seeing her because of Tamara Granot?"

Misha shifted his feet, looking uncomfortable. He lowered his voice, as though afraid Alexios might overhear him. "Nathan saw both at the same time."

If he thought I'd be shocked, I wasn't. "Do you know where I might find her?"

"Nathan said she works at a dance club on Gordon Street. The Toval club. I've never been there myself."

I hadn't either, but it shouldn't be too hard to find.

I said, "The night Nathan was killed, any idea where he was going?"

"No. I didn't even know he was gone until I'd closed up for the night and went upstairs to see if he needed anything. There's a back door. He must have used it."

"Okay," I said. "Thank you." I started for the door, then turned back. "One last thing. Did Nathan have a brother? A younger one?"

"Yes. Peter. Why do you ask?"

"I was just wondering if you knew what happened to him."

Misha spread his hands, fingers splayed. "Like everyone else. He is now ashes."

Chapter 28

The sun was making its presence known, peeking through rifts in the cloud cover. A fast wind swirled about, but it did not have much bite to it. The air was heavy with accumulated dampness. Each breath felt like you were drawing in water.

I boarded a bus heading north. All the seats were taken, so I stood holding the overhead railing, planted my feet wide, and swayed with the bus's constant motion.

I got off on Dizengoff Square, walked north to Gordon Street, and accosted a young man who was staring into the display window of a clothing store. I asked him if he knew where the Toval club was and he pointed west toward the sea.

The club took up a wide lot just west of the corner of Gordon and Hayarkon Streets. The air was saltier here, the wind sharper. Waves burst in foam and thunder against the sand less than a hundred meters away.

From inside the club floated the sound of modern music. Lots of drums and horns. I went inside and found myself in a large, mostly empty space. Tables on the right and along the back wall, a bar on the left, and, in the middle, nothing but scuffed floor tiles. A dance floor, though at this early time of day no one was dancing.

There were a few customers. Two couples taking up tables and one solitary drinker occupying a stool at the farthest end of the bar. A waitress was serving drinks to one of the couples. The bartender had his eyes closed and was drumming on the bar top with all ten fingers in rhythm with the music.

I stepped over to him and loudly cleared my throat. He opened one eye, looked me over, and then added the other. His fingers tapped a few more bars, then stopped. He smiled. "Get you anything, mister?"

"A soda," I said, taking another look around.

He brought me the bottle and an empty glass. I poured and took a sip.

I said, "Kind of slow, isn't it?"

"For now. It will fill up quite a bit over the next couple of hours. Not like in summertime—people dance more when it's hot—but still busy enough to keep me hopping."

"Is that the sort of music you usually play here?"

"Big band? I wish. I like it a lot. Very energetic. But we play all sorts. Modern and old. A lot of European stuff—waltzes, things like that. Many of the customers prefer that. Makes them remember their old homes, I guess."

He shrugged, mystified. I could tell by his accent that he'd been born here, in Israel. He had not suffered the loss of home and family, had not lived through the disillusionment of being cast out of a country you considered your homeland by people you thought of as your compatriots. He was the new Jew, reborn, one who did not carry the baggage of torment and loss. I envied him.

I took another sip. "Is Iris Rosenfeld here, by any chance?"

This time, his smile had a tinge of roguishness to it. He was young, no more than twenty-three, fresh-faced and broad-shouldered and trim. A good-looking man. The smile sat on his face as though it belonged there.

"If I had a lira for every man who asked me that question over the past week..."

"Oh?"

"I'm afraid the lovely Iris no longer plies her trade in this establishment."

"Her trade? Waitressing?"

He laughed, but then his face turned serious. "Since you've obviously never been here before, I gotta ask you what this is about."

"I want to ask her a few questions. That's all."

"Aha," he said in a disbelieving tone. "Lots of men do. Questions about what?"

"A man we both knew."

"Knew?"

"He died recently." I pulled out the picture of Nathan and Iris. "This guy."

The bartender took a look, frowning. "Hey, I recognize him. His name was Nathan, right? He's dead?"

"Yes. He died a few days ago. How did you know him?"

"He was here pretty regularly. A great guy. Very friendly. What happened?"

"You haven't heard? It was on the radio. In the papers too, I bet."

"I don't follow the news much, and the only thing I listen to on the radio is music."

"He was knifed down on Allenby Street."

The bartender looked stunned and even younger than before.

"I'm talking to everyone who knew him. I understand he and Iris were close."

"More than close, I'd say. He would come here sometimes on nights she worked, drink a beer or two until she got through with her shift, and they'd head out together."

"You said she wasn't a waitress. What was her job?"

"She danced."

"Danced? In a show?"

He shook his head. "She was a house dancer. She danced with customers."

"What do you mean?"

"I mean a lonely, single guy comes in. He can either try his luck, ask a woman customer for a dance, or he can dance with Iris."

"And he pays her for that?"

"Well, yeah. A lot of clubs have someone like Iris on hand. She also gets paid by the owner. The idea is that more men will come in, stay longer, and order more if they can dance with a girl like Iris. And it works. Some of these men, they aren't likely to ever dance with a girl who looks like Iris if they don't pay her."

"An unpleasant sort of job."

"I think so. Especially since most of the customers like slow, close dances."

"Do they ever get out of line?"

"Yeah, but we have a guy around to handle that sort of thing. Iris points him out to anyone who wants to buy a dance. It's rare that someone needs to be thrown out."

I thought of Sima Vaaknin. "Is dancing all she sells?"

He gave me a sly look. "I've often wondered about that myself. I'm sure she was propositioned from time to time. But if she ever accepted, I wouldn't know about it."

"Where can I find her?"

He motioned for the waitress. "Matilda might know."

Matilda did know. It took a bit of cajoling, a touch of persuasion, but when I left the Toval club, it was with Iris Rosenfeld's address written in my notebook.

Chapter 29

The address was for a three-story building on Bar-Ilan Street. Apartment three, second floor. I rapped on the door, heard a "Give me a minute" shouted from inside, and did just that.

She opened the door, wearing a long-sleeved red blouse tucked into an ankle-length blue skirt, and a pair of low-heeled black shoes. A cigarette burned between her lips—one of the long, slim brands that some women seemed to favor.

Her hair was longer than it had been in the picture of her and Nathan. It cascaded down her back in a thick, brilliant mane. Other than that, she looked the same. A striking, oval face, indelicate yet handsome, dominated by a pair of large eyes the color of the sea and the temperature of an iceberg. Her mouth was wide and generous, her neck soaring and powerful, her skin the complexion of alabaster. She had an aquiline nose, long and flaring. She stood five seven and had the straight, easy stance common to dancers. Her shoulders were broad for a woman, her legs long, her hips tapering to a narrow waist. With her athletic build, black mane, strong nose, and straight, rigid posture, she made me think of a thoroughbred mare. Only her breasts didn't fit the image. They seemed to have been borrowed from another woman. They were large for her size and hung loose under her blouse.

She noticed my looking at them and blew smoke in my face.

"Help you with something?" she asked, her tone contemptuous and impatient. Not an auspicious beginning to a conversation.

I waved the smoke away. "Miss Rosenfeld, my name is Adam Lapid. I want to talk to you for a few minutes about Nathan Frankel."

She raised her eyebrows. They were widely spaced, full and prominent. She didn't pluck or thin them out.

"If you're a cop, you're wasting your time. I know nothing about what happened to Nathan."

"I'm not a cop. I was a friend of his."

"I never met you. I don't recall him ever mentioning your name, either."

"He had no reason to. We first met years ago in Europe. He thought I'd died in the war. We ran into each other a few days before he was killed."

She blew out more smoke, this time at the ceiling. "And that random encounter has led you here to my door?"

"Not just to you. I've been talking to people who knew him, trying to learn more about his life, especially his last days."

"Sorry. Can't help you there. Last time I saw Nathan was over two weeks ago."

"Still, I understand you knew him quite well. I'm hoping you'll help me clarify some things."

She tilted her head to the right, studying me with her cool liquid eyes. There was something aloof, almost haughty about her. She was very attractive but gave off an aura of unapproachability. The message seemed to be *Don't think you can get fresh with me, buster. I am not some toy for you to play with.*

Possibly her line of work had made her so. I could see how that would happen. Too many men who let their hands wander about her body or whispered lewd comments in her ear as they pressed themselves to her on the dance floor. It was bound to harden a woman.

"Well," she said, "I don't think I've got much to say to you, Mr. Lapid. I don't wish to discuss Nathan with you or anyone."

She gave me a dismissive little shoo-away wave and was closing the door when I said, "I'll let the police know about you, then."

She stopped, the door half-open, and threw me a sharp look.

I continued, "They asked everyone who knew Nathan to come forward, give a statement. They'd like to get yours, I'm sure. I've had the misfortune to meet the officer in charge of the investigation. He's very thorough. But you shouldn't worry. He should be done sticking his nose into every nook and cranny of your life in no more than five hours."

She said nothing, gazing at me with something approaching fury in her eyes. An inch of gray ash broke free from the end of her cigarette and landed on her shoe. She didn't seem to notice it.

"Or," I said, "you can stop being so goddamn difficult, invite me in, answer some questions, and I'll be gone and out of your life in under thirty minutes."

She lifted her chin, her flaring nostrils bringing to mind the double barrels of a shotgun. She exhaled air forcefully, again reminding me of a mare.

"All right," she said. "You can come in. It'll give me the pleasure of throwing you out."

She turned, leaving the door only partially open so I had to push it the rest of the way. She walked with long, graceful strides. Wordlessly I followed her down a short hallway to a shabbily appointed living room.

There was a sofa, a padded armchair, a radio, a frayed circular rug, and a table with four chairs. None of the furniture matched and all of it was fairly old and showing advanced signs of wear and tear. The radio was an ancient model—fifteen years old or so—and was missing one of its knobs. It appeared that being a dance partner for hire did not earn one a healthy living. An assortment of wet female clothing was draped over the four dining chairs. Some of it did not seem like Iris Rosenfeld's size.

"You have a roommate?"

She eyed me suspiciously, wondering how I knew. Then she followed my gaze and her face resumed its cold detachment.

"Why? Are you planning on forcing her to talk to you as well? If so, you're out of luck. Rina is at work. Besides, she hardly knew Nathan."

One of the windows was open, letting in chilled air and the rumble and buzz of the city. It did little to disperse the thick smell of her cigarettes. She sat in the armchair, crossing her legs. She took a final drag off her cigarette, then mashed it out in an ashtray that was filled to overflowing. She didn't invite me to sit. I settled myself on the sofa. She ran a hand along her long thigh, smoothing out a crease in her skirt, and contemplated me with those icy eyes of hers. A lot of men, I bet, asked her to dance just because of those eyes. They were alluringly cold and distant. Some men, those who were entranced by a challenging woman, would have wanted to see whether they could make those eyes melt. It was no surprise that Nathan had been drawn to her.

She said, "It's not a gentlemanly thing to do, you know, to twist the arm of a lady."

"You didn't leave me much choice, I'm afraid."

"You could have walked away. Why is Nathan so important to you?"

"Let's just say I'm indebted to him."

"You owe him money?" she asked, then laughed. "No. Of course not. If it were money, you would be counting your blessings, wouldn't you? You wouldn't be here, bothering me."

"Unless I was the sort of person who would pay the next of kin."

"A saint, are you?" she said, grinning. Then she leaned a bit forward, her grin fading to be replaced by an expression of thoughtful incredulity. "My God, if I didn't know better, I might actually believe you were serious."

"Know better? We've never met."

She made a who-cares-about-that gesture with her hand. "I've met more than enough men in my life, Mr. Lapid. I am not naive about how you operate."

I studied her, trying to determine her age. It took a moment. Parts of her appeared exceedingly young—her skin, hair, the tautness of her body—while other parts, like her eyes, would have been at home on a woman twice her age. It wasn't the first time I'd met people like her. I'd seen thousands of young men and women with old eyes. War cultivates such people as avidly as it cuts down others.

Still, her youth was unmistakable. She was twenty, maybe twenty-one. Young, but not too young to learn much of the truth about the world. And about men, too.

"Who gave you my address?" she asked.

"Your fellow employees at the Toval club."

She rolled her eyes. "People love to blab, don't they?"

"Some of them. They told me you're a dancer."

"That's right. What do you think of that?"

She was challenging me to express my opinion, doubtless expecting a negative one.

"It's a job, I suppose. No different at its core than most others."

She smiled a humorless smile. "Tell that to most women. The looks I get once they figure out what I do—way they see it, I'm just a prostitute by another name."

"And men? How do they see it?"

"Some make me offers. Sometimes very generous offers."

"Ever accept them?"

Again she raised her chin, showing me the full length of her stately neck. Pride radiated off her like summer heat off asphalt. "Why do you ask? Thinking of making me an offer yourself?"

Possibly she was hoping I would make her an offer just so she could turn me down—in the most humiliating fashion, no doubt.

"How did Nathan see it?" I said.

She blinked. Then her demeanor underwent a transformation. First, a tremor vibrated across her face. Then her eyes changed hue, the ice gone in an instant. Her tongue darted out of her mouth, wetting her lips. With tremulous fingers she fumbled in the pocket of her skirt, fished out a pack of cigarettes, plucked one out, and stuck it between her lips. Then she tried and failed to light a match. She cursed after the fourth unsuccessful attempt.

"Here," I said, holding out my lighter.

Her eyes flashed with irritation, but she took the proffered lighter, ignited her cigarette, and drew a couple of quick drags. She tossed the lighter back to me.

For a moment we were both silent. She smoked, her gaze turned away from me. She was not happy that I had witnessed her display of emotion. It was a show of weakness, of vulnerability, and Iris Rosenfeld was a person who prided herself on her strength. Her life and job had taught her that it was best to have your guard up in the company of men, to show them nothing of your true self. But here she had given me a glimpse of what lay behind the armor, and it made her angry—both at me and at herself.

And it was a simple question about Nathan that had led to this exposure. She had cared about him, and now she was hurting because of him. Probably she'd been hurting for some time, ever since their relationship came to an end, and now she was hurting because he was gone for good.

Only when her cigarette was half gone did she finally answer my question. And for the first time, there was softness in her voice.

"Nathan was not like other men."

"How long were you two involved?"

"Six months or so."

"How did you meet?"

She smiled a wistful smile. "The way you would think. He bought a dance. I remember thinking that he was better looking than most of my clients. And when he took me in his arms and led me across the dance floor, I found myself actually enjoying myself. It doesn't happen often. Most men are clumsy oafs. They step on your toes; they move like elephants. Nathan was light on his feet, graceful. So much so that in the course of our dance, I asked him if he'd had lessons. And he just smiled and said that he was merely following my lead. Which was a lie, but a good lie." She puffed some more on her cigarette. "We danced a waltz, and when the tune was drawing to a close, he asked me if I would have a drink with him. Some nights I get a dozen such offers, and I always decline them. This time I found myself saying yes, against my better judgment. And so it began."

"You were in love with him," I said, making a statement rather than posing a question.

She looked at me as though I had overstepped my bounds, and then surprised me by answering, "Yes. And he with me."

"He told you that?"

"Often enough. But I didn't need to hear the words. I could feel it in his body, Mr. Lapid, when I was in his bed."

There was that challenging tone again. She wanted me to know that she and Nathan had been lovers, and didn't care one bit whether I was shocked by her candor.

"What went wrong?"

She didn't answer. She got out a fresh cigarette and lit it with the burning tip of the current one. She then stubbed out the old cigarette, adding its carcass to the mountain of butts in the ashtray.

"Was it Tamara Granot?" I asked. "Was she why you and Nathan were no longer together?"

It was as if I had lit a fuse. A short one. Iris Rosenfeld's face twisted into something ugly. She pried the cigarette from between her lips and slashed the air with it.

"That bitch," she spat. "Little miss right and proper. Never had to work a day in her life, never lifted a finger. Daddy gave her everything she ever wanted."

And took so much more from her, I thought. *More than you could ever imagine.*

"So it was her," I said.

"Yes, it was her. Don't ask me what he saw in that dry

little mouse. I don't know. And what's worse, I'm not sure Nathan knew either. I asked him once, after he finally told me why he was being distant, why I was seeing him less frequently, and he couldn't tell me. He tried, but he couldn't find the words."

"What did he say?"

"That he hadn't expected to fall in love with another woman. That he was sorry."

Each word came out of her mouth as though coated in venom. Iris Rosenfeld hated Tamara Granot, but she was also very bitter toward Nathan. And his apology for breaking it off with her seemed to have had a similar effect to the false one I had made on his behalf to Tova Wasserman. It put salt on Iris Rosenfeld's wounds, inflamed her resentment and humiliation, and not only failed in its goal of assuaging her soul-crushing pain, but actually aggravated it.

But to what point? My detective's mind asked.

And more by ingrained habit than actual suspicion—for I was certain that Gregor and Dov were the ones who had murdered Nathan—I said, "You seem to be very bitter, Miss Rosenfeld. Very angry."

She scoffed. "You think?"

"Angry enough to kill?"

She stared at me with dilated eyes, and I wondered how the smoke was not bothering her, pluming as it did right by her face.

"You think I killed Nathan?" she asked in a tone of utter disbelief. "Are you insane?"

"It wouldn't be the first time a jilted lover was driven

to murder. They don't call it a crime of passion for no reason."

"But I loved him."

"That's exactly it. You were madly in love with Nathan. You couldn't bear the thought of another woman having him. Once it was clear he was lost to you, you decided no other woman would have him. That also explains why you didn't want me to go to the police. You don't want them to know about you. Because you have a clear motive. You'd be suspect number one."

And as I was saying all this, I could feel my skin prickling from the base of my spine clear up to my scalp. I found myself leaning forward, senses heightened, looking for any telltale signs of deceit or dissembling on her part. Had I been all wrong? Was I sitting before Nathan's killer?

She surprised me by throwing her head back and bursting into a long, unbridled laugh. Her shoulders shook with it. When she finally ceased laughing, her cheeks were merrily pink and her blue eyes glistened. She took one final drag off her cigarette, crushed it out, and looked upon me with a smile stretching her lips. Gone was the vulnerable, hurt woman I had witnessed a moment ago; nor was this the cold, haughty person she'd been at the onset of our meeting. Iris Rosenfeld now bore an expression of high amusement and deep satisfaction, like a child who knows a secret and feels smarter than anyone else because of it.

"That was an impressive display, Mr. Lapid, you playing detective like that. Did that come from some movie or was it a dime novel? For your information, I had no reason to kill Nathan. None whatsoever. Care to guess why?"

"Enlighten me," I said, eying her closely.

"Because I was going to get him back. That little closed-up bitch, she was nothing more than a temporary obstacle."

"You couldn't know that for certain."

"But I could. Believe me I could. They wouldn't have lasted. Before long, Nathan would have come back to me."

"He didn't plan to. He was going to marry Tamara Granot. He had a ring and everything."

The way she flinched when I said this made me think she had no idea how serious Nathan had been about Tamara Granot. Or she was a very skillful actress. Which she had to be, I reminded myself, since her job was to make men she found repulsive believe she relished their company.

"Still," she said when she'd recovered from her momentary shock, "I would have gotten him back. They would have never been married."

"How would you have gotten him to change his mind?" I asked.

She lit another cigarette. This time she got the match going on the first try. She took a drag, the satisfied set of her features once more reminding me of a child cherishing a secret nugget of knowledge.

"That's none of your business, Mr. Lapid. Let's just say I was not powerless when it came to Nathan."

The mention of his name, evoking as it undoubtedly did the fact of his demise, shook the satisfaction off her face. She watched the smoke undulate upward from her cigarette, saying, more to herself, it seemed like, than to me, "He would've been mine again. All mine."

I could detect no doubt in her tone. Sorrow, yes. Profound sadness, too. But not a scintilla of doubt. I had a suspicion as to what tactics she had planned on using to lure Nathan back to her. She was a beautiful woman, and she had given Nathan what Tamara Granot had so far denied him—she'd been his lover, while her rival had not. She was a woman of passion—whether it was anger, hate, or love she felt—and doubtlessly she brought that passion with her into the bedroom. A beautiful, passionate woman, I knew full well, was an intoxicant a man would find hard to resist, even when he thought he would be better off if he did.

It was obvious she was not about to confirm or deny my suspicion. She had made it clear that topic was off bounds. It was time to shift direction. "You know Nathan was killed not far from here," I said. "Just a few minutes' walk from this apartment."

She sighed tiredly. "You're still harping on about that nonsense? I tell you I didn't kill him. I had absolutely no reason to."

"Ease my mind. Tell me where you were the night he was killed."

"Part of the evening I was here; part of it I was out walking, getting some fresh air. If you want to know exactly at what time I did this or that, I'd have to disappoint you. I wasn't checking the time; I didn't think I'd need an alibi." She shut her eyes and pinched her temples between her left thumb and middle finger, rubbing them gently. "But it's none of your business what I did. And I don't want to answer any more of your questions. You've given me a monstrous headache. Give my name to the police if you want, I don't care, but I'm done talking to you."

She rose to her feet in one abrupt motion. It was an unequivocal dismissal. I stood up. Without a word she strode to her door and had it open by the time I got there.

"By the way," I said, stopping just inside the doorway, "I understand you quit your job."

"That's right," she said, one arm curled around her chest, the other holding the cigarette aloft. Her forehead was creased, her mouth tight. She certainly looked as though she was in pain. Maybe that headache wasn't merely an excuse to get rid of me.

"What are you going to do now?"

"I'm going to be a dance teacher," she said. "If you're as ungainly on your feet as you are with your questions, a lesson or two may do you wonders."

She had gone full circle. Once again she was the contemptuous, keep-your-distance cynic she'd been when she first opened her door.

A parting shot felt in order.

"You'd better get your alibi straight, Miss Rosenfeld. You're likely to need it," I said and stepped over the threshold onto the landing.

She responded by slamming the door shut so hard it would have been no surprise to see plaster fall all around me.

Chapter 30

It was evening by now, dark and gloomy and cold as only winter evenings and nights could be. No rain though, which was a blessing. The moon was a sinister grin; the stars sparkled like fool's gold. The wind had kicked up a notch. It roiled the air, sending it down collars and up pant legs, slithering between coat and shirt buttons, touching frosty little tongues to skin.

I put on my new gloves, which had the odd effect of making not just my hands warm, but the rest of me as well.

I walked south down Rothschild Boulevard, stopping along the way for a sandwich and soup. I perused a newspaper while I ate. The Americans were retreating down the Korean peninsula; Chinese and North-Korean forces were in hot pursuit. President Truman was calling for an increase in American military spending and for a separate increase in military aid for Western European countries. Two former Wehrmacht generals were conducting talks with Allied representatives regarding the establishment of new German military units, as part of the coalition of Western countries.

That last report snuffed out my appetite. I pushed my plate away, sandwich half eaten, and reread the article in outright amazement. I couldn't believe that the Allies were willing to even contemplate the creation of a new German army. Especially less than six years since the end of history's bloodiest war. And they apparently planned on placing at the head of this new army some of the leaders of the old German army, which had subjugated Europe and murdered millions. It seemed outlandish, grotesque, perverted. But the Allies now had new enemies. The victims of yesterday were to be sacrificed on the altar of political expediency.

In burning rage and disgust, I crumpled the newspaper into a misshapen ball and dropped it on my plate. I jumped to my feet and stomped out of the café, ignoring the anxious calls of the manager, asking if something was wrong with the food.

I marched downtown, hands balled into fists, my face and neck scorching hot. Slowly, gradually, I cooled myself down. I reminded myself that I had a job to do, that I had to keep a cool head. I could not influence major political events in Europe. I could, however, bring Nathan's killers to justice.

In a side street in Jaffa, I found a dingy hotel that offered cheap rooms. The guy at the desk wanted me to pay a week in advance, but I finally got him to accept a two-day payment.

In exchange for my money, I got a key to a tiny room with a single bed, a small dresser, and a bedside table with a shaded lamp. In addition, the desk clerk grudgingly supplied me with a ratty towel and a quarter bar of soap. No toothbrush was available.

It was pretty dismal—cramped and chilly and smelling of mildew—but it would have to do. I needed a place for the night; I couldn't go home. Now that I had good reason to suspect Gregor and Dov would not be satisfied with searching, and trashing, my place, but had every intention of killing me as well, I had to assume they might get it into their heads to pay my apartment a return visit. I also did not wish to rely on Sima's hospitality. It was best to be on my own until this case was over and done with.

The bathroom was communal, at the end of the hall. I waited twenty minutes for it to become vacant, then showered before climbing back into my clothes. Then I headed out, hiking through the cold darkness until I got to Fyodor's bar.

I didn't go in. Instead, I took up position in the recessed doorway of a shuttered store diagonally across the street from the bar. I tightened my coat around me, raised my collar, and stuck my gloved hands in my pockets. It was still cold, but bearable.

For over two hours, I stood watching the door to the bar, seeing people go in and out. Dov and Gregor were not among them. I had a hankering for a cigarette but didn't dare light one for fear of its glow being seen. I just waited, keeping my eyes peeled, and allowed my mind to drift this way and that, the way it does when you're not actively focusing it on any specific task.

As the night progressed, the flow of people became decisively negative—for every person who ventured inside, three or four or five exited. Then there was a long lull in traffic, following the departure of one stoop-shouldered gray-haired customer who staggered drunkenly down the street. It was now close to midnight, and the temperature dropped a few extra notches.

I waited some more and then, finally, saw Fyodor emerging from the bar wearing a gray coat and black pants. He was whistling a happy tune as he shut the door and fumbled with a set of keys. He had found the right one and inserted it in the lock by the time I came up behind him.

"Hello, Fyodor. Got time for one more drink?"

He turned, began shaking his head, then stopped when he caught sight of my face. I saw recognition flit across his bearded features followed closely by apprehension before he broke into a smile that was too wide to be sincere.

"Hey, it's been a while, hasn't it?"

"Not too long," I said. "Less than a week."

"Yeah?" he said in a surprised tone. He grinned, motioning vaguely at his forehead. "I got no head for dates. And the booze doesn't help either." He laughed too loudly, the laughter devolving into an awkward chuckle and then nothing at all when he saw I wasn't smiling.

"Remember my name, Fyodor? Remember the night we met?"

He made a show of trying, scrunching up his face and scratching his chin. Finally he said, "Afraid not. Anyway, it's too late for a drink. As you can see, I've already locked up."

"Not yet, you haven't. You still haven't turned the key

in the lock."

He sighed, grasped the protruding end of the key, and twisted it counterclockwise. The bolt clicked home. He flashed me an are-you-happy-now smile. "Okay. So now it's locked. And now, if you don't mind, I'll head on home. My bed's calling me. No sore feelings, right? Come back tomorrow night and I'll give you one on the house to make it up to you. Say around nine?"

I shook my head slowly, casting quick glances up and down the street. There was no one but Fyodor and me. "Can't wait that long, I'm afraid. Let's go inside. I promise you it won't take long."

"You don't seem to be listening. I said—"

"I know what you said. Now open the damn door." And I showed him the Luger.

Fyodor stiffened. The keys slipped from his grasp and clattered onto the sidewalk. His rounded eyes jumped from my face to the gun and back again.

I said, "Pick them up. And no funny business. If you want to make it to your bed tonight, or any night for that matter, do what I say when I say it. Now get the keys and open the door."

He bent down, clasped the keys with a shaky hand, and managed after a few failed attempts to work one into the lock. He pushed open the door and half wobbled inside. I gave him some room so he wouldn't be able to catch me off guard with a surprise swing, then followed into the bar. I shut the door.

Inside it was dark and quiet, and smelled of fish, seawater, cheap alcohol, and tobacco. I told Fyodor to turn on a light and he did. I motioned him to a table and told him to have a seat. I sat down on the opposite side of the table, keeping the Luger visible. "Keep both hands on the tabletop and don't try anything stupid," I said. "I've had this gun for a long time, and I know how to use it."

"There's no need for that," he said, sounding peeved. "I ain't done nothing to you."

"No, you haven't. And I have no wish to do you any harm. I need some information, Fyodor. Give it to me and I'll be on my way."

"What information?"

"Let's start with Gregor and Dov. Seen them lately?"

"Not since the night you were here."

"Know where I can find them?"

"No."

I injected some malice into my voice. "You lying to me, Fyodor? Because if you are, I'll get very upset."

He shook his head. His forehead glistened with sweat. "I'm telling the truth, I swear it. Those guys aren't my friends. They're customers, nothing more. But I wouldn't tell you even if I knew. Gregor—I'm not getting on his bad side."

He sounded sincere, but it was also possible he was simply an accomplished liar.

"So you know what they do for a living," I said.

"I know they're criminals. I know they're dangerous. Both have killed men before. You're a fool if you plan on taking them on."

"Thanks for your concern. I appreciate it. Now tell me

what went on here that night, after Nathan and I went out."

"If Gregor finds out I talked to you—"

"Don't worry about him. He's not here. I am, and I have a gun. Worry about me."

He wiped his forehead with the back of his hand, then ran the same hand over his mouth, apparently oblivious of the sweat he was transferring to his lips. "A couple of minutes after you had gone, Gregor came downstairs, looking like he was about to blow up. He gave me the third degree, made me tell him everything you said to me."

"You told him my name?"

"Yes," Fyodor said, barely able to meet my eye.

That explained how Gregor had learned who I was. How he had discovered where I lived was another matter. But once you had a name, with a little time and effort you could get an address.

"What happened then?"

"Then he called me a bunch of names and said to never let anyone go up to the second floor while he was there, before clearing it first with him. He also ordered me not to tell Nathan that he asked about you."

"And I suppose you didn't."

He shook his head. "Like I said, I'm not getting on Gregor's bad side without a pretty good reason."

And, apparently, I thought, *letting Nathan know that Gregor was asking questions behind his back was not such a reason.*

"Some friend you are," I remarked.

He shrugged, keeping his gaze pointed at his hands. "I

liked Nathan. Liked him a lot. But I gotta think of me first."

"Yeah," I said, kneading the back of my neck, thinking that it would have made no difference if Fyodor had told Nathan about Gregor asking those questions. Because Nathan had decided to go into hiding anyway. Evidently, he had sensed that he might be in danger and took precautions. Only they hadn't been enough.

Still, that didn't change the fact that Fyodor had acted cowardly. "They killed him, you know."

He squeezed his eyes shut, as though to keep out an unpleasant sight or truth. "I'm sorry about that. Truly I am."

"Yeah," I said again, knowing I was wasting time, that trying to make Fyodor feel guilty about Nathan's death was pointless. That wasn't why I was here.

"Ever meet a guy called Tadeusz?" I asked.

Fyodor raised his head and opened his eyes. "How do you know him?"

"Never mind how. Do you know him or don't you?"

"Yes. He came around. Twice or maybe three times. Not for a month, though, maybe even longer."

"With Nathan?"

"Yes. Always. He's Polish. Speaks broken Hebrew, like he just got off the boat from Europe."

"Where can I find him?"

Fyodor said he didn't know.

"What's his last name?"

He didn't know that either.

"Is he a criminal like the rest of them? Part of the gang?"

"Oh no. He's an artist."

"An artist?"

"Yeah. A painter. A good one. I have one of his drawings. I can show you." He started to rise but stopped midway with his back bent, hands still on the table, staring worriedly at the Luger.

"Go ahead," I said.

He went behind the bar. I stayed vigilant, keeping the gun aimed at his chest. He opened a drawer and took out a piece of paper, roughly twice the size and width of a paperback page. He held it like a fragile heirloom and laid it gently on the bar after wiping off a section of it.

It was a portrait of Fyodor, made with a pencil. It was better than good. It was true art. Not only was the portrait exquisitely detailed and accurate, it also seemed to tell a story about the man whose face it was depicting. Every line around the mouth, the angle of the eyes, even the dark mess of his beard conveyed an array of emotions. It was the sort of drawing you could look at again and again, and each time find something new to admire. No wonder Fyodor handled it with such care.

"He did this?" I asked, awed. "Tadeusz?"

"Yes. One of the times he was here. It didn't take him long, and he didn't even have me sit for him. He drew it while I was working. I was speechless when he handed it to me."

"It's amazing."

Fyodor nodded. He gazed upon the drawing with a

loving smile, all traces of the fear he'd been displaying since I approached him on the street gone.

I was thinking about the food labels I'd found in Nathan's suitcase and the note written by Tadeusz, asking what Nathan thought of them. Now I had a pretty good idea what Tadeusz had meant by that.

"Did you see any other work by Tadeusz?" I asked.

Fyodor shook his head. "Just this one drawing."

"I need to find him. What else can you tell me about him?"

"I don't know anything else. Like I said, he didn't speak Hebrew very well."

"Think, dammit. Does he live in Tel Aviv?"

"I don't know."

My lips tightened in disappointment. Fyodor must have seen something in my face, because he stepped back from the bar, his expression wary.

I held up my left hand, palm out. "It's all right. You got nothing to worry about from me."

He nodded and let out a breath. I asked him to describe Tadeusz.

"Short, thin, wears glasses. Pale skinned. Has brown eyes and a long, thin nose. A studious sort of face. Looks like a bookkeeper, know what I mean?"

I wasn't sure that I did, but I didn't dwell on it. "Okay, Fyodor. Thank you. And don't worry, Gregor will never know we talked."

Chapter 31

Back at my cell of a hotel room, I stood at the tiny window with a cigarette, watching its smoke drift out into the night sky. My thoughts drifted as well, settling, of all things, on Sima Vaaknin.

For a moment, I could sense her—smell her scent, see her gorgeous face before my eyes, feel her hot skin on my fingertips. Then I thought about the men she'd been with that day and the pleasant illusion was shattered. All I could smell was the mildew in the walls of my room and the smoke from my cigarette. All I could see was the decrepit buildings on the other side of the street and a slice of dark Jaffa sky. All I could feel was the cigarette pinched between my fingers and the heavy tiredness that was weighing on me.

It had been a long and eventful day, and also a fruitful one. Now, at the end of it, a picture was forming. Like a jigsaw puzzle, pieces were connecting. I did not know everything yet, but I felt I was on the verge of it.

The key was Tadeusz. I had to find him and get him to talk to me. I did not know how to do that yet, but tomorrow I would have to find a way.

When my cigarette was done, I went down the hall to use the restroom. I drank a little water from the tap, then went to bed.

I woke up in the early morning with the foggy remnants of a nightmare clawing at me, and also with an idea. The problem was that I had no clue where Tadeusz lived. I assumed he resided in or in the vicinity of Tel Aviv, but this was an area that encompassed dozens of cities, towns, villages, and kibbutzim. Sifting through all of them would take time. Perhaps days. I could not take that long.

But when I woke up, it was with the memory of something I'd seen in Nathan's apartment, a bus ticket to the city of Ramat Gan, a few kilometers east of Tel Aviv.

It could have meant anything. There were plenty of reasons why Nathan might have chosen to travel to Ramat Gan and nearly all of them had nothing to do with Tadeusz. But it was the one lead I had, so I decided to pursue it.

It took over a dozen telephone calls spread across the entire morning and into the early afternoon for me to learn that Tadeusz Urlanski lived in a house in one of the lesser parts of Ramat Gan. "Out on the very edge of the city," a city clerk informed me. The contempt in his voice toward the people who lived there was palpable.

I also learned that Tadeusz worked as a printer. He printed books and other written material for various publishers across the coastal region of Israel. One of these publishers told me that Tadeusz was the best he'd ever worked with and that "I would give him more work, but he doesn't want it. A strange sort of fellow."

Once I had an address, it took me a few more calls to

determine the best way to get there. The closest I could come by bus was a little under a kilometer and a half away. The rest would have to be done on foot.

The bus ride took fifty minutes. I was the only passenger to disembark at that stop. The area was within the city limits of Ramat Gan, but just barely. Every city has such areas, usually on its periphery—sections that the city administration does its best to ignore.

Both sides of the potholed road I walked along were overgrown with weeds, waist-high bushes, and evergreens, whose leaves rustled with the brisk wind that blew in the smell of the nearby river. Isolated little white houses with red-tile roofs stood in the center of large lots of mostly uncultivated land. Animal sounds abounded, both domestic and wild. A few dogs rushed from their kennels to watch me warily as I passed, standing like sentinels at the boundaries of the properties they guarded. They growled deep in their chests if I looked at them funny.

Finding the right house proved challenging, because number signs were few and far between. At some point it started raining. Not heavily, but hard enough to reduce visibility. I began to think that I would have to check each and every house, when my luck took an upturn. I encountered a local resident ambling about with a walking stick, dressed in shirtsleeves and knee-length khaki pants, oblivious to the downpour.

"Oh, the printer," he said when I asked him for directions. "Just keep walking down this road. His is the last house."

It took another ten soggy minutes to get there. The house was set well back from the main road and at a distance of a few hundred meters from its closest neighbor. The Yarkon River, swollen with rain, flowed thickly at the edge of the property.

There were two buildings. Both ugly one-story rectangular shapes without a hint of aesthetic consideration to them. The closer one was smaller and made entirely of stone. The other, set closer to the river, had a metal roof and the appearance of a garage or workshop. There was no car. No person in sight. The steady rumbling of machinery emerged from the second building. I decided to check there first.

The door wasn't locked. Pushing it open, I found myself in a long high-ceilinged workshop lit by six overhanging lamps. Various machines and worktables and printing equipment and supplies were spread out across the room. The place reeked of machine oil, ink, and solvents, but it looked clean and tidy, no dirt on the floor, nothing seemingly out of place.

The source of the noise was a hulking printing press that sprawled across much of the workshop like some primeval black beast. More than twenty feet long and at least half that in width, with its uppermost parts soaring past eight feet in height, it was busily spewing sheet after sheet of what looked like copies of newspaper. The racket drowned out all sound of the rain falling outside. It made my ears ache.

"Mr. Urlanski?" I called, shouting to be heard above the din as I moved past the churning printing press toward the far end of the workshop.

There was no answer.

I walked past metal barrels, type cases filled with wooden blocks of letters and symbols in a variety of fonts and styles, and pigeonhole cabinets holding rolls of white paper and an assortment of instruments and tools.

Near the rear wall, where the light from the ceiling bulbs fell weaker, I came upon a scarred and ink-stained worktable, on which stood a desk lamp, now switched off, and a large magnifying glass on a stand. I located the lamp switch, turned it on, and looked at the papers on the table.

They were a work in progress, less than half done, but I could tell what they were going to be. Labels for canned beef. A new design, similar, but not identical, to the first.

I took off my hat, set it aside on a nearby wooden chair, and bent down to peer more closely at the drawing of the beaming cow at the center of the label. It was meticulous, intricate, exact work. Not the sort that would ever hang in a museum, but one done with the talent to produce other work that could.

The worktable came with three drawers. In the first I found a selection of fine brushes alongside pens and pencils in various widths and shades. In the second were stacks of paper holding unfinished sketches that seemed to have been abandoned mid-stroke, like partially formed thoughts or interrupted dreams.

The third drawer contained completed drawings. I recognized the style immediately; they'd been done by the same hand that had drawn Fyodor's portrait.

These drawings—there were a few dozen of them— were not all portraits. Some were landscapes, some captured small slices of domestic life, while others depicted fantastical sceneries and worlds, figments of a fevered imagination or the rendering in ink or lead of some legend or myth.

All the drawings had that special element that exalted them from the mundane to the transcendent, a blend of rare talent and tangible, tightly controlled emotion. But of the lot, it was a number of realistic drawings, done in a subdued and gentle hand, that were particularly powerful.

In one, an emaciated woman with a star sewn on the breast of her dress was cradling a baby in her arms. She appeared to be weeping, making me think that the baby she was holding was dead. In another, an old bearded Jew cowered at the feet of two German soldiers. Both of them were laughing.

A third drawing showed a brick wall topped by coils of barbed wire. In the center of the wall was a gate guarded by a number of German soldiers bearing rifles. Two of the soldiers were frisking a Jewish teenager. He had his hands up and an expression of abject defeat on his face. I could see why. By his shoes lay a loaf of bread and a bottle of milk, both of which he had been trying to smuggle past the guards. His punishment was not in question. He would be put to death for attempting to feed himself and his family.

There were other pictures in a similar vein, images of ghetto life, dark and brooding and suffused with fear and despondency. All were hauntingly beautiful.

And there were more portraits, of men and women and children. Most of them were done with a regular pencil, but a few were in color. I recognized none of the faces but one.

Nathan Frankel.

His drawing lay at the bottom of the drawer. Tadeusz had caught Nathan's face at a slight rightward angle, though his eyes stared right at me. Even though the only colors in the drawing were the black of the pencil and the white of the paper, Tadeusz had managed to create the impression that Nathan's eyes were twinkling mischievously, and this was supported by his roguish grin. Unlike the other portraits, this one did not convey a sense of tragedy and doom. Nathan's expression was optimistic, happy, upbeat. It was the Nathan who could beguile even the most suspecting of persons. It was the Nathan who had charm enough for ten men, even though sometimes he lacked the common sense of one.

It was the Nathan I had known only for a sliver of time, but to whom I was indebted for life.

I was still immersed in his portrait when I sensed the presence of another person in the room, somewhere behind me. I turned and saw the man.

Then I saw the gun in his hand.

Chapter 32

I knew who he was the instant I saw him. Fyodor's description had been dead-on.

He was five six, scrawny, with wet, thinning black hair spread unevenly across a pale, bumpy scalp. His narrow shoulders, hips, and limbs all appeared to be completely devoid of muscle and were baggily wrapped in a thick brown shirt and faded blue overalls. A pair of heavy work boots, scuffed and muddy, covered his feet and calves.

His face was thin and angular, the skin stretched tightly over protruding bones. His nose, sharp and long as a letter opener, supported a pair of round wire-rim glasses. His chin was bony and tapered, his eyebrows sparse and widely spaced. His serious dark eyes, black in the imperfect lighting of the workshop, were set very deep, each looking like a coin at the bottom of an empty glass.

At that moment, with those clothes and the gun in his hand, he did not look like any bookkeeper I'd ever run across. In fact, I could not tell precisely what he looked like. His expression was impossible to read. But he did not seem the least bit perturbed by my presence. His hand did not shake one bit as it pointed the gun at my midriff.

The gun was a small model, a .25 caliber, I thought. It would make a much smaller hole than the Luger could, but a small hole in the right place would still make me a dead man.

I had not heard him approach due to the rumbling of the printing press. Now I wondered how long he had been standing there watching me poke through his things.

He said something, but it was swallowed up by the noise. He made a motion with his free hand and had to repeat it before I understood that he was directing me to come toward him.

I let go of Nathan's portrait, lifted my hands in surrender, and stepped forward slowly. He mirrored my advance by retreating into the space between the side wall and the printing press, maintaining a distance of about eight feet between us.

After about fifteen paces, he gestured for me to halt. He reached out a hand toward the printing press and with the heel of his palm pressed a large black button. The big machine groaned to a stop.

For a split second there was an illusion of total silence. Then outside noise rushed in to fill the void. Rain clattering on the metal roof of the workshop. Thunder bellowing in the distance. The thumping of my heart, fast and jumpy.

"Who are you?" he asked. "A thief?"

His accent was very thick and his pronunciation atrocious. It was clear he was not yet fluent in Hebrew and perhaps never would be.

"My name is Adam Lapid. I'm here to talk to you, Tadeusz."

His eyes narrowed at my mentioning his name. "Do I know you?"

"No. But we both knew Nathan Frankel."

"Nathan? Where you know Nathan from?"

"From Auschwitz."

"Nathan dead," he said, speaking with such finality that it sounded as though he believed that these two words were the last that would be uttered before the world came to an end.

"I know. That's the reason I'm here."

He frowned. "You not with police. You come into my workshop uninvited, search through my things. Why? What you wish to find?"

"Something that would tell me how you made counterfeit dollars."

This time his expression was easy to read. I had stunned him. His arm tensed, and he raised his gun, leveling it at my head. "How you know about that?" he demanded.

"A little bit of it I learned from Nathan. The rest I discovered myself through deduction, and by talking to people who knew Nathan. And you're right. I'm not with the police. I'm not here to arrest you or steal from you."

"You want me to make you dollars, is that what you want?" He shook his head resolutely, his sharp nose and bony chin looking like a pair of fins in motion. "No way. Forget it."

"I don't want you to make me anything, Tadeusz. Not

dollars and not food labels either. All I want is to punish those who murdered Nathan."

His thin eyebrows jumped. "You think I—"

I shook my head. "If you were involved in his murder, you would know who I am. I was Nathan's friend, Tadeusz. Just like you were his friend, weren't you?"

"Yes. Good friend. Very good friend."

He lowered his gun a bit. Now it was aimed once more at my torso. He could still shoot me dead, but he did not look as ready to do so as thirty seconds ago.

"Where did you and Nathan meet?" I asked.

"In ghetto. His family and me, we lived in the same building. Sixty-eight people in six apartments."

"Were you in Auschwitz too?"

"No. I got away before ghetto was liquidated. I made myself fake identification papers. Different name, different religion. I escaped ghetto, lived rest of war as a regular Polish Catholic." He smiled a proud smile. "No one ever questioned my papers." Then his smile faded and his face turned grim. "I offered to make Nathan papers, and for his brother, too, but he refused."

"Why?"

"His mother was sick. He would not leave her. I told him he was being fool, she was close to death, he could not save her. He not listen."

"So he and Peter stayed in the ghetto?"

His eyes widened. "Now I'm sure you knew Nathan. Otherwise you not know his brother's name." He lowered the gun the rest of the way, looked at it for a second, then slipped it into his overalls. He said, "Yes, both Nathan and Peter stayed in ghetto. Their mother died soon after I left. Nathan and Peter were sent to Auschwitz. Peter not survive."

"When did you and Nathan meet again?"

"A year ago, in Tel Aviv. It was—how you say?—by accident. I was surprised to see him and he me. We both thought the other was dead."

"Was it then that he asked you to forge dollars for him?"

"No. That happened only recently. About five weeks ago. Before that, he ask me to do the labels."

"The food labels?"

He nodded, smiling proudly again. "They're good, eh?"

"Excellent. I doubt anyone would suspect they did not come from a genuine beef vendor, but they're worthless without a product to accompany them. Where does the meat come from?"

"An Arab from up north in Galilee. I don't know name. I never met him. Nathan found him somehow, got him to go along with plan." He appeared about to add something but thought better of it. His eyes went to his shoes.

I had an idea as to why he was being reticent. I decided on a direct approach.

"What sort of meat is it?"

His eyes sprang up to my face. They looked like deep wells bored into the bony landscape of his face. The ceiling lights flickered and dimmed, flickered and dimmed, as a series of lightning bolts snaked from heaven to earth. Then came the thunder roars, one after the other, in rapid succession, a tidal wave of all-encompassing noise.

When it was possible to be heard again, I continued. "Because it's not cow, is it? Not unless that Arab has some secret herd that the government has failed to notice, or he's able to drive a large number of cattle across the border from an enemy country. So what kind of meat is going into those cans, with those labels?"

"Horse," Tadeusz said, first with obvious reluctance, then more freely. "It's horse meat. The Arab has horses, Nathan said, and most of them are good for nothing. More cars every week; not as many horses needed."

"And the government isn't likely to expropriate horses with the excuse of some national emergency," I said, "because horses aren't kosher. Still, it could have been worse, I suppose; you could have sold pork." I sighed, marveling at the beauty of it. Take meat no one wants, meat that is dirt cheap, and market it as the sort of meat every mother in Israel is eager to feed her children. All you'd need to do is package it right. And with Tadeusz for a partner, you had that bit covered. "With such a lucrative scheme, why would you need to forge dollars?"

"It would take long time," Tadeusz said, "to butcher animals, put meat in cans, package everything correctly. And you could not sell it all at once or price will be lower and you'd draw unwanted attention. Nathan said he could not wait. He needed lots of money fast."

"Why?" I asked, but then the answer came to me. "For Tamara Granot."

I had not said it as a question, but that was how Tadeusz must have heard it.

"Yes. Nathan said she comes from wealthy family. Her father not approve of him unless he has plenty of money. So he asked me to help."

"And you agreed."

Tadeusz shook his narrow head. "Not at first. I told him I could not do a perfect forgery. Too much small detail, too little time, and I did not have right ink. But Nathan insisted, so I gave in."

"You did an excellent job; you managed to fool me."

He waved the compliment away. "Anyone with good eyes would have seen through it." He paused as the implication of his words sank in and hurriedly added, "I did not mean to suggest—"

"That's all right. I took no offense. How much did you make?"

"Not much. Less than a thousand."

"Did Gregor know about the dollars?"

He tilted his head. "You know Gregor too?"

"We've met." It was not me who had spoken those words. The raspy voice had come from the half-shadows behind Tadeusz. And from those shadows two figures now emerged. The thick-muscled Dov and the ginger-haired, green-eyed Gregor. Dov's mouth was open in a wide, all-but-imbecilic grin; Gregor smiled a tight-lipped, triumphant smile. Each carried a handgun. Gregor held a compact snub-nosed pistol, while Dov gripped a fat revolver with a four-inch barrel.

Judging by their relatively dry clothes, I concluded that

they had arrived by car. Inwardly, I cursed the heavy rain and frequent thunder. Both had covered up the sound of their car's engine and whatever noise they'd made entering the workshop and coming upon Tadeusz and me.

Tadeusz swiveled to face the two criminals. "Gregor, Dov, what you doing here?"

"We've been looking for Mr. Lapid," Gregor said, "and now we've finally found him."

There was no mistaking the gleam in his eyes. He had bloody murder on his mind and I was the intended victim. He was relishing the prospect of my imminent death. It was part payback for how I'd interrupted his card game, part cleanup. Because I knew about the fake dollars, I had to be eliminated.

Gregor said, "To answer your question, Mr. Lapid, I did know about the dollars. Nathan told me himself. He wished to have Tadeusz make fifty thousand of them and he asked me if I knew any money changers he could lay the forged bills on. I made it clear to him that it was a stupid idea and forbade him to make or distribute any forged currency. Now raise your hands slowly and lace your fingers on top of your head."

He and Dov had stopped about twelve feet away. The Luger was in my waistband, pressing insistently into my side. I could make a grab for it, but it wouldn't work; they already had their guns out. I interlaced my fingers and placed both hands on the crown of my head.

Tadeusz said to Gregor, "You don't need guns. This man is friend of Nathan."

Gregor chuckled. "Is that what he told you? He is not one of us, Tadeusz, and he knows about our business. Dov, search him."

Dov brushed past Tadeusz, who turned to look at me. The uncertainty was plain on his face. He did not know what to make of this situation. He believed I had been Nathan's friend, but he'd known Gregor and Dov for longer and was in business with them.

Dov jammed the barrel of his revolver into my waist hard enough to hurt and began patting me down with his other hand. He stank of cigarettes and dank body odor. He quickly discovered the knife and the Luger and held them up for Gregor to see. Then he stuck them in a jacket pocket. He took a step back, withdrawing the gun from my side. He half turned, then spun and rammed his fist into my belly.

I had not seen it coming and was unprepared for it. The blow folded me in half, and I fell to one knee, smacking my shoulder against the printing press on the way to the floor. I gasped for breath, pain cramping my stomach and chest. Dizziness swept over me, and for a moment I was on the verge of throwing up.

Then, bit by bit, my head cleared. I coughed and retched, but managed to keep the contents of my stomach where they belonged.

An acidic, digestive taste filled my mouth. I worked some saliva around and swallowed it. Lifting my head, I saw that Tadeusz had shrunk back against the side of the printing press. He wore a stunned expression on his face. I watched him release a pent-up breath as he saw that I was more or less okay. Angling my head, I saw Dov handing my Luger to Gregor. The ginger-haired man's lip curled into a nasty smile. He made his snub-nosed pistol disappear into his jacket and now held the Luger with the business end pointed in my direction. From my vantage point, the muzzle hole looked as big as a cannon's. "Thoughtful of you to bring your gun with you, Mr. Lapid," Gregor said.

"How did you know where to find me?" I asked, hoping to exploit the natural tendency of criminals, especially those who regard themselves as something akin to masterminds, to put their genius on public display. Down on one knee, unarmed, with two guns leveled at me, I posed no apparent threat. I was hoping that Gregor would see it that way, and that it would encourage him to fill in the few blank spots that remained in my understanding of the events surrounding Nathan's murder. Another benefit was that as long as we were talking, he and Dov weren't shooting.

"Fyodor. He told us all about the visit you paid him. I think he was frightened that we would learn of it some other way."

Gregor said all this deadpan, his face revealing nothing; but Dov's grin widened, showing a set of wayward teeth. A dreadful realization descended upon me.

"You killed him, didn't you?"

"We had to," Gregor said. "He wasn't one of us any more than you are. And after talking to you, he knew way too much."

He was saying Fyodor's death was my fault, like Nathan's death was my fault. I felt a great rage for Gregor then. A bubbling cauldron of boiling fury. But I couldn't let it consume me. I had to keep a level head.

I said, "Which is also why you killed Tova Wasserman."

"For that I should thank you. If you hadn't barged in that night, looking for Nathan, I would never have known that he had exchanged those forged dollars. When you said the name Tova Wasserman, I knew I'd heard it before. It took me a while to recall what she did for a living. Once I did, I knew I had to get rid of her."

"You tortured her."

His cruel mouth twisted in psychopathic amusement. "Only roughed her up a bit. We had to know whether she still had any of those dollars around, or if she'd told anyone about them. The only name she gave us was yours. But we already knew about you, of course."

"So you went to my apartment to look for the dollars."

"Yes."

"You were taking a chance, coming there in the middle of the day. If I'd been in the apartment, you would have had a real fight on your hands for once."

Gregor sneered. "But you weren't there, were you? Lucky us. I'm sorry about your icebox. I just couldn't hold it in a second longer."

As we were talking, I'd been glancing left and right, looking for anything I might use as a weapon. There was nothing. But from where I was half-kneeling, I noticed that there was a gap between the floor and the bottom of the printing press—four feet wide and about one and a half high—about five feet to my right. It was cover, if I could get to it before being blown full of holes.

I said, "But why were you opposed to Nathan's foreign currency idea? Isn't it a good way to make a lot of money fast?"

Gregor's expression suggested that he considered me to be possessed of the intelligence of a woodworm. "It's an even better way to land in a jail cell."

"Why?"

"Because it's the sort of crime you can't bribe yourself out of, that's why. It's not like black marketeering, where you can always grease a few palms and have the cops look the other way. Get caught forging foreign currency— especially that of a friendly superpower—and they'll throw the book at you. Even our regular police contact said he couldn't protect us from that kind of charge."

"Your contact? Who?"

Gregor smiled enigmatically, oozing self-satisfaction. But I didn't need to hear the name from his lips. It came to me almost as soon as I had finished voicing the question. It was obvious, really. Now I knew why he'd been so eager to know what I'd taken from Nathan's apartment; he thought I'd found more fake dollars.

It also explained why he had given Reuben strict instructions to report any calls from me, and why he had let me go free when he'd had me locked up and under his control. It might have been easier to have me killed in prison, but that would have taken some time and effort to organize and might have attracted a measure of unwanted attention his way. But out on the street I could be dispatched by Gregor and Dov with no chance of his complicity coming to light.

"Leibowitz," I said. "It's Leibowitz, isn't it?" And in that moment I hated the greedy, worn-out inspector more than I had hated any man since I'd killed my last Nazi officer.

Dov and Gregor both laughed.

"Isn't he a smart fellow, Dov?" Gregor said through his raspy gasps of laughter. "There's no fooling him."

"So that's why you killed Nathan," I said, "because he put you at risk by exchanging counterfeit dollars with Tova Wasserman."

Tadeusz had been standing to the side, listening attentively to all of this, his dark eyes flicking back and forth between Gregor and me, all the while bearing a tortured look of confusion and indecision. Now his head jerked to stare at me and his body drew taut as a bowstring.

Gregor said, "We've talked long enough. Dov." He made a slicing motion with his hand in my direction. Dov brought his left hand up to curl around his right, which was wrapped around the revolver's grip.

Tadeusz stepped between me and his two associates, blocking Dov's aim. "Wait! Is what he is saying true? You killed Nathan?"

Gregor's tone was impatient, curt, dismissive. "Step aside, Tadeusz."

The little printer did not budge. His voice rose. "I

want an answer, Gregor. Did you kill Nathan?"

I was still on one knee—my left—and now I tilted my body forward a bit, raising my right ankle, my hands on the floor to either side of me, ready to push myself toward that gap while Tadeusz gave me cover.

"Of course not," Gregor said. "He's lying through his teeth. Now get out of the way."

Tadeusz shook his head. "I don't believe you." And he reached a hand into his overalls and drew out the small gun he'd stashed there.

"No!" I shouted, a split second before Dov's revolver roared. Tadeusz's body jerked, a large red stain appearing on the back of his overalls. The gun dropped from his hand and bounced once on the concrete floor before sliding deep into that gap I'd been eying.

I launched myself right after the gun with the desperation of the condemned. I landed hard on my elbows and stomach, my chin scraping against the floor, skin tearing. I scrambled forward in a frenzied crawl, ignoring the pain in my chin as well as the one that flared up in my stitched side. Behind me Tadeusz's lifeless body crashed to the floor, and I heard first one blast and then a few more as both Gregor and Dov discharged their weapons. Bullets pinged off the metal hide of the printing press, but I was already underneath it, squeezed between its metal bulk and the floor.

It was dirty under there and almost completely dark. I choked on the thick dust disturbed by my slithering body. My eyes frantically scoured for Tadeusz's pistol. I had two seconds at most. Where the hell was it? I didn't see it.

It had been swallowed up by the darkness. I heard Gregor cursing in Russian and the sound of feet stomping closer. I scrabbled for the pistol with both hands, brushing my fingers in a wide arc across the grimy floor. One second, no more.

The fingers of my left hand touched cold metal. I curled them around the grip of the gun, my palm so sweaty I was sure it would slip from my grasp, and worked my forefinger into the trigger guard just as Dov's thick face appeared at the other side of the gap, the barrel of his revolver before him, seeking me out.

I was not accustomed to shooting with my left hand and had no time to brace myself or aim. I fired four rapid shots, the reports amplified by the tight space, the muzzle flashes like tiny blooms of fire.

For a moment I was sure all four shots had missed. Then a red bubble formed on the left side of Dov's neck. It popped and out streamed a thin trail of blood. Dov's mouth opened, but if a sound emerged from it, I did not hear it over the ringing in my ears. Dov blinked in baffled incomprehension, but then his face hardened. His mouth clamped shut and he slowly brought his gun to bear on me.

By this time I had adjusted my position and was bracing my left hand with my right. I let out a breath and squeezed the trigger. Dov's right eye turned to pulp.

That was the good news.

The bad news was that the slide of Tadeusz's gun had not retracted after ejecting the spent cartridge. It remained locked in the open position.

Which could only mean one thing.
I was out of bullets.

Chapter 33

I ejected the magazine and ran my thumb over its open end.

Empty.

Ramming the magazine back into place, I cursed silently. The little pistol had served me well, but it was now useless.

"Dov?"

Gregor sounded nervous, almost panicked. Things had taken an unexpected, disastrous turn for him. Little did he know just how much more desperate my position was compared to his.

"Dov?"

I didn't bother informing him that his partner was dead. He was smart enough to figure it out for himself.

"Lapid! Listen to me, Lapid!" Gregor's voice echoed strangely, distorted by the mass of metal machinery that now stretched above me. It was impossible to tell which direction it came from, nor from how far. "You got nowhere to go. The moment you show your face, I'll blast it off. But I'll make a deal with you. You come out now and I'll give you a thousand liras if you promise to leave Tel Aviv today and never breathe a word about any of this to the cops. What do you say?"

He should have offered a lower, more reasonable sum, but he wouldn't have convinced me either way. I was under no illusions. It was either me or him.

I touched a finger to my chin. It came away slippery and wet. The cut wasn't serious, but maybe I'd have a new scar for Sima Vaaknin to admire. That is, if I ever had the chance of seeing Sima again.

Dim light was visible in all four directions where the bottom of the printing press did not reach the floor. In each case, the gap was the same width and height as the one I'd crawled into.

Gregor could choose any of these four gaps and pick me off. The only thing that was holding him back was the fear that I'd shoot him like I had Dov.

How long, however, before he worked up the courage to come for me? No more than five minutes, I wagered. Wouldn't he be in for a pleasant surprise when he found me unable to return fire? He'd get a kick out of that for sure.

"Lapid?" Gregor's voice boomed. The panic had gone from it. He was recovering from the shock of losing his partner. He was becoming himself again. A cold-blooded killer. "Come on, Lapid, dealing with me is the only way you make it out of here alive. What's your answer?"

I didn't waste my breath on answering him. Thirty seconds of quietness ensued, and then he said, "Fine, you son of a bitch. Have it your way."

In the confined space between printing press and floor, the air was redolent of burnt gunpowder. My side hurt like hell, but it felt dry. Sima's stitches continued to hold.

Lying there helpless, with a ton or more of metal poised above me like a boot ready to crush a bug, I began to feel the icy tendrils of panic close around me.

It wouldn't be long now. Either I found a way to fight back or I would die. I had to ward off the panic. I had to think. And I needed to start doing both right this instant.

I sensed Gregor moving, but I could not tell where. I glanced toward each of the gaps in turn. No sign of the ginger-haired killer. Rain continued pummeling the roof high above me. Thunder roared. The concrete beneath me was cold and hard.

Was this where I died, in this tomblike space, as powerless as the camp inmate I'd once been? I'd promised myself countless times that I would never be like that again, but here I was.

No. This was a different place, a different time. I could still do something. I could still resist.

But how?

My eyes roamed about for a solution, and also for the shadow of Gregor as he came to finish me off. They skimmed over Dov's body, stopped, returned.

The big man was lying on the floor like a kit bag filled with rocks, half blocking the gap through which I had crawled to temporary safety.

His head lay on its side, facing my way. His ruined eye was leaking blood across the bridge of his nose and cheek. The other eye was open, staring vacantly at nothing in particular.

One of his arms was out of sight, on the far side of his body; the other was wedged beneath his torso. It was his gun hand, I realized, and, presumably, his gun was right there with it.

There was no time to waste. I belly-crawled over to Dov, worked my fingers under his body, and lifted. Or tried to. He was heavy as hell, and from where I lay, I could barely get any leverage.

Knowing that failure meant death, I wormed my fingers farther under Dov's corpse, managed to grab his belt with one hand, and, putting all I had into it, pulled and lifted.

His body shifted a little, and I dug deeper into myself and lifted harder. I managed to hoist the near side of his body five inches off the floor. I grunted with the effort, the muscles in my arms and shoulders screaming with agony.

It seemed to take forever, though it must have been just a couple of seconds. Then I saw the revolver stuck between the floor and his sternum. Planting my left elbow on the floor, grabbing a fistful of his shirtfront, I propped up his body with my left hand, like the side of a tent. Lying on my back, I slid my right shoulder and chest under his corpse, my right hand groping for the gun.

I had almost gotten my fingers around it, when the report of a pistol boomed. A spark flew off metal an inch from my temple. Gregor had positioned himself on top of the printing press, where he could see all four sides of it, and had spotted me.

Instinct yelled at me to pull back, under the cover

afforded by the printing press. But that way lay certain death. Bellowing with effort, every muscle straining to the point of ripping, I pushed myself farther out from under the printing press while pulling Dov's body over mine.

Gregor fired again. Dov's body jerked as the bullet smacked into his back. He covered me like a shield, and I felt the impact of the bullet reverberate through his body like a dull whack. The fingers of my right hand closed around the grip of the revolver. Another shot. Dov's body jerked again. His head flopped, his forehead banging on my torn chin. I clenched my jaw against the pain and tugged harder on the body, freeing my right arm from under it. Gregor was coming down the side of the printing press, as nimble on his feet as a mountain cat, firing twice. One bullet whizzed past my ear, chewing into the concrete. The other punched into Dov.

Gregor was now six feet above me. I raised the revolver and fired. The revolver bucked against my hand, its recoil formidable. The shot went wide. Gregor's gun blazed. Dov's neck burst open. Blood spilled onto my shirt. The stench of blood and death was nearly overpowering. Gregor was screaming something incoherent. His face was a nightmarish mask of hate. His gun roared. My left shoulder erupted in fiery pain. I let out a cry of agony. Gregor's green eyes were flashing like fireworks. His thin mouth was grinning. He was in the heat of battle, and he had drawn blood. I pulled the trigger again. Another miss. But this time I had seen where the shot went. Higher and to the left of where I had aimed.

I lined the gun sight on empty space a little to Gregor's right, taking an extra half-second to make sure, even as I saw Gregor adjusting his own aim so his next shot would find my head.

I squeezed the trigger first. The bullet punched into Gregor's right clavicle bone, spinning him around. He lost his footing, tumbling down the side of the printing press onto the concrete floor. He landed hard on his back but managed to roll to his side and up on one knee. Blood soaked his jacket. He still gripped the gun.

I put one bullet in his chest and another in his mouth. He went down and was still.

For a minute or so, I stayed where I was, under Dov's body, trying to catch my breath and get my heart to slow down. Then I let go of the revolver, rolled Dov off me, and stood up shakily. My shoulder hurt, but I found that I could move my arm freely. Wincing, I shucked off my coat and peered at the wound. The bullet had grazed the skin, leaving a red furrow of blood. It would hurt for a while, but it would heal.

Blood, mine and Dov's, soaked my shirt. My pants and shoes were gray with dust. My legs felt weak, rubbery. Leaning with one hand on the printing press, I minced over to where Gregor lay.

A large hole gaped in his chest. His head was a disfigured mess of blood and torn tissue, the bullet having entered his mouth at an upward angle, gone through his brain, and punched its way out of the top of his skull. You could still recognize him, though. Both of his eyes were intact.

I lowered my chin to my chest, eyes shut, breathing slowly. It was over. I had avenged Nathan's death. I had repaid my debt. And survived.

Then came the voice.

"Hold it right there. Don't move."

I lifted my head and opened my eyes. For the third time that day, I had a gun aimed at me.

Chapter 34

Two guns, actually. One held by Officer Elkin, the other by Inspector Leibowitz.

I raised my hands quickly, splaying my fingers to show I was unarmed. I didn't want to give them—Leibowitz in particular—any excuse to shoot me.

Leibowitz's bulging eyes went to each of the three bodies in turn. He shook his head gravely.

"Mr. Lapid, you're in even bigger trouble than I thought. What the hell happened here?"

You know it all, you dirty bastard. But I told it as if he didn't. Maybe if I played it as if I were ignorant of his corruption, I might make it out of there alive. I'd settle with him later.

I explained the partnership between Gregor, Dov, Nathan, and Tadeusz; the scheme with the horse meat; the way Nathan went behind Gregor's and Dov's backs with the fake dollars Tadeusz had made for him and how that gave Gregor and Dov the motive to kill him. I described the gunfight that had taken place in the workshop and showed Leibowitz and Elkin the half-finished food labels on Tadeusz's desk.

"If you look around enough, you'll find some evidence

of the currency forgery."

"How did you learn about it?"

"I'm a detective, remember?"

Leibowitz gave a thin smile. "A little more detail if that's not too much trouble."

I told them about being hired by Mrs. Wasserman to get her money back, about finding Nathan in the company of Gregor and Dov, and how I'd concluded that they were the ones behind his murder. I did not tell them about Tamara Granot, Zalman Alphon, Iris Rosenfeld, or the two men Tova Wasserman had sent to kill me.

"Tova Wasserman is dead," Leibowitz said.

I nodded. "Gregor and Dov killed her. They wanted no one left alive who knew about the forged dollars. That's also why they ransacked my apartment."

"Why didn't you tell us all you knew the night of the murder?"

"Nathan Frankel saved my life once, during the war in Europe. I owed him a debt. And I didn't think I could trust you guys to exert yourselves once you learned that he was a criminal. Also, I didn't want to get Mrs. Wasserman in trouble with the law."

"I'm sure she thanks you for that," Leibowitz remarked, with enough acid in his voice to burn a hole through steel. With his free hand, he rifled through Tadeusz's papers. The other hand still clutched the gun. It was no longer aimed at me but at the floor. Elkin, however, had his trained on my chest.

"A talented guy," Leibowitz said, holding up one of Tadeusz's drawings. "A great painter. These would have fooled me." He turned to Elkin. "A good plan, wouldn't you say?"

Elkin looked nervous. Beads of sweat dotted his brow. He didn't appear comfortable with the gun. He kept his eyes on me as he nodded.

Leibowitz looked again at the papers. "Yes. A good plan. It would have worked, too. They would have made a bundle. And if Frankel hadn't gotten greedy, they'd have gotten away with it without anyone knowing." There was a note of admiration in his voice. I wanted to clobber him.

Instead, I asked, "You didn't know they were in business together?"

Leibowitz gestured at Dov and Gregor. "We knew about these two. We've been looking for them, raided their apartments yesterday. They weren't there. We couldn't find them."

They probably got early warning from you, I thought.

Leibowitz pointed at Tadeusz. "We didn't know about him. I bet he didn't even have a record." He gave me an inscrutable look. "Lucky for you he stepped in when he did."

I felt a stab of guilt and did my best not to show it. My veins throbbed with unadulterated hatred toward Leibowitz. I kept that hidden as well. I said, "I don't think Gregor was aware of how close Tadeusz felt toward Nathan. Otherwise, he wouldn't have talked so freely in front of him. If you didn't know about Tadeusz, what made you come here?"

"An anonymous tip," Leibowitz said. "Some guy

called and said we'd find Gregor and Dov here. He didn't mention you."

He doesn't exist, I thought. *Never has. You invented him.*

"You came alone? Just the two of you?"

"Don't worry. Backup should be here any minute." His sloping forehead creased in a frown. To Elkin he said, "Go radio in, see what's keeping them."

Elkin blinked in surprise. He motioned at me with his gun. "What about him?"

"It's okay. He won't try anything. Not while I have a gun and he doesn't."

Still Elkin hesitated, but when Leibowitz repeated his order, he reluctantly lowered his gun, turned, and walked off toward the door.

Leibowitz had his pistol up, a sleek model, a .38 caliber. *He's going to shoot me the instant the door closes after Elkin*, I thought. *He'll say he didn't have a choice, I rushed him, tried to grab his gun. I have to make a move.* But he wasn't looking at me. He was staring at the bodies. The door of the workshop opened and banged shut. Leibowitz gave a small shake of his head.

"I should never have let you out of that cell," he said. "You've certainly made a mess of things. I'm surprised Elkin didn't throw up or faint. These poor bastards look much worse than Frankel did."

He was right. They did. Dov with his ruined eye and Gregor with his blown-up head. There was brain matter on the floor beside Gregor's body. Not the sort of sight a man with a weak stomach could withstand.

Something stirred in my mind. A hazy suspicion. Then

it solidified to a perfect, mind-boggling clarity.

"It's Elkin," I muttered.

"How's that?"

"Elkin's dirty. He's their partner."

Leibowitz smirked. "Nice try."

"No, listen," I said, urgency tightening my voice. "Listen. Gregor told me they had a police contact, someone who was on their payroll. When I said it was you, he and Dov both laughed."

"Me? I—"

"You were the obvious choice. Why would you let me go otherwise? But it's not you. It's Elkin."

"Quit your nonsense. Whatever you're trying to pull, it won't work."

"They knew I wouldn't be in the apartment. That's why they searched it when they did. Someone told them I was in police custody. It was either you or Elkin. And remember how he reacted when he saw Nathan's body? Like he was going to throw up. But he sees these three and no reaction whatsoever. He wasn't sick, but surprised. He had been searching for Nathan, too, but Gregor and Dov hadn't gotten word to him that they'd already found him."

"None of this is proof," Leibowitz said, but his tone was no longer derisive.

"Who got the anonymous tip? You or Elkin?"

His silence was answer enough.

"And who was supposed to make sure you had backup?"

"Me."

Leibowitz and I turned. Elkin was standing seven feet away, gun pointed in our direction. He had not gone out to the squad car. He had not radioed in to check on the backup. He had banged the door shut without leaving and padded his way back to us.

"So it's true," Leibowitz said.

Elkin nodded. "It's true. More than once I thought of telling you. I know I should have. I knew you could help us, that you'd appreciate the idea. You said yourself it's a good plan."

"It is."

Elkin looked tense. He spoke rapidly, urgently. "We can still pull it off. You and me. I know the name of the Arab with the horses. We can use the labels Tadeusz made and find another printer to make new ones. The money would be great."

"It would," Leibowitz agreed.

Elkin grinned in relief. "I knew you'd see it that way." Then he turned his attention to me and his grin gave way to a glower. "If not for him, everything would have been fine. We have to get rid of him. We can't go forward with this if he's alive."

"You're right," said Leibowitz. "We can't." And he raised his gun and fired.

Chapter 35

The bullet took Elkin in the chest. He staggered backward into a wall and slid down the side of it till he was sitting slumped on the floor. The gun had slipped from his hand and skittered past his reach.

He wore an expression of shocked incredulity.

"Why?" he gasped.

"You know why," Leibowitz said. "You brought me here for a reason. You and your pals were going to do me in. Probably planned on blaming it on Lapid here. Get rid of two nuisances in one elegant swoop."

Elkin didn't protest. Maybe he didn't have the strength. Or maybe he knew it would be futile. His face screwed up in pain. Air wheezed out of his mouth. Then the light flickered out of his eyes and his head fell forward.

Leibowitz looked bleak. "Damn. The first criminal I shoot and he's a cop."

I said nothing.

"I had high hopes for him. I thought he'd grow to be a good detective one day. But he crossed the line."

"Yes," I said.

Leibowitz appraised me with narrowed eyes. "If this ever got out…"

"I'd be in the cell next to yours. Don't worry. If you keep me out of it, I'll do the same for you."

He nodded and holstered his gun. Pursing his lips, he considered the dead policeman. "Well, young Elkin will go down as a hero cop, cut down in the line of duty. There are worse ways to go. Perhaps the heroic nature of his demise will provide some comfort to his widow. If not, the pension his death will earn her likely will." He sniffed the air loudly and made a face. "Let's go outside. It stinks in here."

Outside, we ran over to Tadeusz's house and stood in the shelter of the doorway as the rain came down in torrents. I lit a cigarette for myself and one for him. We smoked in silence for a while, watching the downpour.

Eventually he said, "What happened to your chin?"

"Scraped it on the floor back there."

"And your shoulder?"

"Gregor shot me. Just a graze. I'll live."

He grunted in a manner that made it unclear whether he found that bit of news to his liking.

I looked at his profile. He seemed pensive. Killing Elkin troubled him.

"I apologize for thinking you were dirty."

He smiled with little humor. "I am dirty, as you very well know, so no apology is warranted. How much money did you take from Frankel's wallet?"

"Two hundred liras."

He turned his head to stare at me. "Say that again."

"I didn't keep it. I gave it all to Tamara Granot."

"Why?"

312

"I guessed that was what he would have wanted." I told him about the ring that Nathan had entrusted me with.

He shook his head in disbelief. "You are a damn fool." He flicked the remains of the cigarette into the rain and stuck both hands in his coat pockets.

He said, "I suppose you'll look unkindly on me if I go through the pockets of the dearly departed back there."

"Would it stop you if I did?"

"It wouldn't even slow me down."

"I didn't think it would. I'm afraid, though, that you'd have to settle for half of whatever you find."

That surprised him. "Have you come down with a case of greed?"

"No. Nothing like that."

"What is it, then?"

"I don't take money off murder victims. Those who try to kill me are another matter."

"Ah, I see. Spoils of war."

"Not exactly, but close enough."

Something approximating a smile played on his lips. "You are a strange one."

"Just to be clear," I said. "Tadeusz, the printer, is off-limits to both of us."

He nodded. "Understood."

"As for Elkin, he's all yours."

He didn't speak for thirty seconds or so. Then he said, "No. I'll let his widow keep whatever he's got on him."

"How generous of you."

"Go to hell, you rotten bastard."

I smiled. "Speaking of money, you've got some of mine."

"What are you talking about?"

"The hundred dollars you took. I'd like to have them back."

"Oh, no." He wagged a forefinger. "That's my compensation for all the trouble you've caused me."

I was about to argue the point, but ended up deciding not to. Leibowitz wasn't entirely wrong. Besides, he had saved my life. And such a debt must be repaid, one way or another.

"I still don't understand why you let me go free," I said.

"You've got a reputation. Stubborn, tenacious, honest. I knew you didn't rob Frankel's apartment. You were there, but not to rob it. I didn't know why you'd taken such an interest in this case, but I figured if I let you go, there'd be another detective working to solve the murder. Worst case, I'd arrest you again."

"Why would you care so much about the death of a criminal?"

He turned to face me. Gone was the weary cynicism that normally marked his features. In its place was unyielding resolve.

"I'm no pure lily, Lapid. I take the occasional bribe, pick the pocket of the occasional corpse, look the other way when it suits me. But some crimes I don't like. Murder is one of them. No amount of money will buy my complicity in a murder case. No matter who the victim is. That's why Elkin and his cronies planned on having me killed tonight. Elkin knew I'd never let up until I solved this murder."

I offered him another cigarette and he accepted. I lit a fresh one for myself as well.

"One of the guns inside there is yours?"

"Yes," I said. "The Luger."

"You used it?"

"Gregor did, after they took it off me."

"You'll need to leave it behind. It'll be easier that way."

I felt a pang of loss. That Luger was precious to me. But Leibowitz was right.

"By the way," he said, "we're done with Frankel's body. He's to be buried tomorrow. I figured you'd want to attend."

"I do. What about his belongings?"

"We'll hold them for a while longer. Why?"

"There's something there I want."

"What?"

"A photograph of Nathan and his brother. It was in his apartment."

"Ah, a confession at last. Why didn't you take it when you were there?"

I didn't know and admitted as much.

"Come by the station tomorrow morning; I'll give it to you. Any other requests?"

There was one. I told him what it was when we went back inside the workshop to tidy things up. He raised an eyebrow but nodded.

I chose one of Tadeusz's drawings. A landscape that

had caught my eye earlier. Rich, detailed, magnificent. I rolled it carefully and tucked it under my coat to protect it from the rain.

I would have it framed, I decided. It would fit nicely on one of the two empty nails in my apartment. One of these days, I'd find something to hang on the other.

Chapter 36

Nathan Frankel was buried in the shade of a Cyprus tree in Kiryat Shaul Cemetery. Attendance was surprisingly sparse. Misha, myself, two neighbors from Nathan's building. For such a likable man, Nathan had had almost no true friends in this world.

The ceremony was brief. No teary eulogies, no drama, just the interment of a dead body in the earth of his homeland.

A lanky rabbi with weak eyes recited the customary prayers, and we in turn mumbled amen in all the right places. It all sounded hollow, meaningless, done by rote, with no purpose other than the maintenance of tradition.

Misha had supplied Nathan's date of birth and the names of his parents, and these had been scribbled on a small marker that was then thrust into the head of the grave, until a proper headstone could be made. At some point in the far reaches of the murky, distant past, Misha's and Nathan's families had been bonded by marriage. It was a tenuous relation, no doubt, but it made Misha the only blood tie that Nathan had had in this world. As such, he was asked to read the *Kaddish*, which he did slowly, in a choked voice, barely able to contain his tears.

After the funeral, I handed Misha the photograph of Nathan and Peter Frankel that I'd collected from Leibowitz earlier that morning. He wept at the sight of it.

I was not surprised by Tamara Granot's absence. No doubt her father forbade her from coming. But I had expected to see Iris Rosenfeld. Perhaps her grief had been too great for her to attend. Or, and this I felt was more likely, it was the pain of her rejection by Nathan that had kept her away.

I felt pity for her. She had lost the man she loved not once, but twice. The first time was when he'd left her for another woman; the second was when he died soon after. And I had only augmented her pain by subjecting her to an interrogation, treating her as a suspect in the murder of the man she had loved and lost.

She lingered in my mind long after the funeral was over, and I made the decision to go see her, to apologize for having suspected her.

My knock on her door was answered by a short, pear-shaped woman, black-haired and olive-skinned, who peered up at me with curious brown eyes.

"Iris isn't here," she said.

"You're her roommate?"

"That's me. Rina Ben-Simon." She thrust out a hand and gave mine a solid pump before releasing it.

"I'm Adam Lapid. Any idea when she'll be back?"

She shrugged her round shoulders. "Not a clue. I don't keep tabs on her. But it probably won't be too long."

"Can I wait for her inside?"

She examined my face and found no threat in it. "Sure.

318

Come in. You look like you could use a glass of water. I can also make you some tea if you like."

"Water's fine. Thank you."

I sat on the sofa in the living room while she filled a glass at the kitchen sink. She handed me the glass and watched me drain it.

"My, my, you were thirsty. Want another one?"

"No, thanks. One was all I needed."

She took the empty glass from my hand and gave me a sympathetic look. "Can I give you a piece of advice?"

"Sure."

"Forget about Iris. You seem like a nice man, and you're good looking, too. Go find some other woman. You're wasting your time with her."

"You don't seem to like her very much."

She smiled. "You noticed, huh?"

"It must be hard, living with a roommate you dislike."

"It's no picnic. I just make it a habit to be in when she's out and out when she's in. The good news is I won't be her roommate for long. Sweet Iris has given me notice. She's moving out in two weeks."

"Oh?"

"Yes. And it fills my heart with joy that no innocent soul will have to endure the agony of sharing a home with her."

"She's moving to her own place?"

"A two-room apartment on Dizengoff. Not too far from the square, according to her bragging."

"That sounds expensive," I said. "I didn't think she made that kind of money dancing in a bar."

"But sweet Iris is a bar dancer no longer, or haven't you heard?"

"I heard. She told me she was taking a job as a dance teacher."

Rina Ben-Simon laughed. "How uncharacteristically modest on her part. She's not going to be a mere dance teacher. She's opening her own dance studio. Close to where she's going to live, actually. Prime location."

I frowned at her. "Are you sure about all this?"

"Why wouldn't I be? I heard it all from the mare's mouth."

"Where did Iris get the money for all this—to live by herself and open her own business?"

Rina Ben-Simon flashed a wide smile. She took a distinct pleasure in telling me all this. "From the deep pockets of her rich lover, I imagine."

"Lover? Who?"

She studied me closely. "Please tell me you're not the sort to fly off into an envy-induced rage."

I saw no point in wasting time and effort in explaining to her that I was not romantically interested in Iris Rosenfeld. "I'm not. You have my word."

"Well, the truth is I don't know the man's name. I've only seen him twice. I can tell you he's old enough to be her father. I call him Old Mr. Tomato."

"Why do you call him that?"

"Because of his face. It has this reddish tint to it. On another man it might have been funny; on him it's downright scary. He looks like a humorless man. No wonder he has to pay Iris for her time and company. I wouldn't spend five minutes with him for all the money in the world."

She prattled some more, but I had stopped listening. The image of a man hovered before my eyes. A ruddy-faced man. A man I had recently met. And in the depths of my brain came a sound similar to the one made by tumbling blocks of dominoes, as one mental construction of assumptions and false conclusions came crashing down, and a new one was beginning to assemble itself.

It took a minute before I realized she had ceased talking and was peering worriedly at me.

"Say, are you all right?"

I inhaled deeply. "I'm fine. About this man you said you saw with Iris…"

Chapter 37

I had just about finished asking Rina Ben-Simon all the questions I had when we both heard the sound of the front door being opened.

"Speak of the she-devil," Rina Ben-Simon said with a wink. She rose from the chair she'd been perched on just as Iris Rosenfeld appeared at the entrance to the living room. She froze when she saw me.

"Oh, not you again."

"Afraid so," I said.

Rina Ben-Simon clapped her hands once. "Well, I've got to rush off. It was a pleasure meeting you, Adam. You're welcome to drop by again any time." She brushed past Iris, who gave her not a gesture nor a word of farewell, and stuck her tongue out at her hated roommate's back before giving me a frilly wave with her fingers. She was whistling by the time she went out of the apartment.

Iris Rosenfeld remained rooted in place. She wore a black pleated skirt into which she'd tucked a cream-colored blouse. She must have removed her jacket when she came into the apartment. Her mouth was set in a dissatisfied line.

"I thought I told you I did not wish to speak with you again."

"But I wanted to talk to you," I said. "I missed you at the funeral today."

"I couldn't make it. Not that it's any of your business. I suppose my not coming only confirmed your deranged suspicion that I had something to do with Nathan's death. Is that what you're here for? To accuse me again of murder?"

"No. Actually, the reason I came here was to apologize to you."

She gave me a dubious frown. "Apologize?"

I gestured at the armchair she had occupied on my previous visit. "Why don't you sit down?"

She hesitated, then shrugged, and walked over to the armchair. She lowered herself into it with her customary gracefulness, then cast her eyes about, searching for something.

I guessed what it was. I handed her my lighter and almost-depleted pack of cigarettes. She plucked one out, lit it, took a puff, and made a face.

"This is rough stuff," she said, making a motion with the cigarette, but she took another draw. She handed me back the pack and lighter. "Well, apologize away."

"I'm sorry I treated you like a suspect. I know you had no hand in Nathan's murder."

She blew out a jet of smoke. "What made you come to your senses?"

"You have an alibi."

"An alibi?"

"Yes. You were with someone the night of the murder."

Iris Rosenfeld paused with the cigarette on the way to her lips. She lowered her hand so that it rested on the armrest of her chair. "What are you talking about?"

"You told me you spent part of that night here and part of it out walking. You must have gotten the dates mixed up, because at about ten o'clock that night, you were picked up by a car on the street outside this very building. You returned home a little after midnight. Care to tell me the name of the driver?"

She gave a theatrical sigh. "I see that you've not really rejoined the land of the sane and sound of mind. What a shame."

"Stop playing games. Your roommate saw you get into the car."

Her mouth twisted in irritation. She smoothed out her features and said, "Maybe it's Rina who's gotten her dates mixed up. The poor dear, her mind does tend to wander."

"She also saw the driver. This was not the first time she'd laid eyes on him. He paid at least one visit to this apartment not long after Nathan ended your relationship. She didn't know his name, but she did furnish me with his description. Mind telling me what you were up to with Shlomo Granot, the father of Tamara, the girl who took Nathan from you?"

She brought the cigarette to her mouth and took a very long drag. It proved too much for her and she coughed out a mouthful of smoke and waved it away from her face. She rose, grabbed the ashtray from the dining table, brought it back to the armchair, and took a final pull before methodically crushing out the cigarette. She crossed her legs, plucked at a piece of lint on her skirt, and let it drop to the floor. She wouldn't answer me.

"Your roommate thinks he's your lover, that he gave you money for a new apartment and your own dance studio in exchange for sex. She thinks you're a mistress if not a whore."

Her eyes were a blaze of blue fire. "I'm no whore."

"I believe you. So tell me what service you performed for Shlomo Granot."

She lowered her gaze, biting her lip. Her hands had joined in her lap. She began twisting them.

"Maybe he paid you to kill Nathan?"

Her head jerked up. "You don't believe that! You said—"

"I know what I said." I sprang to my feet, crossed over to her, crouched down, and grabbed her by the arms just above the elbows, bringing my face close to hers. "I don't believe that's what he did. He certainly hated Nathan enough to have him killed, but he would either have done it himself or hired a professional. He wouldn't use you for that. So what was it?"

"You're hurting me," she said, trying to break free from my grasp. I held on tight.

"It was something else, something to do with the relationship between Nathan and Tamara Granot. When I spoke to Mr. Granot, he made it clear that he would never have allowed the two of them to marry. He's not a man to leave things to chance; he must have made a plan.

And you made it clear to me that, had Nathan not died, you would have gotten him back. You were pretty sure of that. I think you and Granot conspired to end Nathan and Tamara's relationship. How?" I shook her hard. "What did you do?"

"Pictures," she shouted into my face. "I gave him pictures."

"Of who?"

"Of me and Nathan. Together. In bed."

"To show his daughter?"

She nodded. Strands of hair fell across her face. I let go of her and she slumped in her chair and began rubbing her arms. I leaned back on my haunches, feeling ashamed of myself. I ran a hand through my hair. It was damp with sweat when a moment ago it had been dry.

"When were they taken?"

"A week before Nathan was killed. I asked him to come over, just to talk. When he got here, I seduced him. A photographer I knew was in my bedroom closet. He took the pictures."

"Whose idea was it?"

"His. Granot's. He came to me, said we could work together, that we shared the same goal. I loved Nathan so much. I couldn't let him go without a fight."

"You didn't do this for love. You did it for money."

Her face hardened in defiance. "I did it for both those things—for love *and* money. I've never had much of either, so when I saw an opportunity to have them both, I took it."

"When did you give Mr. Granot the pictures? How

long before Nathan was killed?"

"Four days."

"So why did you meet again the night of the murder?"

"He only paid me half when I gave him the pictures. He said he'd have to see if they had the desired effect on his daughter before he paid me the rest."

"And did they?"

Iris shrugged. "That's what he said. He was in high spirits that night. He insisted on taking me to a fancy restaurant, to celebrate our successful venture. He said I could order anything I wanted. He drank quite a bit of wine, expensive wine, and that brightened his mood further. I was sure he was going to make a pass at me, but he didn't. He wasn't interested in that. He'd gotten what he wanted."

"His daughter," I said, more to myself than to her.

"Yes. His daughter. I almost pitied her that night, for having him for a father, despite all his money."

And I pity you, I thought, *for feeling that you had to do what you did.*

I rose to my full height and looked down at her. She met my gaze full on. There was no hint of shame or remorse anywhere on her face. She was a hard woman who had done a terrible thing, but she viewed it as a necessary action, one of many she'd had to take in her life simply to get by. There was nothing more I needed from her. I turned to leave.

"It would have worked," she said to my back. "If he hadn't died, he would have been mine again."

I thought of hurling the truth in her face, but it would

have done neither of us any good. I did not turn around. I just walked out and left her sitting there.

Chapter 38

Three hours later I knocked on her door. I waited for a full minute before hearing the sound of soft footsteps approaching on the other side. Her voice came, tiny, brittle, asking for my identity.

"It's Adam Lapid, Tamara. I'd like to talk to you for a moment. Can you open up, please?"

"Father said I shouldn't speak to you."

"Is he home?"

"No. But I don't know when he'll be back."

"This won't take long. It's important."

When she opened the door, I had to make a conscious effort to keep the shock from showing on my face. Judging by her wan smile, it was evident that I had failed.

"I look terrible, I know," she said.

"Not terrible. Only tired."

Which was a gross understatement. What she looked like was a woman who was utterly wrung out. Her hair hung listless; her eyes were bloodshot. Her face was gray and marred by lines that hadn't been there when I'd last seen her. She appeared to have aged a decade or more. Dark bags underlined her eyes, and she looked thinner, the skin on her cheeks and neck a bit loose. Her bearing had also changed; she'd developed a slight stoop, like that of a woman in the midst of the shift between middle-adulthood and old age.

"I haven't been sleeping very well," she said. Then she asked me to come in and led the way to the living room. She plopped into a chair with a sigh, arranging her long dress so that it covered every inch of her legs. She half-heartedly brushed a hand through her hair, as if knowing the effort was a futile one. I remained standing.

"I did not mention your name to the police," she said. "Neither did Father. He said it would be best if we didn't."

"Thank you. That was kind of you."

She gave an almost imperceptible shrug. She sat slumped in her chair, her legs touching, a thin-boned hand on each thigh. "It was the least I could do. You did right by me and Nathan, bringing me his ring."

She did not mention the two hundred liras that I'd also given her. The money was so unimportant as to be insignificant. What she cared about was Nathan's ring.

"I've hidden it," she suddenly said, her tone conspiratorial. "He'll never find it."

"Who? Your father?"

"I won't let him take it. It's mine."

I peered more closely at her. Tears had gathered in her eyes, and beyond them I saw a glimmer of something that verged on madness. Then she blinked three times in rapid succession, and the glimmer was gone. Now only the hopeless fatigue remained.

"But that's not what you're here for, is it, Mr. Lapid?

You said you had something important to discuss."

"I'm afraid so," I said, not wanting to give voice to the words that had to come next, but knowing that I must. Inside my chest, I felt something cold grip my heart and give it a painful squeeze. "I know you killed him, Tamara."

There was a long silence, and a stillness. I might have shifted a bit on my feet, but Tamara did not move a muscle. Her gaze was directed at something outside that room and that time. Perhaps she recalled the horrible act itself. Or maybe her mind had taken pity on her and had served her a joyful memory, an hour she'd spent with Nathan in which she'd known true love. I hoped it was the latter but suspected it was not.

When she finally spoke, all she could utter was a single word before her voice failed her. "How...?"

At the sound of that word, relief flooded my body. I closed my eyes and floated on its tranquil waves. Tears lapped against my closed eyelids. I opened them a crack and dried my eyes with a sleeve. I was not guilty of Nathan's murder. He, at least, would not weigh on my overburdened conscience.

But with the relief had come also grief. A deep mourning for Nathan, for all he'd lost in his short life— his family, his childhood home in Poland, and his life at the hand of the woman he loved, with whom he had planned on starting a new family and building a new home. But not all of the grief was for Nathan. Some of it was for the young woman sitting here with me. She had never had a family in the true sense of the word. And she had a lifetime ahead of her to blame herself for killing her chance at creating one.

She'd asked me how I'd known she had slain Nathan, so I told her. I related my meeting with Iris Rosenfeld and how I had discovered that Tamara's father had offered the dancer a great sum of money in exchange for pictures of her and Nathan in bed.

"He procured these pictures for the purpose of showing them to you, to persuade you to end your involvement with Nathan. They were proof that Nathan had deceived you, that he'd been seeing another woman behind your back, that, at least physically, he and this woman were more intimate than you and he had ever been."

A single tear dribbled out of her left eye. She made no move to wipe it off as it made its way down her cheek.

"That's not what Father said. He told me the pictures had been taken by a private detective he'd hired."

"He lied to you, Tamara. He couldn't stand the thought of losing you, especially to someone like Nathan."

She accepted her father's guilt without further protestation. She knew him better than anyone, knew what he was capable of.

"I thought I was going to die when I first saw those pictures," she said. "My heart stopped beating and I could not draw air. It was as though the sky itself had crashed down upon me. Nathan was my life, not just my love, and he betrayed me."

"Yes, he did. But he hadn't planned to. He yielded to

temptation, to a carefully arranged trap. But you didn't know that."

"No, I did not."

"And when he asked to meet you that night, you went to see him with vengeance on your mind."

"No. Not vengeance. I wanted him to have no one else, and for no one else to have him."

"He asked you to meet him at Café Kislev, on Yohanan Hasandlar Street, not too far from Allenby, where he finally succumbed to his wounds. This taken in that café, wasn't it?" I showed her the picture of her and Nathan. She nodded shakily. I said, "It's an out-of-the-way sort of place; I almost missed it when I was walking by it earlier today. The owner recognized the two of you from the picture, said you came by a number of times, that you looked very much in love."

"It was our place," she said. "One of them, anyway."

"That night, I think you told Nathan not to wait for you inside the café, but to meet you on the street somewhere. You didn't want any witnesses. Your father had told you he was going out. It was the perfect opportunity. What knife did you use?"

"A kitchen knife. One used to slice vegetables. I threw it away afterward."

"Did you tell him about the pictures? Did you give him a chance to explain?"

She gave a small shake of her head. Now the tears fell in profusion, carving wet lines down her face. "When he saw me, he opened his arms to hug me. He smiled broadly, as if he'd done nothing wrong. I felt outside

333

myself, pushed out of my body by a sudden, overpowering hatred. I was looking at myself from a distance, like an audience at a play. I had the knife in my right hand, hidden behind my back. When he wrapped his arms around me, I whispered in his ear, 'Traitor. How I hate you!' and I brought the knife forward, into his body. Twice."

She paused to take a shuddering breath before continuing. "He took a few faltering steps backward, staring down at his bloody torso, then at the knife in my hand, and then right into my eyes. On his face I could see shock, horror, and so much pain that I almost came to pieces then and there. Without a word he staggered back, his eyes latched to my face, until he turned around and shambled off. I stood transfixed for a minute, maybe more. I thought of rushing after him, but he was no longer mine. He had made his choice; he had chosen her. So I went home, got rid of the knife somewhere along the way; I don't remember where. I fell into a deep, black sleep, and when I awoke, I heard Nathan was dead. You know something strange?"

She was looking at me. Her large brown eyes looked dull. Like two marbles that had lost all their luster.

"What?" I asked.

"I was surprised to hear he was dead. Somehow, what I'd done had not sunk in until I heard it on the radio the following morning."

We were both silent for a few moments. Outside, a truck horn bellowed and the sound of voices raised in argument filtered into the room.

At length she said, "What now?"

"Now," I said, "we'll go together to the police station. You'll tell them everything, Tamara."

"I don't think Father would like that."

"You're not under his thumb. Not anymore."

Soon, I thought, *you'll be under someone else's. A prison warden and guards. But that might be better for you. Because they will likely not be as harsh as your father.*

She appeared to mull it over. Then she gave a tiny nod. "All right. But can you wait a moment? I'd like to get something from upstairs."

I hesitated, fearing that she was planning on doing something rash—slashing her wrists, perhaps. But for some reason, I didn't think she had suicide on her mind. "Of course. I'll wait for you here."

She rose and left the room, climbed the stairs, and was back within a minute. It took me a second to tell what she'd gotten. Then I saw Nathan's ring glittering on her finger.

"I'm ready now," she said. "We can go."

We were halfway to the door when it opened. On the threshold stood Mr. Granot. Upon seeing me, his face contorted in anger, his natural ruddiness turning a deeper red.

"You again! How dare you enter my home, talk to my daughter without my permission?" Then it dawned on him that we were on our way out. "Where do you think you're going?"

"To the police station, Mr. Granot."

"Whatever for?"

"Tamara is going to turn herself in, make a full confession."

"Confession? What—" Then it struck him, not just the crime in question, but the motive, too, and his role in supplying it. His gray eyes got bigger and some of the color drained from his cheeks. "No," he said in a hoarse voice. "No."

I took Tamara gently by the elbow and steered her toward the door. "Let's go."

Mr. Granot blocked the doorway.

"Step aside," I said.

"Tamara," he pleaded, "you don't have to do this. We can work something out."

She didn't deign to look at him. She simply continued walking as though he wasn't even there. And something undefinable compelled him to step aside and let her through.

"Tamara," he said, using the authoritative tone that had always worked to bend her will to his, "I'm talking to you."

She did not respond, nor did she turn around. She was already on the sidewalk when Mr. Granot gripped my forearm.

"Lapid, don't do this. I'll pay you not to. I have money."

I grabbed his hand and unhooked his fingers from my arm. "Use your money to get your daughter a good lawyer."

Then I stepped past him, joined Tamara on the street, and together we walked away.

Chapter 39

That night, a little after nine o'clock, I finished telling Greta the whole story. We were sitting alone in the café, all the other customers having gone home to their beds. Two cups stood on the table next to a solitary brass pot. The cups were empty. The pot was about a quarter full of coffee.

Greta had not spoken throughout my narration. Now she took a long breath and turned to stare through the front window at Allenby Street beyond.

"So tragic," she said.

"Yes."

"True happiness was within their reach and they allowed it to slip through their fingers, he by tumbling into bed with his former lover, she by committing murder." She shook her head. "I feel sorry for them both."

"I do too."

She turned her head to look at me. "How did you know she was the one? Even after you learned about the pictures, you couldn't be sure."

"You're right, I couldn't. But it made certain things fit that wouldn't have otherwise."

"What things?"

I poured the remainder of the coffee into my cup and took a long sip, swirling the liquid around my mouth before swallowing it. It was lukewarm but still good.

"The first thing was Elkin's reaction when he saw Nathan lying dead in the street. It wasn't disgust or horror, but surprise. At first, when I believed Gregor and Dov had killed Nathan, I assumed they'd simply not had time to inform Elkin of what they'd done. That wasn't it, of course. Elkin was surprised to see Nathan dead because he knew that Gregor and Dov had yet to find him. In fact, they had no idea where he might be. Elkin himself had been on the lookout for Nathan, and now here the man was, dead. Killed, Elkin knew, by someone other than Gregor and Dov.

"The second thing—which has bothered me since the night I came upon Nathan's body—was why he had received no help between the time he was stabbed and the moment he collapsed on Allenby Street. He could've made a racket, knocked on doors, shouted for help. It seemed odd that no one heard him, that no one called the police. I believe I know the reason that didn't happen."

"Which is?"

"I think that Nathan did not cry for help, did not knock on any door. Hell, he might have come across other people out on the street, but if so, he didn't enlist their help. He simply kept on hobbling forward until he dropped from lack of blood."

"But why would he do that? It makes no sense. Did he think his injuries were not serious?"

"On the contrary. He probably knew he was dying."

"Then why?"

"You need to remember that Nathan had lost his entire family in Europe. His mother, his brother, and God knows who else. He had a friend in Misha, but that's not quite the same thing as a family, is it?"

Greta, sensing that I had posed a rhetorical question, waited silently for me to continue.

"In Nathan's eyes, and in his heart, Tamara Granot was more than a love interest, more than a potential wife. She signified the rebirth of his family. With her he would one day have children, a home, a meaningful future. She was not as exciting as Iris Rosenfeld, perhaps, not as passionate, but she was everything he had longed for over the past few years. She was what he needed, what he dreamed about, even if he hadn't known it himself until he met her. Now you see why he didn't cry for help?"

Greta shook her head slowly. "No, I'm afraid I don't."

But I did. I had seen that sort of thing before. Many times. In Auschwitz. Men who had given up, in whom the will to live had been extinguished. Driven to despair by loneliness, by the knowledge that their children, wives, brothers and sisters and parents were all dead, these men simply guttered out. Sometimes it took weeks from the moment the light died in their eyes to the instant they perished altogether. There was a temptation in that, I knew, an alluring prospect of escape and peace. I had felt its tug during my time in Auschwitz, and, on occasion, since then as well.

"When she sank that knife into his body," I said, "Tamara did not merely injure Nathan. She murdered his hopes, his dreams, the things that kept him going, his reasons for living. Now he had no one. And what made it even worse was that this time it wasn't a group of evil strangers who had taken everything from him. This time, it was the one person he viewed as his family—a future one, but still his family. She was the one who had stabbed him with a knife, who had sought to kill him. He didn't call for help because he didn't want to live anymore."

Neither of us said a word for several moments. Outside it had begun to drizzle. Tiny rivulets of rain slithered down the face of the front windowpane like the tears that had coursed down Tamara Granot's cheeks.

"So much death," Greta said, almost too faintly to hear. "I can't bear the thought of it." Which was probably why she chose to change the subject. "What was Inspector Leibowitz's reaction when he received Tamara's confession?"

"Nothing much. He didn't expect it, but he's seen much over his career. Too much to be truly surprised by anything. What cops learn, and what most civilians never imagine, is that people kill for the oddest of reasons. Sometimes, those reasons linger in your mind longer than the actual victims do."

"Did he say anything to you?"

"After Tamara signed her statement and was taken away, he turned to me and said, 'See? I knew I'd have a better chance of solving this murder with you on the loose.' I asked him to do what he can for her, and he said he will."

A little later, I sauntered alone through the drizzle. I

headed uptown, ignoring the turn to Hamaccabi Street and my apartment, and continued up King George and Dizengoff, past shuttered storefronts and trees with naked limbs, the pavement glistening in the rain. I took my time. I was in no hurry. My watch told me it was not yet ten o'clock. She would be busy. She would have company.

It was a quarter to eleven when I got to her building. Still I dawdled. I lit a cigarette and smoked it with strained leisure, staring at the light in her window. The drizzle dampened my hair, soaking into the fabric of my jacket. My skin was cold, but the heat of the cigarette smoke kept my insides warm.

Soon, once I'd finished putting off the inevitable, I'd climb the stairs to her apartment and knock on her door. She would gaze upon me with those deep dark eyes and remark bitingly on my appearance, likely focusing her words on the cut on my chin. I would say I came for my box and she would invite me in. And in that instant she'd begin her barrage of enticement.

Would I be able to resist her? Did I even want to?

I finished my cigarette and fired up another. It was the last one in the pack.

Five minutes, maybe six if I stretched it out, and then I'd go to Sima Vaaknin and see where the night took me.

THE END

Flip the page for a personal message from the author

Author's note

Dear Reader,

Let me start by thanking you for reading *A Debt of Death*. I write both for the sheer pleasure of creation and for my work to be read by as many people as possible. I treasure each and every one of my readers, so thank you!

I thought you might like to know how *A Debt of Death* came to be. I first wrote the scene in which Adam is hired by Mrs. Wasserman many months ago (I don't recall exactly when) and, at the time, could not find a way to push the story forward. I set that scene aside and forgot about it—or at least thought I did.

But, evidently, that scene stuck in my subconscious, because when it came time for me to begin writing the fourth Adam Lapid novel, I recalled that scene and decided to explore it again. The problem was that I couldn't find it.

My old computer had gone the way of all electronic things, and either I neglected to back up that scene or was unable to find exactly where I had saved it. So I wrote it from scratch.

And this time, I found myself able to plow on with the story, to add new words each day, to create characters that I found interesting, and to slowly form the book that you've just read.

Most of *A Debt of Death*, like all my other novels, was not planned in advance. When I began writing, I did not know who the culprit would turn out to be, nor did I have a clear notion of the characters involved or how the plot would unfold. I allowed myself to discover the story as it developed, much like you did when you read this book. At times, I found myself grinning at the screen as characters such as Inspector Leibowitz and Mrs. Wasserman acquired shape and motivation and the traits that make them memorable. There were some tough spots during the writing process (there are with every book), but overall, I enjoyed writing *A Debt of Death* immensely. I hope you enjoyed reading it just as much.

I love hearing from readers, and I answer every reader email I get. If you've got any feedback, questions, or you simply want to reach out and say hi, write to me at contact@JonathanDunsky.com.

If you enjoyed *A Debt of Death*, could you do me a favor and leave a review on its Amazon page? Good reviews are very important. They help persuade potential readers to try out new books. I'd be grateful if you could spare a moment to write your review of *A Debt of Death*.

I also invite you to join my VIP readers club where you'll be the first to know of new releases and special deals. All new members get a free copy of my short story, The Favor. Join the club here: jonathandunsky.com/free/

You may be wondering what the future holds for Adam Lapid. I have a few ideas percolating in my head for future novels in the series. Adam will continue solving crimes and trying to rebuild his life. So rest assured, you will be seeing more of him.

I hope to meet you again soon in another one of my books.

Yours,

Jonathan Dunsky

p.s. You are also welcome to contact me on Goodreads:

goodreads.com/author/show/15942284.Jonathan_Dunsky

or Facebook:

facebook.com/JonathanDunskyBooks

About the Author

Jonathan Dunsky lives in Israel with his wife and two sons. He enjoys reading, writing, and goofing around with his kids. He began writing in his teens, then took a break for close to twenty years, during which he worked an assortment of jobs. He is the author of four novels and a handful of short stories, mostly in the mystery and crime genres.

Printed in Poland
by Amazon Fulfillment
Poland Sp. z o.o., Wrocław